"I'm not that kind of woman."

"And what kind of woman might that be?" he asked.

"The kind who...one who..." Unable to force out the right words, she saw the glint of devilment in his eyes then and almost threw her sack of new clothes at him. "What are you laughing at?"

"Me? Nothing," he claimed innocently. "I just thought you might like to get a room and clean up. But if you've got sex on your mind..."

"I never said that!"

He arched a masculine brow at her. "Didn't you?"

He had her, and they both knew it, but she would rather die than admit it. "I told you—I'm not that kind of woman."

"But I'm that kind of man, right?" When she refused to answer, he chuckled and leaned close. "You're damn right I'm that kind of man, sweetheart," he taunted softly. "And with the right man, you'll be that kind of woman."

Dear Reader,

Wow! What a month we've got for you. Take *Maddy Lawrence's Big Adventure*, Linda Turner's newest. Like most of us, Maddy's lived a pretty calm life, maybe even too calm. But all that's about to change, because now Ace Mackenzie is on the job. Don't miss this wonderful book.

We've got some great miniseries this month, too. *The One Worth Waiting For* is the latest of Alicia Scott's THE GUINESS GANG, while Cathryn Clare continues ASSIGNMENT: ROMANCE with *The Honeymoon Assignment*. Plus Sandy Steen is back with the suspenseful—and sexy—*Hunting Houston*. Then there's Beverly Bird's *Undercover Cowboy*, which successfully mixes romance and danger for a powerhouse read. Finally, try Lee Karr's *Child of the Night* if you enjoy a book where things are never quite what they seem.

Then come back again next month, because you won't want to miss some of the best romantic reading around—only in Silhouette Intimate Moments.

Enjoy!

Leslie Wainger
Senior Editor and Editorial Coordinator

Please address questions and book requests to:
Silhouette Reader Service
U.S.: 3010 Walden Ave., P.O. Box 1325, Buffalo, NY 14269
Canadian: P.O. Box 609, Fort Erie, Ont. L2A 5X3

Linda Turner

Maddy Lawrence's Big Adventure

Silhouette® INTIMATE™ MOMENTS®

Published by Silhouette Books

America's Publisher of Contemporary Romance

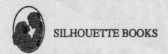 SILHOUETTE BOOKS

ISBN 0-373-07709-2

MADDY LAWRENCE'S BIG ADVENTURE

Copyright © 1996 by Linda Turner

This edition published by arrangement with Harlequin Books S.A.

® and TM are trademarks of Harlequin Books S.A., used under license. Trademarks indicated with ® are registered in the United States Patent and Trademark Office, the Canadian Trade Marks Office and in other countries.

Printed in U.S.A.

Books by Linda Turner

LINDA TURNER

began reading romances in high school and began writing them one night when she had nothing else to read. She's been writing ever since. Single and living in Texas, she travels every chance she gets, scouting locales for her books.

Prologue

A cold wind raced down the dark, wet street, dragging soggy leaves and trash after it. Shivering, Maddy pulled the collar of her jacket closer around her neck, pushed her glasses farther up her nose and wondered if she dared close the newsstand early. After all, it wasn't as if the world was beating a path to her little corner of Manhattan. She hadn't had a customer in nearly an hour. The first cold front of the season had sent most people rushing home right after work, and those unlucky enough to live on the street had long since found shelter from the cold bite of the wind. There wasn't a soul in sight. She could close up the place and head home and no one would notice or care.

But even as she toyed with the idea, she knew she couldn't do it. Maddy Lawrence didn't take chances. Ever. She didn't cheat or fudge on her taxes or even nibble on the grapes she bought at the market before going through the checkout. She was dependable right down to the tips of her plain brown hair, which was why she was working at the news-

stand in the first place. Tommy Lazear had needed someone he could depend on to run the place in the evenings
without supervision, and she'd been in desperate need of a
second job. The salary she made as an elementary school librarian hadn't been enough to help support her mother after she'd fallen last month and broken her hip, and she
couldn't jeopardize the much-needed money Mr. Lazear
paid her just because the night was cold and she wanted to
be home in bed, curled up with the newest Ace MacKenzie
book she'd bought on the way to work.

A wistful smile curled her mouth at the thought of her
favorite fictional character. The creation of Susannah Patterson Rawlings and the star of his own wildly successful
series of men's adventure novels, Ace MacKenzie was an irreverent hero and everything that Maddy was not. Bold,
daring, courageous, outrageous. From page one of his
books, she lost herself in his exploits and dreamed of one
day meeting a man just like him. The only problem was that
men like Ace MacKenzie didn't exist, at least not in her
tame, uneventful world. And even if they had, they
wouldn't have spared her a second glance. She was too
plain, too ordinary, too shy. So she had to be content with
reading about a man who didn't exist . . . and dreaming.

Casting a quick look around to make sure that she was
still the only one crazy enough to be out on such a lousy
night, she grabbed the new paperback from where she'd
stuffed it in her purse. Mr. Lazear wouldn't care, she assured herself as she settled down on a stool behind the
counter and once again pushed her glasses into place. What
harm could it do? Turning to the first chapter, she began to
read. . . .

She was one of those women who shouldn't have been
let loose on the street alone. Dreamy and innocent and
lost in her window-shopping, she didn't have a clue as

to the kind of danger she was in. Golden eyes watched her from the shadows, following her every movement, waiting . . . just waiting. She was his—she just didn't know it yet. But she would. Oh, yes, she would know it any second now. The alley was just ahead, the one she took every day on her way home from work when she cut across to Broadway. Anticipation burning like a fire in his belly, he slowly, patiently, began to eliminate the distance between them. And still she had no idea that she was being hunted like a lamb by a big cat.

Her thoughts on John and the special dinner she was going to cook for him at her place, Cheryl turned into the alley and hurried past a Dumpster. She would wear something that would knock John out of his socks, she decided, her dimples flashing at the thought. Maybe that new angora sweater that she'd been saving for a special occasion. . . .

Lost in her thoughts, she heard the footsteps behind her too late. Her heart suddenly in her throat, she started to turn. She never had a chance. In the next instant, pain exploded at the back of her head. Without a sound, she crumpled like a broken doll.

An eternity later, it was the pain that she became aware of first. Burning hot, it throbbed unmercifully, dragging her slowly, ruthlessly, back to consciousness. Afraid to move and possibly increase the pain, she lay perfectly still, tears stinging her eyes and her breathing tense and measured as she tried to collect herself and get her bearings. It was then that she realized she was in a moving car. Surprised, she gasped and struggled to sit up. But she was tied, her arms bound behind her. And from out of the darkness that had fallen while she was unconscious, sinister golden eyes watched her every move—

At the far end of one of the racks that formed narrow aisles across the width of the newsstand, a sudden gust of wind caught a magazine and knocked it to the floor. Pages fluttered wildly in the silence. Startled, Maddy jumped, her heart thundering in her ears. "Silly," she chided, shaking her head over her own foolishness. "Don't be such a baby. It's just the wind."

The words were hardly out of her mouth when another gust, this one accompanied by an unexpected deluge of rain, sent two more periodicals to the floor. Within seconds, they were soaked through.

"Oh, no!" Tossing her book on the counter, Maddy hurried toward the fallen magazines, her only thought to pull down the overhead metal door on that side of the shop before any other merchandise was ruined. But the thick cord attached to the end of the garagelike door was out of her reach. Jumping for it, the wind whipping her long brown hair in her eyes, she didn't see the magazine-laden rack behind her start to topple toward her. A heartbeat later, it slammed against her unprotected head. She never knew what hit her.

Chapter 1

The second-floor apartment was small and cold and bare. A naked light bulb hung from the ceiling, but the man who stood at the window preferred the obscurity of darkness. As comfortable with the night as a thief who silently scurried down unlit side streets and alleys, he stood in the shadows at the window and watched, with gathering rage, the scene unfolding at the newsstand across the street.

Maddy Lawrence lay in a soft, unconscious heap on the cold floor of the shop, her beige, colorless clothes darkening in the rain. And over her stood Cement Johnny Dempsey, the lowlife scum who had knocked the magazine rack over on her unsuspecting head.

A man of many faces, many names, the watcher at the window swore long and low. He'd been scoping Tommy "Sneakers" Lazear's newsstand for weeks now, recording every transaction on his surveillance equipment, and there was no question that the place was a front for something far more sinister. The word on the street was that Lazear was into fencing, and he didn't mess around with penny-ante stuff like hot TVs and VCRs. Oh, no, Tommy had a taste for museum-quality jewels and precious art, and the word was he had a whole warehouse full of the stuff for sale to those who could afford the price.

And the watcher wanted the contents of that warehouse. As did Cement Johnny, who was Sneaker's sworn enemy. Only one of them knew the location of the warehouse, and it wasn't Johnny.

His dark blue eyes as cold as ice, the watcher never took his gaze from the thug across the street as he hunkered down beside Maddy Lawrence, rolled her to her stomach and efficiently tied her hands behind her back. Still out cold, she never knew when her attacker lifted her limp form and carried her around the corner to a black Riviera that was nearly concealed by the shadows of the night.

It didn't take a genius to figure out what the man was going to do next—kidnap Maddy and force her to tell him where the warehouse was. It was, the watcher had to admit, a smart move. If he hadn't already figured out the location of the warehouse, he might have considered doing the same thing himself. He'd been studying the lady for weeks now and there was no question that Maddy Lawrence was as much a part of the front as the newsstand itself. And she was good. Damn good. As prim and proper as an old-maid schoolmarm in her long brown dresses, ankle boots and wire-rimmed glasses, she had Innocent stamped all over her. But innocents didn't work for known Mafia bosses. And Mafia bosses didn't put innocents on duty right in front of a multimillion-dollar illegal operation.

No, she knew what was going on, all right. And Cement Johnny had her. The watcher was well acquainted with Johnny's reputation, knew what he was capable of. He hadn't earned his nickname for nothing, and had, according to reliable rumor, dropped more than one poor sucker in the East River with a pair of concrete shoes for not giving him what he wanted. If Maddy Lawrence decided to be loyal and hold her tongue, she was in for a long night and a lot of pain. And it would all be for nothing. Because in the end, she would talk. Johnny would make sure of it. And when he had what he wanted from her, the lady would go for a nice, cold, permanent swim.

The watcher swore long and low in the darkness and told himself that Maddy Lawrence's health and well-being were none of his concern. Anyone who had the guts to be in cahoots with Sneakers Lazear had to be a tough cookie. She could take care of herself.

Oh, yeah? his conscience jeered. *Then if she's so tough, why did she let a lead foot like Cement Johnny creep up on her and knock her into next week?*

The taunt struck a nerve, irritating him no end. His gaze lingering on the slumped figure in the front seat of the darkened Buick, he grimly reminded himself that there was too much at stake for him to leave his post now. It had taken him months to figure out that Sneakers was behind all the museum thefts, then longer still to discover the whereabouts of the warehouse. Through careful, round-the-clock scrutiny, he'd learned the movements of everyone connected with the place, waiting for just the right time to strike himself. And tonight was the night, dammit! He wasn't blowing months of work to play a goddamn knight to Maddy Lawrence's damsel in distress. She'd gotten herself into this mess; she'd just have to get herself out of it.

The decision made, he deliberately turned his attention back to the abandoned newsstand, ignoring the well-tuned car that quietly roared to life. In the darkness, brake lights flashed for just an instant, then went out as the Buick pulled away from the curb and headed north. For the span of a heartbeat, the watcher stood his ground, fighting his conscience. But it was a battle he couldn't win. Snarling an oath, he rushed for the door, cursing Maddy Lawrence all the way.

The blackness of the night pressed down on Maddy, weighing her down, swamping her dulled senses. Her breath hitching through her parted lips, she frowned and tried to open her eyes, but that simple motion set the pain at the back of her head throbbing like a red-hot blinking light. Stifling a moan, she lay perfectly still, trying to remember what had happened. The wind...

The lines furrowing her brow deepened as her memory returned in bits and starts. The wind had knocked some magazines from the rack and it had started to rain. The garage door... She'd tried to shut the one on that side of the building, but something had hit her. The rack, she thought dully. The wind must have sent one of the racks crashing into her and knocked her out. She had to get up—

But when she tried to move, the fog shrouding her brain abruptly lifted and for the first time she became aware of the unnatural position of her arms behind her back and the rough bite of the rope around the tender skin of her wrists as the car she had somehow been spirited away to hit a chughole. Horrified, she froze, her blood turning to ice as realization hit her like a slap in the face.

She'd been kidnapped.

Her eyes flew open, panic seizing her by the throat as questions backed up in her bruised brain. How? Why? Things like this didn't happen to women like her. She was a thirty-four-year old virgin with no man in her life, an elementary school librarian who was timid and bookish and spent most of her adult life looking after her frail mother. The only exciting thing that had ever happened to her was when she got lost on a trip to D.C. for a librarian workshop and ended up in Richmond without quite knowing how.

This had to be a dream, she told herself in growing desperation. That was the only logical explanation. She'd slipped and fallen at the newsstand and knocked herself senseless. Even now, she was probably lying in a wet heap on the floor, out cold.

But her eyes were open.

She slammed them shut, telling herself to calm down and think. Her imagination was just working overtime. But when she opened her eyes again, nothing had changed. She was still in the front seat of a strange car and slumped against the passenger door. Her vision blurring, she stared unseeingly at the distorted, shadowy buildings that flew past her window as the car raced down an unknown street. Frowning, she tried to focus and only then realized that both lenses of her glasses were a web of spidery cracks.

"Well, well, looky here," a gravelly voice drawled out of the darkness beside her. "Sleeping Beauty awakes. Turn over, sweetheart, and meet Prince Charming."

Startled, Maddy froze, her blood turning to ice in her veins. Afraid to breathe, to move so much as a muscle, she squeezed her eyes shut, desperately promising herself that any second she was going to wake up and the nightmare would be over. It was just a bad dream. It had to be!

But the car continued to race through the night, and the man at the wheel refused to fade into her subconscious where he belonged. Not the least concerned that she refused to even acknowledge him, he laughed softly, menacingly, and said, "So you don't want to talk, huh? That's okay. You will later. In fact, by the time I'm through with you, sweetheart, you'll beg me to let you spill your guts."

His words were oil slick, his tone confident enough to strike fear in the bravest heart. And bravery was something

Maddy had never had in spades. She wasn't one of those adventuresome women who struck off on her own to explore the world, afraid of neither man nor beast. Oh, she dreamed about doing such things every time she read an Ace MacKenzie book, but those were just the dreams of a fanciful woman who preferred the pages of her favorite books to the harshness of the real world. She could deal with children, with a sick mother who complained about every ache and pain and worried when she was more than a few minutes late, but she had no experience with men who broke the rules at their own discretion, men who cavalierly made threats and wouldn't bat an eye at carrying them out.

Her teeth starting to chatter with icy anticipation, she locked her jaw, struggling for a control that was momentarily beyond her. Sick fear twisted deep inside her like a coiling rattler. Spill her guts about what? she wondered in growing confusion as her head throbbed painfully with every beat of her heart. What could she possibly know about anything that this man would be interested in?

"I don't know what you're talking about," she whispered hoarsely, forcing the words through her dry throat. "Who are you? What do you want?"

He laughed at that, the sound low and mocking and dangerous. *"What do I want?"* he mimicked. "How stupid do you think I am, lady? I want the location of that damn warehouse and you're going to give it to me. So save the innocent act for somebody who appreciates it. I ain't got time for it."

Her upper arms numb from the unrelieved pressure of her position and the tight bindings at her wrist, she shifted in her seat to face him. "But—"

Her gaze lifted to his . . . and widened in confused horror, familiarity pulling at her, teasing her, taunting her, scaring her spitless. He had golden eyes, she thought wildly, swallowing a sob as her head started to spin. Golden, sinister eyes—just like the villain in the newest Ace MacKenzie book.

And she was bound and kidnapped—just like Susannah Rawlings's latest heroine.

No! she cried silently, the roar of her blood loud in her ears. This was crazy. *She* was crazy! There was no other explanation. People only fell down rabbit holes in *Alice in Wonderland.* It had to be that blow to the head she'd taken—it had scrambled her brains. This might look and feel real, but she was still unconscious, still flat on the floor at the newsstand, dreaming about the last thing she'd read before she'd somehow knocked herself silly. Any minute now, she'd wake up and laugh at her own foolishness.

But long seconds passed, and with every tick of the clock, the nightmare became more and more real. With her eyes closed and all her senses attuned to her surroundings, she could feel the car sway as it took a corner, smell the heavy, cloying cologne of the man who sat next to her in the driver's seat. Bile backing up in her throat, threatening to choke her, she started to shake.

She wasn't dreaming!

She didn't have a clue as to how it had happened, but she was at this man's mercy, and one glance at his ruthless face told her that was one virtue he was fresh out of. If she so much as looked at him wrong, he would make her wish she'd never been born.

Think! she ordered herself sternly. This was all just a mix-up, a stupid mistake that could be easily corrected. The man obviously had the wrong person. Once she convinced him of that, surely he'd let her go.

Grabbing on to that thought as if it was a lifeline, she turned pleading eyes to his wicked, golden ones and tried not to show her revulsion. "I don't know what you're talking about," she said shakily, shattering the chilling silence. "Really, I don't!" she cried when he only snorted in disbelief. "I just work nights at the newsstand and don't know anything about a warehouse. The shelves are stocked by the time I clock in every evening. I don't even know where the inventory is stored."

"I don't give a damn about that inventory," he snapped impatiently, "and you know it. It's the other I want. And you're going to give it to me. You hear?"

"What other?" she asked, frowning in bewilderment. "I don't know of any other."

The look he shot her was hard and brutal and sharp as a well-honed knife. "You damn well better know, sister, 'cause that's the only thing that's keeping you alive. You hear me? If you ain't got what I need in that pretty little head of yours, then I ain't got no use for you. *Capishe?*"

She blanched, panic closing as tight as a strangler's hands around her throat. He was going to kill her. Snuff her out like a candle. Dump her lifeless body in the woods somewhere or, worse yet, fit her with cement boots and toss her in the river while she was still kicking and fighting and begging for her life. There would be no one to hear, of course, no one to help. He'd choose a secluded spot on the Jersey shoreline, somewhere that was dark and deserted, and with her hands bound behind her, there wouldn't be a thing she could do to stop him. The water would close around her with terrifying swiftness, cutting off her screams, her air....

No!

A silent scream of denial echoing through the canyons of her head, she violently shoved the graphic scene out of her head. She wouldn't let him do this, wouldn't let him demoralize her with her own fearful imaginings so that she was virtually helpless with terror by the time he decided to make his move. She had to do something, had to keep her wits about her and find a way to escape. Because there was no superhero out there in the dark, no caped crusader just waiting for the chance to swoop down and rescue her.

She was thoroughly and completely on her own.

Her heart thundered at the thought, the frantic beat echoing all the way down to her toes. Feeling herself start to shake again, she dragged in a quick breath, but it did little to calm her jittery nerves. God, she had to do something, come up with a plan. Don't just sit there like a bump on a log, for heaven's sake! she told herself fiercely. There had to be a way out of this mess. If she could get her hands untied without her kidnapper knowing, then grab the door handle, she could jump out the next time he slowed down for a corner.

Yeah, right, a voice drawled sarcastically in her head. *And then what? You're going to make a run for it? Gimme a break. You get winded just climbing the stairs to your apartment.*

She winced, knowing this was no time to lie to herself. She wasn't athletic, and if it came to a footrace, she could be in big trouble. But her kidnapper wasn't exactly a long-distance runner himself, she decided, studying him through lowered lids in the darkness. Not if the beer gut hanging over his belt was anything to go by. And she was quick—for short distances. If she was lucky, she'd be safely hidden in the night by the time he was able to stop the car and come after her.

If she could get her hands free.

Never taking her eyes from his harshly carved profile in the darkness, she carefully twisted her hands and wrists, silently pulling against her rope bindings. But they held tight. Her teeth clenching on a surprising oath she hadn't even realized she knew, she tried again. And again. The rough flax rubbed her skin raw . . . and didn't give so much as an inch.

Swallowing a sob, she blinked back hot tears, despair swamping her, threatening to drain the fight right out of her. No! She couldn't do this! She couldn't give up. Because if she did, she'd be dead.

All her concentration focused on finding a way out of her bindings, Maddy never saw the battered pickup truck that came flying out of a dark alley on the left. But her kidnapper did. Swearing, he jerked the steering wheel to the right, but he was a split second too late. The pickup slammed into them, crashing into the Riviera's left front fender.

With her arms bound and no seat belt in place to protect her, Maddy went flying. She slammed against the passenger door, her head and right shoulder cracking the window before she went careening back the other way toward her kidnapper. She only had time to cry out in fright and pain before the car started to spin. A blur of dark colors swirling before her dazed eyes, she groaned and weakly tried to brace herself for the next blow.

It happened so fast, she didn't have time to do anything but gasp. One second the car seemed to be spinning on an axis of its own, and the next it smacked headfirst into a light pole that refused to budge so much as an inch. Hurtling toward the windshield, Maddy screamed as her glasses went flying and she found herself face-to-face with certain death.

Later, she never knew if she actually hit the windshield or not. Battered and bruised, blood trickling down her forehead from a cut near her hairline, she collapsed against the seat like a broken doll. How long she lay there, shuddering, she couldn't have said. It could have been seconds, minutes. Urgency pulled at her, nudging her to get out of there. Now! While her kidnapper was too stunned to realize she was escaping!

Her heart thundering with panic, she jerked upright and shot a quick, apprehensive glance at her companion. Without her glasses, everything was fuzzy, but she could just make out his blurred figure slumped over the steering wheel.

Run! a voice screamed in her aching head.

But the punishment her body had taken finally hit and she was suddenly very uncoordinated and moving in slow motion. The door handle, she thought groggily, feeling blindly for it. She had to reach the door handle....

But before she could find it in the dark with her cold, stiff fingers, the door was wrenched open. Startled, she glanced up... and gasped at the sight of the stranger standing in the V made by the open door and the car body.

In the shadows of the night, he was larger than life, a giant of a man who towered over her like a dark, avenging angel. Dressed in black from his booted feet to the well-worn leather biker's jacket that encased his impossibly broad shoulders, he looked hard, stern, dangerous. There was no softness to him, not in the long black hair that curled around his collar or in the lean, angular planes of his rough-hewn face or a jaw that appeared to be as rigid as granite. Still, Maddy might have thought he was a good-looking devil... until she got a good look at his eyes. Dark as pitch, they could have been black or indigo or any color in between and were the eyes of a man who let nothing get in his way. Razor sharp with purpose, they were cold, determined, as unyielding as a brick wall.

Transfixed, too shocked by his sudden appearance to move, she could only stare at him. Then she heard a hissing click in the silence and saw the knife he clutched like a street fighter in his right hand. Small and deadly, it caught the light of a distant streetlight, its well-honed blade four inches long if it was an inch.

Her heart stopped dead in her chest. Her gaze locked on the switchblade, she felt hysterical laughter gurgle in her throat. First a kidnapper, and now a knife-wielding bandit.

Talk about having a bad night! This couldn't be happening. Not really. It was just a result of the combination of the pastrami she'd had for supper and a blow to the head. Any second now, she was going to come to her senses before this ridiculous dream got completely out of hand.

God, oh, God, please let me wake up now, she pleaded silently. Let me be safe and sound in my own bed and not worry how I got there.

But in spite of her prayer, the man before her didn't disappear in a puff of smoke as she had vainly hoped. Instead, he appeared frighteningly real and solid. *And he was reaching for her!* Horrified, she whimpered and pulled back, shaking her aching head. "No! Please—"

"Look, honey," he growled in disgust, "I don't play Superman for just anyone, so don't give me a hard time, okay? We've only got a few seconds before your friend there comes around and I'd just as soon be long gone before that happens." Not giving her a chance to argue further, he jerked her around until her back was to him, inserted the knife between her wrists and neatly slit the rope that bound her. "C'mon. Let's get out of here."

With the assurance of a man who was used to giving orders and having them obeyed, he pocketed the switchblade with a smooth, practiced motion, grabbed her by the wrist and hauled her out of the Buick as if she were a particularly bothersome child. Tugging her over to his pickup, which sat arrogantly abandoned in the middle of the street and looked none the worse for wear despite a head-on confrontation with the Riviera, he hoisted her up into the passenger seat. At her gasp, he flashed her a wicked grin and slammed the door.

Her pulse skittering and her temples throbbing with pain, Maddy tried to grab on to one of the outraged objections buzzing around in her head long enough to force it through her dry throat, but she couldn't quite manage the task. She had to get out of here! So what if her rescuer claimed to be the next best thing to Superman? He said himself he didn't do it for just anyone, and talk was cheap. No decent man handled a switchblade with such practiced ease, let alone carried one in his pocket.

And he had a gun.

Her breath lodging in her lungs, she stared in horror at the pistol he pulled from inside his black leather biker's jacket as he walked around the hood of the pickup to the driver's side. It was small and ugly and seemed to fit the palm of his hand as if it was made for it. And he knew how to use it. Turning suddenly, he fired three times at the Riviera.

Startled, Maddy screamed and instinctively flinched, covering her ears, but her companion didn't so much as blink. Continuing around the front of the pickup, he jerked open the driver's door and climbed inside.

Alarmed, Maddy almost jumped from the vehicle right then and there. She didn't know this man, had no reason to trust him. Sure, he had saved her, but for what? Himself?

Torn by indecision, the throbbing in her head intensifying so that she could hardly think straight, she glanced at the incapacitated Buick and saw the man slumped over the steering wheel groggily lift his head. A shudder of revulsion rippled through her. If she made the mistake of stepping out of the pickup, she knew he would be on her like a snake on a baby chick. And this time, no dark stranger would come crashing to her rescue. She'd be on her own. And with her glasses gone and her shoulder and head one big ache, she'd never stand a chance against him. Sinking back against the seat, she jerkily reached for her seat belt.

Beside her, she had no idea that the man at her side was watching every nuance of her expression until she glanced over and found him studying her with eyes that missed little. She didn't say a word, but she apparently didn't have to to have him read her like an open book. His mouth quirking with a tight, approving smile, he nodded as if she'd just passed some hidden test.

"Smart move, Snow White," he murmured in a raspy voice. His dark eyes still trained on hers, he reached over and hit the electronic door locks, locking her kidnapper out...and her in. A second later, they were racing off into the night.

With total disregard for traffic laws, he darted down side streets, took corners at the last minute and even, on one occasion, raced the wrong way down a one-way street, weaving in and out of the oncoming cars like a marine darting up a beach littered with mines. Or a thief who had vast experience eluding the police, a voice whispered in Maddy's head.

Her eyes locked in horrified fascination on the man at her side, she whispered, "Who are you?"

He had been expecting the question for some time and could have, had he chosen, given her any one of a dozen different names. He had IDs for all of them in his wallet and had, when the occasion demanded it, been known to go by two or more at the same time. Then he remembered the book she'd been reading when Cement Johnny had sent the magazine rack slamming down on the back of her head. Grinning slightly at the ironies of fate, he told her the truth...sort of. "Ace."

Whatever reaction he was expecting, it wasn't the one he got. The last of the blood drained from her cheeks, leaving her eyes huge in her suddenly ashen face. Looking at him as if he were some kind of monster who had just stepped out of her worst nightmare, she shook her head dazedly, the trembling fingers of one hand coming up to rub at her temple. "No. It isn't possible. My head . . . I hit my head. That explains it. . . ."

The angry blare of a horn snapped his attention back to his driving, and with a muttered curse, he dodged another car before swiftly turning into the correct flow of traffic on another one-way street. By the time he turned back to the woman at his side, her eyes were rolling back in her head.

"Whoa, babe, don't pass out on me now!" Lightning quick, he grabbed her by the back of her slender neck and forced her head down to her knees. "Just take slow, easy breaths. You're going to be fine."

"I'm not your babe."

The faint protest was dignified and indignant . . . and murmured into her lap. His grin flashing in the darkness, Ace had to agree with her. No doubt about it, she wasn't his type, thank God. He preferred blondes, ones with a little meat on their bones who couldn't handle too much machinery. The kind who didn't ask questions or expect anything more from him than a couple of hours of mutual pleasure. From what he'd seen of Maddy Lawrence, she missed on all counts. Skinny as a rail, with mousy brown hair, she made no attempt to hide the intelligence in her eyes. As for pleasure, Ace had watched her every night for a week now and there was no question that she was as prim and proper as an old-maid schoolteacher. If a man wanted warmth, he'd do well to go looking for it somewhere else.

But the skin at the back of her neck was soft under his hand, her hair silky as it brushed his fingertips—which was something he'd rather not have noticed. Scowling, he released her abruptly and jerked his attention back to his driving. "Right," he said flatly as she popped upright like a jack-in-the-box. "You belong to Sneakers, don't you?" His mouth twisted with distaste. "I guess there's no accounting for taste, but I tell you, brown eyes, I don't know how you climb into bed with the slimeball. He must be really good between the sheets.''

"Between the—ooh!" Suddenly realizing what he was accusing her of, Maddy gasped as if he'd struck her. "How dare you!"

Not the least perturbed, he shot her a crooked grin. "You stick around me long enough, *babe,* and you'll learn there's not a whole helluva lot I *won't* dare. So save the innocent act for someone who appreciates it. I'd rather hear about Sneakers."

"Sneakers who?" she demanded, confusion warring with anger in her eyes. "I don't know anyone by that ridiculous name."

"Sure you don't," he mocked cynically. "And I suppose you don't know anything about the warehouse, either, do you?"

Surprised, Maddy blanched, fear sliding like a chunk of ice down her spine. "Oh, God," she whispered, cringing away from him. "Not you, too. Has the whole world gone crazy? I don't know anything about a warehouse—I swear it! I told the other man, but he didn't believe me. He was going to..." Just thinking about what the fat little toad had planned for her sickened her stomach. Dragging in a cleansing breath, she said faintly, "This is all some kind of weird dream—it has to be."

"If it is, you're in it right up to your pretty little neck," he retorted, unimpressed by her theatrics. "So save the act for someone who appreciates it. I know what's going on at the newsstand. I've been watching the place for weeks now."

He'd been watching her at the newsstand? Why? Her overactive imagination, always at the ready, was more than willing to supply her with a series of twisted images. "Who are you?" she choked, wildly wondering what kind of depravity she'd stumbled into. "What do you want with me?"

"Obviously not what you're thinking," he drawled. Irritated with the way she was looking at him—as if he was a pervert trying to get in her pants, for God's sake!—he shook his head in reluctant admiration. "Boy, lady, you're really good. If I didn't know better, I'd swear you were as innocent as Shirley Temple in her heyday. The problem is...my momma didn't raise any idiots. So let's just cut the crap, okay? We both know you know about the warehouse behind the newsstand—"

"But I don't—"

"The one full of stolen museum pieces," he continued through his teeth, trying to hang on to his temper. "The one that Lazear fences hot goods out of during the day..." He watched her eyes widen with recognition and grinned nastily. "Bingo. And you said you didn't know Sneakers. Finally, we're getting somewhere. What else don't you know?"

Hugging the door, she shook her head. "N-nothing. Just Mr. L-Lazear. T-Tommy Lazear."

"Tommy Sneakers Lazear," he corrected as he turned the corner onto the street where the newsstand was located. Glancing down the block to where the shop took up the northeast corner at the next intersection, he swore and swiftly pulled over to the curb, cutting his lights. "Speaking of the devil..."

"What?" Following his gaze, Maddy gaped at the sight of her boss, Tommy Lazear, rushing out of a door that she'd never seen before. A door that, she realized with a jolt of shock, had always been hidden by a magazine rack that she'd thought was bolted to the wall but now stood open like a door, revealing the warehouse behind it. Harried and unkempt in a way she had never seen him before, Lazear tossed a large, stuffed plastic bag into the front seat of his gray Mercedes, which was illegally parked at the curb, then turned back to what must have been the hidden warehouse. Seconds later, he reappeared, his hands dripping with jewelry as he jammed the items into the pockets of his silk suitcoat.

"Son of a bitch, he must have had somebody watching the place just in case his cover was blown," Ace muttered.

"I didn't know anything about this," Maddy told him earnestly. "Honest to God, I just thought it was a newsstand. I never sold anything but newspapers and magazines."

That much, at least, was the truth, Ace silently acknowledged. All the nights that he'd watched her, he'd never seen her do anything the least bit suspicious. That didn't, however, mean she was the innocent she proclaimed to be. "We'll have to discuss that later," he said grimly and put the pickup in gear.

To Maddy's growing horror, he pulled away from the curb and headed right toward the newsstand. "What are you doing?"

"Going after a snake in the grass," he said with a bold grin as he hit the gas. "Hang on to your hat."

Chapter 2

The bullet came out of nowhere, blasting through the windshield to the accompaniment of breaking glass, and slammed into the seat just to the left of Maddy's shoulder. Wide-eyed, she stared in macabre fascination at the small, still-smoking blackened hole that ruined the previously unmarred vinyl of the seat. Two inches, she thought numbly. Two inches farther to the right, and the bullet would have buried itself in her skin. A low moan working its way up her tight throat, she whimpered and suddenly couldn't stop shaking.

"Get down, woman! Dammit, do you want to get shot or what?"

Grabbing her, he jerked her down, bringing her head level with his thigh on the bench seat. "Hell, I just had that windshield replaced," he muttered. "Bastard!"

Another shot rang out, this one hitting Ace's side mirror and shattering it. Maddy screamed and cowered closer to him, her heart jackhammering in her breast like a frightened rabbit's. Above her, she heard Ace swear, then felt him duck so that he was hovering over her protectively, and it was all she could do not to crawl right inside his skin. He would stop now and forget this wild idea about going after Mr. Lazear, she told herself frantically as she buried her head against his rock-hard thigh with a boldness that would have horrified her if she hadn't been trembling with fright. He'd pull over and let the police handle this before he got them both killed. It was the only sane thing to do.

But instead of hitting the brake, he stomped on the gas, and the pickup lurched forward like a thoroughbred out of the gate. "What are you doing?" she cried, clutching at his leg with both hands. "Trying to get us killed? You've got to stop!"

"And let your boyfriend get away?" he mocked. "I don't think so." Nobody—especially a slimy bastard like Lazear—took potshots at him and got away with it.

"I told you—he's not my boyfriend!"

"Right." Tearing his eyes away from his driving for only a second, he grinned suddenly and reached down to ease her tight grip on his thigh. "Whatever he is, you're not going to save him by cutting off the circulation to some of my more vital parts, babe. Watch the hands, okay?"

Mortified, Maddy snatched her hands back and snapped upright, a hot, painful blush sweeping up from her toes all the way to the roots of her hair. Dear God, what had she been thinking of, touching him like that? She could still feel the heat under her fingertips, the incredible strength of those hard muscles....

Abruptly realizing that her gaze had wandered to his lap, she quickly jerked her eyes to the front, her cheeks burning, and prayed he couldn't hear the mad pounding of her heart. Lord, what was wrong with her? "I'm s-sorry. I didn't mean to... I didn't realize..."

She sounded so mortified, she could have convinced Saint Peter himself that she was as pure as the driven snow, Ace thought with reluctant admiration. Hell, she almost had him convinced that he'd misjudged her. And he knew better! But she was good—he had to give her credit. Better than good. She hadn't broken character once since he'd pulled her from Cement Johnny's car, and that made her damn dangerous. A woman who could lie that easily, that completely, had her own agenda and would say anything, do anything, to get what she wanted. If she said it was raining, a smart man would run to the window and check the current conditions for himself. He'd do well to remember that.

More shots rang out, sending the woman at his side diving under the dash with a startled shriek. Dodging bullets, Ace swore and spun the wheel sharply to the right, then the left, sending the pickup careering back and forth across the street like an out-of-control Ping-Pong ball. It took all his concentration just to miss the cars parked at the curb, and by the time he lifted his gaze to the Mercedes in the distance, he caught only a glimpse of its taillights as it disappeared around the next corner.

"Damn! The son of a bitch is heading for the thruway."

Peeking over the dash, Maddy pushed the long strands of her hair out of the way. "He got away?"

Ace grinned at her hopeful tone, not a trace of humor in his hard eyes. "Don't you wish. Sorry to disappoint you, sweetheart, but it's going to take more than a few wild shots and a fast car for your boss to lose me."

He hit the gas again and reached the intersection where Sneakers had turned, taking the corner on what felt like two wheels. By the time he turned onto the freeway entrance ramp a half a block away, the speedometer was at seventy-five and climbing. His only thought to catch Lazear, he burst into the first lane...only to discover four lanes of traffic backing up in front of him.

"Watch out!"

His reflexes lightning quick, he slammed on the brakes even before Maddy gasped the frightened warning. Tires squealed and shuddered. Biting out a curse, he swerved to miss a van full of people, and almost sideswiped a little green sports car that came out of nowhere on his left. At his side, Maddy made a squeak of protest, but Ace didn't dare take his attention away from the road to reassure her that he had everything under control. "Jackass!" he yelled at the young punk as he darted around him. "Where'd you learn how to drive? A go-cart track?"

For an answer, he got an obscene hand signal that he cheerfully returned. Blaring his horn, he scowled at the cars that stretched four lanes deep all the way to the horizon. "Dammit to hell, the place looks like a damn parking lot. Where'd all these cars come from at this hour of the night?"

"The Knicks game," Maddy mumbled, rigidly clinging to the door handle at her side as the car in front of him forced him to finally come to a complete stop. "They played Orlando tonight at the Garden."

Grinding an oath between his teeth, Ace hit the steering wheel with the palm of his hand. For as far as he could see, there was nothing but wave after wave of red taillights, and in the dark, it was impossible to distinguish one car from another. Sneakers and his Mercedes could be anywhere ahead of him...or the bastard could have taken the exit immediately after he got on the freeway and be halfway to Brooklyn by now, where Ace knew he had a brother who would hide him until things cooled off.

If he wasn't going to lose the bastard completely, he had to make a choice, and damn quick, Ace thought grimly. Common sense told him to take the next exit and circle back—Lazear would have never allowed himself to get stuck in traffic—but Ace's gut was telling him that a freeway full of cars was a perfect place to hide in the dark. Going with his gut, he wrenched the steering wheel to the right, gunned the accelerator and sent them shooting onto the shoulder. "Watch out for Lazear," he told Maddy tersely. "He's got to be around here somewhere."

Sitting as stiff as a poker in her seat, braced for the collision she knew was going to happen any second, she looked at him as if he was crazy. "You've just escaped from Bellvue, haven't you? That must be it. Oh, God, why did I come into work tonight? I should have known better. The nuts always come out when there's a full moon."

Not the least insulted, her companion only chuckled. "I'm crazy, all right, but not certifiable. Hang on. We're going around this truck."

Distracted by the husky sound of his laughter, it was a moment before she realized they were racing right toward a wreck between a moving truck and a Jeep that blocked the shoulder and the entire far right lane a hundred feet in front of them. Cars, bumper to bumper, crawled around the disabled vehicles, and to the right of the shoulder there was a steep concrete embankment that jutted steeply up into an overpass.

There was nowhere to go!

"Oh, God, oh, God," she whispered when Ace showed no sign of slowing down. "We're going to die. Right here and now. And I've never done anything, never been anywhere. Oh, Lord, does Mother know where my insurance papers are? This is going to kill her...." Covering her eyes with her hands, she rocked back and forth and started to pray.

Over the frantic pounding of her heart in her ears, she heard Ace laugh softly. An instant later, she felt the pickup swing to the right and shoot up the side of the embankment. Her stomach lurched, then did a free-fall to her knees. "Yea, though I walk through the valley of death..." she chanted hoarsely.

"You can save the rest," he said dryly, humor lacing every word as he safely circled around the broken-down truck and brought the pickup safely back to the shoulder on the other side. "You're not cashing in your chips tonight. Not if I—" Suddenly spying the Mercedes darting down the next exit, he spit out a curse. "The son of a bitch is heading for the airport!"

He floorboarded the accelerator and started to shoot over from the shoulder onto the regular pavement, only to nearly lock bumpers with a BMW whose driver didn't seem inclined to let him in. When the other man blew his horn at him, he took it as a personal insult and muttered, "Yeah, yeah, I see you." He gave him a wave as if in apology, but instead of pulling back onto the shoulder, he forced his way in, just daring the guy to hit him. The other driver was still laying on his horn when Ace took the ramp to the airport.

Due to the lateness of the hour, the airport wasn't nearly as crowded as it usually was, but Lazear had the advantage of knowing where he was going—they didn't. And by the time they reached the parking area, he and his gray Mercedes were nowhere in sight. Hurriedly scanning the lot, Maddy sighed in relief. Finally, this madness was about to end! They'd lost him.

But her savior—or abductor, she hadn't decided yet which category he fit into—apparently had no intention of giving up so easily. Instead of swearing and heading back to the newsstand as she'd expected, he pulled up with a loud squeal of breaks in front of the United terminal. Ignoring the no-parking sign, he hopped out, then leaned back inside the pickup to grab Maddy by the wrist.

"C'mon," he growled, tugging at her arm. "Let's go."

Caught off guard, she instinctively stumbled out of the pickup, never thinking to protest until it was too late. "Go?" she echoed in alarm. "Go where?"

"After Lazear," he retorted, and pulled her after him into the terminal.

"But he could be anywhere!"

"He's gonna be halfway to China if you don't hurry up. C'mon! Get the lead out!"

Given half a chance, she would have pointed out that she was hurrying, but his legs were six inches longer than hers and she had to practically run to keep from being jerked along like a puppy on a leash. Breathless and growing more indignant by the second, she hurried to catch up with him, only to run into his broad back when he stopped suddenly at the first boarding area they came to. Staggering, she would have fallen if he hadn't still gripped her wrist like a wayward child's. "What—"

All his attention focused on the tall, eye-catching stewardess at the check-in desk he'd stopped in front of, he didn't spare Maddy a second glance. Quickly flashing some kind of badge, which he pulled from his pocket with practiced ease, he said, "Hi, darlin'. I could use your help if you've got a minute. I'm looking for a little weasel of a man—short, round, pock-faced. Wearing a suit and a bad toupee. He came through here a few minutes ago and would have been in a big hurry. Have you seen him?"

He spoke with a rough charm that no female with an ounce of estrogen in her blood could have failed to respond to, and the stewardess was no exception. Her blue eyes sparking with interest and a slow, inviting smile curling her mouth, she considered his description for all of two seconds and regretfully shook her head. "Sorry, not that I re-member. But it's been a hectic night, and after a while, all the passengers start to look alike." With a boldness that Maddy would have never dared emulate, she looked him up and down and made no attempt to hide the fact that she liked what she saw. "Now, if he'd have looked anything like you, I'd have noticed. Some people you just don't for-get...if you know what I mean."

There was no way not to know what she meant, Maddy thought, perversely annoyed as she watched Ace—God, could his name really be Ace?—grin like an idiot. The girl all but had Easy Pickup stamped on her forehead, and Ace was eating up her blatant flattery with a spoon. Wanting to hit him without really knowing why—she couldn't care less who he flirted with!—she wouldn't have been surprised if he'd asked the girl out then and there.

But Ace hadn't forgotten for a minute why they were there. Winking at the girl, he handed her a business card. "If you do remember seeing him, call this number, okay? It's important. Thanks, sweetheart." Tightening his grip on Maddy's wrist, he started down the concourse again, his long strides quickly making up for lost time as he headed for the next terminal. Then the next.

At each check-in counter, he quickly gave the same de-scription, asked the same questions...and received the same answers. No one had seen hide nor hair of Tommy Sneak-ers Lazear.

"Dammit, he's got to be around here somewhere," he grated half to himself. "He couldn't have just disappeared into thin air."

"Maybe he didn't take a plane at all—he could just want you to think he did," Maddy suggested as they hurried past a wide expanse of plate glass that gave a commanding view of the runways. "He could be hiding in the rest room or one of the restaurants until you leave."

Outside, a late-night flight lifted into the night sky and was quickly lost in the stars. Following it with his eyes, Ace considered her suggestion, then shook his head. "Lazear's not that clever. The second he realized we were on to him, he ran right here, and it wasn't to hide."

They reached the TWA terminal, where a crowd was lined up and waiting to check in with the lone stewardess at the check-in desk. Looking slightly harried, her smile strained, she greeted each passenger and quickly processed their paperwork. She was working as fast as she could, but Ace could practically feel lost time slipping through his fingers as he and Maddy claimed a spot at the end of the line. Checking his watch, he bit out a curse as the line slowly inched forward. At this rate, the damn sun would be coming up before he even got to question the woman, he thought irritably.

It did, in fact, take nearly ten minutes. Frustrated enough to chew lead, Ace finally stepped up to the counter, flashed his badge and quickly gave her the same description of Sneakers he'd given everyone else. "He's an ugly little guy in a hurry," he added. "He should have stood out like a sore thumb. Any chance you've seen him?"

"As a matter of fact, I have," she said promptly. "He came through about ten minutes ago with a boarding pass for a flight to Caracas, Venezuela. I wouldn't have noticed him, but he was sweating like it was a hundred degrees outside. I thought he was sick."

"All right!" He would have kissed her but there was no time. "Has he already boarded? Where is he? I've got to stop him—"

"I'm afraid that's impossible," she cut in, her professional smile sliding from her face. Nodding to the windows behind him and the plane steeply climbing into the sky, she said, "You just missed him. He's already in the air."

Ace swore, his jaw rock hard. Of all the miserable luck! Jerking out his wallet, he slapped a credit card on the counter. "When's the next flight?"

"To Caracas? Tomorrow morning at nine," she said smoothly, turning her attention to her computer monitor. "Will you need two tickets?"

"Nine!" he growled incredulously. "You've got to be kidding! Don't you have anything for tonight?"

"Just to Mexico City. And it's boarding now. If you're going to buy a ticket, you'll need to do it now, sir. We're running out of time and still have a lot of passengers to board."

Ace hesitated for all of two seconds. "Two coach seats to Mexico City," he said flatly.

At his side, Maddy choked. "*Two?* Are you out of your mind? I can't go to Mexico City with you!"

The stewardess, her hands on her computer keys, looked up sharply, her gaze bouncing from Ace to Maddy and back again. Arching an inquiring brow at Ace, she said with growing impatience, "One ticket or two, sir?"

"Two," he snapped, and shot Maddy a glare that clearly said, *Don't mess with me, lady.*

Her heart thundering in her breast, she shut her mouth . . . but only because the check-in counter was no place to argue with the man, especially when they were already drawing the eye of everyone in the place. But, Lord, it was hard! Heat climbing in her cheeks, resentment sparking in her eyes, it was all she could do not to tell him exactly what she thought of him. The man was crazy, demented. There was no other explanation. Why else would he think he could haul her out of the country without so much as a by-your-leave?

Fuming, she bit her tongue and waited with growing indignation for him to sign the credit card receipt and the stewardess to give them their boarding passes. Still holding her wrist, he didn't so much as spare her a glance as he started toward the gate with her in tow. After everything else Maddy had been through over the course of the past hour, it was too much. Digging in her heels, she stopped cold.

"What the hell—"

Brought up short, he growled a curse between his teeth and glanced back over his shoulder, his ice blue eyes locking on hers. Her palms damp, she paled, wondering too late if this was a man she wanted to cross. He had a fierce look to him, a hardness that went bone deep and told her more strongly than words that he had fought and won tougher battles than any she could ever hope to give him. But she couldn't just stand there like a wimpy mouse and let him drag her off to Mexico City.

"I can't do this," she said defiantly, throwing up her chin even as her knees started to knock. "I have a job...a sick mother—"

"Sure you do. I bet you're a regular Cinderella complete with wicked stepsisters," he drawled in that caustic way she was coming to positively detest. "And I've got the Easter bunny waiting at home for me. But we're still going to Mexico City after your friend."

"I told you, he's *not* my friend! He signs my paychecks—that's all."

"And considering what you do for him, I'm sure he pays you pretty damn well." Cavalierly assuming the matter was settled, he turned back toward the boarding ramp. "C'mon. You're holding up the plane."

Later, she couldn't say where she got the gumption. Timid by nature and the only child of a strong-willed mother, she'd given way to the more forceful personality all of her life.

Following orders was as ingrained and instinctive to her as breathing, and she was never less sure of herself or more uncomfortable than when she was forced to stand up for herself. Her stomach twisting in knots, she stood her ground and jerked against his hold on her wrist. Caught off guard, he let her go.

Surprised, her success going to her head, she met his fierce look with one of her own. "I'm not going anywhere but home," she said curtly, and turned away.

Searching for the nearest exit, she never saw him move. She took two steps, and he was there beside her in the blink of an eye. Grabbing her arm, he clicked something around her wrist.

Stunned, Maddy stared in disbelief at the handcuffs circling her wrist. "What are y-you d-doing?" she stuttered. "Get those things off me!"

For an answer, he snapped the connecting end of the cuffs around his own wrist.

"You can't do this!" she cried, clawing at the cold metal. "Do you hear me? Take it off."

"I can do any damn thing I want to," he retorted mockingly. "I've got the key, remember? Now get your little butt in gear. We've got a plane to catch."

He didn't give her time to argue, but simply hauled her after him and there wasn't a thing she could do about it. "You won't get away with this. This is America! You can't just drag me onto a plane against my will. I'll scream—"

"You do that," he taunted, unperturbed as he pulled her back to the boarding gate without sparing her a glance. "Let her rip, sweetheart. Give it your best shot. My ears can stand it if yours can."

"Ooh! You . . . you bully! You chest-beating, arrogant Neanderthal . . ." Words failing her, she would have given the last twenty dollars she had for the chance to smack him in the back of the head with something, *anything*. Then she saw the stewardess at the boarding gate arch a brow at the handcuffs stretched tight between her wrist and Ace's. "Please," she pleaded frantically, turning to her as Ace handed the woman their boarding passes. "You've got to help me! This man is kidnapping me—"

Ace chuckled, giving the other woman a smile that would have charmed the devil himself. "She's really something, isn't she?" he marveled, shaking his head as he lazily pulled his badge out of out his pocket and flashed it at the stewardess. "You wouldn't know it to look at her, but she's a lying little thief—"

"I am not! He's the liar—"

Ignoring her, Ace leaned close to the stewardess and confided, "She cons little old ladies. And slick—damn, she's smooth! She makes friends with the old folks faster than you can wink, then manages to get keys to their apartments and robs them blind when they're not looking. And she's not particular where she does it, either. Here, Canada, even Central America. She took a bundle out of Mexico City and made the mistake of leaving prints. That's how we nailed her. I'm taking her back to stand trial."

"That's a lie!" Maddy gasped, outraged. "I haven't robbed anyone—I swear it. I've never even been to Mexico City. You've got to believe me!" she told the stewardess in growing desperation. "I'm an elementary school librarian. I can prove it—I've got my school ID." She fumbled for her purse, only to remember that it had been left behind at the newsstand when she'd been kidnapped. "I—I don't s-seem to have it with me right now. But that doesn't mean I'm lying! If you'll just call security..."

It was a futile hope—she could see the sympathy she'd been able to stir in the other woman's eyes abruptly fade to skepticism and knew she'd lost her. Chilled to the bone, she wanted to hug herself, but the handcuffs chaining her to the man at her side made that impossible. "Oh, God," she whispered to herself, "what am I going to do?"

"Go to Mexico City and stand trial just like you deserve," Ace lied without an ounce of compassion. The glint in his eye warned her she couldn't win when it came to a battle of wits with him, but when he turned his attention back to the stewardess, he was wise enough not to let his triumph show. "I hate these kind of cases, but I've got a job to do. Can we board now? I'd like to get her settled before she can cause any more of a ruckus than she already has."

"Your seats are on the left at the rear," the woman said quietly, handing him their boarding passes. "You can stow whatever carryon luggage you have under the seat or in the overhead compartments."

If Maddy hadn't been so filled with despair, she would have laughed. Luggage? Couldn't the silly woman see they didn't have so much as a toothbrush between them?

But it was too late to protest, too late to scream for help. The stewardess was already turning to the passengers in line behind them, turning her back on them, on *her*. Glancing around wildly for help, she saw nothing but censoring eyes from those people who had been close enough to hear Ace's lies. Mortified, heat burning her cheeks as despair settled like a rock in her stomach, Maddy could do nothing but meekly follow Ace onto the plane and down the central aisle to their seats.

But with every step, her resentment grew. When he stopped at the second to the last row of seats in the tail and mockingly stepped aside to allow her to take the window seat, she said tightly, "You're not going to get away with this. My mother will call the police when I don't show up at home at the usual time. The second they check out the newsstand and realize I've been kidnapped, my face'll be all over the news. That stewardess will see it and remember—"

"That stewardess won't see jacksquat," he cut in coldly as he settled into the seat beside her and tried to stretch out his long legs in the cramped space. "She's on her way to Mexico City just like we are, and by the time she works the return flight, your disappearance will be old news and buried at the back of the paper. Face it, lady. You're good and caught and there's not a damn thing you can do about it."

"But I haven't done anything!"

"Yeah, that's what Lizzie Borden said, too, after she whacked her old man with that ax," he said irritably, tired of her protests. "I never met a crook yet who didn't claim to be as innocent as a newborn baby, so just give it a rest, okay? I've got you and I'm not letting you go until I get my hands on Sneakers."

"Fine," she retorted just as irritably. "You're the one who's going to get sued for false arrest, not me."

A cold silence fell between them then that was broken only by the flight attendant as she welcomed everyone aboard and began her standard speech on emergency procedures. Shifting several times to find a more comfortable position, Ace cursed as his knees slammed into the back of the seat in front of him. "I swear they make these seats for midgets!" he muttered. "There's no leg room at all. I can't even unlock my knees. Damn! This is the last time I fly coach!"

If he expected any sympathy from Maddy, he could have saved his breath. Staring out the window, her seat belt already snug across her lap, her seat in the upright position for takeoff, she stared pointedly out the window, stiffly ignoring him, animosity rolling off her in waves as the plane raced down the runway and lifted steeply into the air.

Perversely bothered by her attitude, he scowled at the back of her head, noting, without meaning to, the slenderness of her neck, the soft tendrils of mouse brown hair that had escaped their confinement to tickle the lily white skin of her nape. She looked so damn fragile....

The thought caught him off guard, irritating him no end. The lady might look as if she'd blow away in a strong breeze, but appearances were deceptive. She hung around with thugs, and that made her a lot tougher than she looked. So what if she turned up that little nose of hers and gave him the silent treatment? They weren't exactly going on vacation together. And he didn't like chatty females, anyway.

Satisfied that he'd put her firmly in her place, he jammed his seat back and closed his eyes with a sigh. Three hours, he thought tiredly. If he could just catch three hours of uninterrupted sleep, he could go the next thirty-six if he had to to catch Sneakers.

Then he heard her sob.

It was only a faint whimper, quickly stifled, but he heard it, nonetheless. Stiffening, he told himself not to be a fool. He'd witnessed the lady's acting abilities firsthand; crying on cue would be a piece of cake for her. Let her try that old trick on somebody else—he wasn't buying it.

But as much as he tried to ignore her, he just couldn't. She didn't make another sound, but she didn't have to. Opening one eye, Ace squinted at her, scowling. She just sat there, huddled against the window, like some kind of waif cowering from a storm in a deserted building. Occasionally she swiped at the silent tears that trickled down her pale cheeks, but other than that, she didn't move so much as an eyelash. And what made it worse was that she didn't even seem to expect a response, let alone sympathy from him or anyone else. Staring blindly out the window at the night, she didn't make eye contact with anyone.

If this was a guilt trick, it was a dandy. Ace felt something twist in his gut, something he had no business feeling for her, and he didn't know which he wanted to do more—hug her and comfort her or paddle her backside. The latter would have been no more than she deserved, and the former... Hell, he didn't even want to think about it. Snarling a curse, he reached into his pocket and pulled out a clean handkerchief. "Here," he said gruffly. "If you're going to start a flood in here, at least mop up after yourself."

"I'm not crying." She sniffed. Still stubbornly presenting him the back of her head, she blindly reached for the handkerchief, murmuring a soft, husky, "Thank you," when he placed it in her hand.

His expression impassive, Ace refused to be taken in by the poor-little-girl act. But she looked so pathetic, he felt like a damn heel. Frowning, he asked dryly, "What exactly are you *not* crying about, if I may ask?"

It was, apparently, the wrong question to ask. She tried to answer, only to swallow thickly. Swiping at her drenched eyes, she folded in on herself like a deck of cards. "Everything!" she choked in what was very nearly a soft wail. "I h-have no clothes, no passport. I don't even have my purse—"

"You don't need it. I'll take care of whatever you need."

"But what about my mother? She doesn't have a clue where I am and she'll be so worried. Who's going to take care of her? She's recovering from a broken hip and can hardly get around. She needs help. And there's nobody but me to look after her."

Ace scowled at her, determined to believe that this was just another part of the act. But if the lady was acting, she had what it took to make it on Broadway. Did she really have a sick mother at home? Doubts plagued him, annoying the hell out of him. She was probably playing him like a damn violin, but it was the possibility that she wasn't that had him muttering a curse and signalling the stewardess for a phone.

"What's your address?" he asked Maddy curtly when he was brought a cellular. When she gave it to him, he quickly punched out a number, waited all of five seconds, then, without bothering to identify himself, repeated the address to someone on the other end of the line. "Check out the mother and make sure she's okay," he said, then hung up and returned the phone to the stewardess.

He told himself he didn't want an innocent woman's poor health on his conscience and he was just covering his bases. But when he returned his attention to the woman at his side and found her looking at him as if she'd like to throw herself into his arms in gratitude, it wasn't the lady's mother he was thinking of. Alarm bells clanging in his head, he said curtly, "There. Your mother's taken care of, so quit your bawling and go to sleep. Once we reach Caracas, we won't stop until we catch up with that slimeball of a boss of yours, so you'd better get some rest while the gettin's good. Tomorrow's going to be a long day." The warning given, he laid his head back and closed his eyes. Within seconds, he was softly snoring.

Unable to believe he could fall asleep so quickly, Maddy turned to stare at him suspiciously, but there was no doubt that the man was out like a light. His breathing was slow and even, his lips slightly parted, his face softened by sleep in a way she had yet to see when he was awake. Fascinated, she knew she should have turned away, but her eyes seemed to have a will of their own when it came to this man.

Who was he? *What* was he? There was no question that he was a man of authority—but that didn't necessarily mean he was on the right side of the law. For all she knew, he could be as bad as that horrible man who had kidnapped her from the newsstand. But she didn't think so.

A dream, she thought shakily. This had to be some kind of weird, twisted dream. *He* had to be a dream. But as much as she wanted to cling to that explanation like a pillow and float back to wakefulness in her own bed, she knew he was real. And that only made the situation that much more bizarre. Because men like Ace were totally outside the realm of her experience.

Without an ounce of self-pity, she silently acknowledged that the few tall, good-looking, assertive types who strayed by accident into her world never stayed long. They looked through her or past her, never at her, simply because she was as different from them as night was from day. Her face was quite ordinary, her figure much less than voluptuous. To put it frankly, she hardly had the kind of beauty that was going to stop traffic, let alone a good-looking man.

Once that had bothered her. But as her mother had wisely pointed out, she could never be anything but a plain daisy in a world full of much fancier hothouse roses, and trying to change what she was would only make her miserable.

Practical all the way down to her white cotton underwear, Maddy had recognized the truth when she heard it and accepted the inevitable. Other women had hot dates and passionate relationships, not her. A plain, thirty-four-year-old spinster, she was an anachronism, the last of her kind born into the wrong era, the only virgin left in a freewheeling, moral-free world.

And there was nothing wrong with that. She had her own little niche, and if her life was steady and uneventful, she reasoned that that was better than rocky and turbulent. And while she might long for adventure, that was for the bold at heart, which was something she could never, ever be. But there were times, like now as her gaze lingered on the tempting contours of Ace's mouth, when she wondered just what she was missing.

Chapter 3

"Time to rise and shine, Sleeping Beauty," a husky male voice murmured teasingly in her ear, tickling her. "Naptime's over."

Safely wrapped in the dark, comforting warmth of slumber, Maddy groaned, a frown rippling across her brow as she resisted the pull of that deep, intoxicating voice. No, she thought sluggishly. She didn't want to wake up, not yet. It was too early, still dark out—she could feel it in her aching bones. And she was so comfortable, more relaxed than she could ever remember being. If she could just lay here a little longer...

Burrowing into her pillow, she mumbled, "In a minute... just a minute. S'tired."

Her hard pillow shifted under her cheek as a soft chuckle rumbled up from somewhere underneath her shoulder. "Suit yourself. Mexico City's dead ahead and we'll be landing any minute. It's no skin off my back if the stewardess finds you draped all over me like a heat rash."

Still more than half-asleep and drifting deeper into much-needed oblivion, Maddy hardly heard the amused taunt. Then the words registered. Her memory returned with a jolt, recognition of *that* voice hitting her like a sudden, unexpected dousing of ice water. Her eyes flew open, only to widen in horror. She'd unconsciously moved in her sleep and now lay with her cheek comfortably cushioned on Ace's shoulder. Her mouth mere inches from his, she was eye to eye with him, caught in the trap of his wicked blue gaze, so close that every breath she took mingled with his.

His grin devilish, he looked pointedly at where her shackled hand rested against his thigh. "If I'd known you were going to sleep in my lap, I'd have stayed awake to enjoy it. Was it good for you, sweetheart?"

"Oh, God!" Flustered, horrified, she jerked upright, scooting as far away from him as the confines of her seat and the handcuffs would allow. It wasn't nearly far enough. Sure he could hear the thundering of her heart, she said tartly, "Don't flatter yourself. I didn't know what I was doing."

"And here I thought you couldn't keep your hands off me," he quipped, chuckling. "I'm crushed."

She shot him a withering look that would have been much more effective if she hadn't had to fight the sudden urge to smile. Darn the man, he was incorrigible. And enjoying every second of her discomfort. Against her will and all the dictates of common sense, she found herself liking him, and that worried her more than she wanted to admit. He'd virtually kidnapped her, for heaven's sake! And what did she know about him, anyway? He'd come charging to her rescue from out of nowhere, flashing a badge and claiming to be one of the good guys. But good guys had last names and didn't drag innocent women off in the middle of the night to Mexico in handcuffs after lying to a stewardess. And they always answered to someone. From what she'd seen so far, Ace Whatever-his-name-was didn't answer to anyone but himself.

And that, more than anything, scared the stuffing out of her. She only had his word that he was who he said he was... and the flash of a badge she had yet to get a good look at. For all she knew, he could be the real villain of this wild adventure. He'd never actually said he was a law enforcement officer, and in the Ace MacKenzie books, the characters who were smooth and charming were usually rotten all the way through to the core. Dear God, what had she gotten herself into?

She had to get away.

Panic and urgency roiled in her stomach at the thought, each fighting for dominance. Any minute now they were going to be landing in Mexico and she might only have one shot at making a break for it. He couldn't keep her hand-cuffed forever—he'd have to release her at least long enough to go to the bathroom. When he did, she had to be ready.

Then... she paled, stricken. What *was* she going to do then? She had no money, no clothes but the ones on her back, and the only Spanish she spoke was taco and burrito. She couldn't buy herself a Coke, let alone airfare home. And even if she could somehow come up with a ticket, they were never going to let her back in the country without some form of identification.

Wracking her brain for a plan, she still didn't have a clue what she was going to do when the stewardess walked down the center aisle, checking to make sure everyone was buckled up and had their seat backs in the upright position. Then it was too late. The landing gear came down, the captain thanked everyone for flying with them and, within a few short minutes, they were safe on the ground again and everyone was jostling shoulders in their hurry to deplane.

If it hadn't been for the handcuff around her wrist, Maddy would have found a way to lose Ace then. But even when the crowd was at its thickest and other passengers tried to crowd between them, she couldn't move without being aware of the fact that he was attached to the other end of her arm. Never more than a step away from her, he was as tenacious as her own shadow.

There was, however, still customs to get through once they finally burst free of the plane. But the hope that lifted her spirits died a quick death as Ace greeted the agents in what sounded like fluent Spanish and flashed that infuriating little badge of his before presenting his passport. She didn't have a clue what he said to the Mexican officials, but from the way they looked her over with amused interest and knowing eyes, then waved her and Ace through without even bothering to look at Ace's paperwork, she knew she'd rather not know.

Left with no choice but to accompany him down the crowded concourse, she winced when a trio of nuns passed them and noted the handcuffs shackling her to Ace. "Can't you take those things off now?" she whispered, crowding closer so that the sleeve of his jacket helped hide the offending bracelet when the nuns looked at her askance. "They've served their purpose—you got me here. And it's not like I can go anywhere without you," she reminded him with a trace of bitterness. "I haven't got two pennies to rub together, let alone any pesos."

She had a point, but Ace was a cautious man, especially when it came to trusting women. "In a minute," he hedged, and ushered her over to the ticket counter of a small commuter airlines that he knew from his frequent trips to Mexico in the past was, all things considered, fairly reliable. Quickly greeting the sleepy clerk, he learned that the next flight to Caracas was scheduled to leave in two and a half hours, which suited his purposes perfectly. Whipping out his credit card, he booked him and Maddy each a seat.

"Oh, God, don't tell me we're getting right back on another plane." She groaned when the clerk handed him the tickets. "It's the middle of the night!"

"Not quite," he chuckled, leading her farther down the concourse once he'd tucked the tickets into the inside pocket of his jacket. "We've got more than a two-hour layover, so it'll be dawn before we get out of here. If we're lucky, it'll be enough."

Her steps decidedly unwilling, she eyed him warily. "Enough for what?"

Amused by her suspicions, he grinned down at her. "Did anyone ever tell you you have a suspicious mind?"

"After what I've been through over the past eight hours, I figure I've got a right." Her eyes held steady on his, she repeated, "Enough for what?"

"To do a little shopping. Unless you want to wear these same clothes for the next week or so."

"What? I can't be gone a week!"

His grin turned mocking. "I don't remember asking your preference one way or the other, baby doll. In case you hadn't noticed, you gave up all rights to a say-so the day you hooked up with Sneakers." Coming to a stop in front of one of the airport's retail shops that was still open despite the lateness of the hour, he studied the contents of the display window and nodded. "This looks like it could have what we'll need. Let's check it out."

The shop was small and intimate, the kind of place that would have made most men distinctively uncomfortable. Decorated with antiques and scented with potpourri, it looked like a woman's boudoir from another era. Dainty lace and satin lingerie was tastefully displayed to draw the eye and the touch, and the open doors of old-fashioned armoires revealed clothes that were designed for women who enjoyed their own femininity. Fine cotton, linen, silk. For those with discriminating taste, it was a shop that seemed to have it all.

And, to Maddy's dismay, Ace was as sure of himself in the feminine atmosphere as if he were in a hardware store. Quickly choosing several bras and pairs of panties for her, he then moved to the armoires. With the eye of a man who knew what he was doing, he picked out designer shorts and slacks and several scoop-necked tops, then handed everything to the clerk, who was eagerly chattering to him in Spanish, her smile flashing broadly as she clutched the intended purchases to her breasts and hurried to the cash register.

Not once in the entire procedure did either of them spare Maddy so much as a glance!

Stunned, she couldn't believe it. He was actually buying her clothes without even bothering to ask her if he'd chosen the right size, let alone something she liked. Talk about nerve! She'd known the man had more than his fair share of arrogance, but this was incredible!

Cocking her head to the side, she studied him through narrowed eyes. "Don't you think you'd better try those things on first? They look a little small."

In the process of signing the credit card receipt, he looked up and couldn't miss the annoyance in her eyes. His lips started to twitch. "Actually, I thought they'd look better on you than me. They're not really my color."

"Oh, really? And how do you know they'll fit me?"

It was the wrong question to ask a man who had made it his business over the years to know just about everything there was to know about women. Picking up a pair of panties and one of the lacy bras that the clerk had laid on the counter to ring up for him, he handed them to Maddy without a word, a challenging grin gleaming in his eyes.

She had no choice but to take them. But as her gaze dropped to the intimate items that looks so delicate against his strong, tanned fingers, she had a sudden, unbidden image of those same hands brushing over her with devastating care, slowly caressing her, heating her skin inch by inch until she melted like hot wax.

"Maddy?"

Her name on his lips dragging her back to her surroundings, she looked up to find him watching her with a crooked smile on his lips. Hot color flooded her cheeks. Wishing she'd never started this, she jerked the underwear from him and almost dropped the delicate pieces in the process. Mortified, she caught them before they fell, discreetly checking the size as she did so. "These couldn't possibly be right..." she began.

But not only were they right, they were perfect. And sheerer than anything she'd ever worn in her life.

Chagrined, she would have given anything to have a hole to crawl into at that moment. Underwear, *her* underwear, wasn't something she discussed with any man, especially this one. He had a cockiness about him, a sureness that was, she hated to admit, vastly appealing. Obviously, he knew women—the scent and size and feel of brunettes and blondes and everything in between. And that included her. Just thinking about him sizing her up, knowing what she looked like under her clothes, made her heart do funny things in her breast.

"I'd rather pick out my own clothes, if you don't mind," she said stiffly. "These aren't my style."

"Actually, I do mind," he replied as he motioned for the clerk to bag the items. "We don't have time to run all over Mexico City when these'll do perfectly well." The sack of new clothes in one hand, her handcuffed wrist in the other, he hustled her out of the boutique and into the beauty shop next door.

Stuffing her purchases into her arms, he reached for a small key in his pocket and unlocked the handcuffs. Maddy couldn't have been more surprised if he'd slung her over his shoulder and bodily carried her off down the concourse. "What are you doing?"

"Leaving you—"

"What? No! You can't drag me all this way and just leave me here! How am I going to get home? I have no money, no—"

"You don't need any money. I told you I'd take care of everything."

"But you're leaving me!"

"Only to get something done to your hair while I buy some clothes for myself," he replied in a voice that was as calm and reasonable as hers was frantic. "Sneakers is no fool. He knows I'm on his tail and you're with me. If he decides to send someone back for us, I plan to make sure he has a hard time recognizing us."

Not giving her time to protest further, he turned to the beautician, who was patiently watching the exchange between them and didn't appear to understand a word they said. "We want a complete makeover," he told the woman in Spanish. "Do what you have to with her hair—I don't want her own mother to recognize her when you get through with her."

"*Sí, señor.*" Nodding eagerly, the stylist lifted Maddy's long silky tresses consideringly. Chattering in growing excitement, she told her exactly what she was going to do to her as she urged her to the back of the salon.

"Ace?" Caught in the woman's friendly but firm grip, Maddy looked wildly over her shoulder for help. "What is she saying? What's she going to do to me?"

"Just take a little off the ends," he lied, grinning. "Relax. You won't feel a thing."

Feeling like a prisoner standing before the firing squad, Maddy stared at the mirror on the wall and saw nothing but a blurred image of herself that scared her to death. What was the silly woman doing to her? She could feel her cutting her hair at the nape, feel the weight that had been with her for as long as she could remember slowly being lifted from her shoulders, leaving her feeling naked and exposed.

Where was Ace? She couldn't believe he'd left her like this, at this woman's mercy, when he knew she couldn't speak a word of Spanish. And, as usual, he hadn't even bothered to give her a choice in the matter, she thought resentfully. She didn't want her hair cut. She liked it long— long and straight so that she could pull it back with a clasp and not worry about it. If anyone would have taken the time to ask her, she would have told them that it was too fine for a shorter style, too wispy and flyaway to ever hold a set.

"Please," she said desperately, lifting her fingers to her bare nape. "This isn't going to work...."

The beautician might not have been able to understand her words, but the language of panic was universal the world over. Smiling, she patted her shoulder and murmured reassurances in a soft, soothing voice. And all the while, she continued to cut steadily away until every last strand was cut and layered and the longest hair on her head barely reached her shoulder.

And she didn't stop there. With mounting dread, Maddy watched her study her from all directions, fingering the texture of her hair between her fingers, studying it with who knew what kind of wild ideas bouncing around in her head. When she reached for a tray of perm rods from the shelf behind her, Maddy stiffened in alarm. "I think you'd better wait till Ace comes back...."

For an answer, the woman parted her hair on one side and began to wind it on the curlers. As helpless as a fly caught in a spider's web, Maddy could do nothing but sit there and watch, praying that she wouldn't be bald by the time she got out of there.

The men's clothing shop that Ace finally discovered in the airport's shopping area didn't have nearly the selection that the women's did. Catering mostly to businessmen, it offered an assortment of ties and silk boxers, as well as standard dress shirts that he knew would be highly uncomfortable where he was going. Ignoring them, he headed straight for the sales rack at the back of the shop. There he found a pair of khaki pants in his size and a few cheap T-shirts. It was the brightly colored cotton shirts he added to the pile, though, that was going to draw people's eyes to his clothes instead of his face. Wild and crazy, they were the kind of shirts that tourists wore on fishing trips and in the tropics and wouldn't be caught dead in at home.

Pulling out his charge card, Ace grinned, picturing Maddy's expression when she saw what he'd bought. The hokey shirts weren't his usual style—in his line of work blending into the woodwork was a necessity, so he invariably wore black T-shirts and jeans that wouldn't draw attention to his presence and allow him to all but disappear in plain sight. Sneakers, however, would be looking for a man in dark clothes who clung to the shadows and was accompanied by a plain-Jane woman with long, fine hair who dressed like an old maid. He would never think to ask about a wildly dressed tourist escorting a long-legged, short-haired lady in shorts and T-shirts.

Just imagining her expression when she realized he'd told the stylist to cut her hair made him chuckle. She was going to be madder than a wet hen. She'd get all stiff and prickly in that way she did whenever she was annoyed, then give him a look that could freeze his underwear. The same one that just dared him to stir her up a little. If the lady learned nothing else during their time together, she'd figure out soon enough that he was a man who couldn't resist a dare.

A crooked grin splitting his face as he anticipated the coming confrontation, he hurried toward the beauty salon, his thoughts already jumping ahead to the other things he had to do before they caught their flight to Caracas. There wasn't much he could do about his own hair, but a hat would help conceal his face. And Maddy was blind as a bat without her glasses. He'd have to make some calls and get her some of those throwaway contacts or he'd have to lead her around by the hand all the way to Venezuela and back. Josh Presley might be able to help with that. He'd always been a resourceful son of a bitch.

Stepping into the salon, he borrowed the phone from the receptionist and punched out Josh's number, hardly noticing his surroundings as he wondered how he was going to talk his old friend into leaving his bed—and the blonde who was invariably in it with him—to do him a major favor in the middle of the night. He'd remind him of that time in La Paz when he saved his butt from that perverted little general who liked—

"This better be damn good."

A slow grin sliding across his face at Josh's raspy growl, he laughed. "Caught you at a bad time, did I? Tough. Get your pants on, Presley. I need your help."

For a moment, there was nothing but surprised silence, then a pleased chuckle. "Hey, amigo, where the hell are you? And what do you mean you need my help?" he demanded suspiciously. "The last time I came to your rescue, I spent two months in traction."

"*You* came to *my* rescue? The way I remember it, you had your back to a cliff and a dozen Uzis aimed right at your gut. If I hadn't taken you over that cliff, you'd be pushing up daisies right now."

A snort told him what his friend thought of his version of the story. "All right, let's hear it. What do you need?"

"I've got a plane to catch in an hour and I've got an errand for you to run." He told him what he needed, then made arrangements to meet him at the information desk. "Don't be late, man. I can't wait for you."

"Twenty minutes," Josh promised. "I'm already on my way."

Ace hung up as excited feminine chatter from the back of the shop caught his attention. Glancing up, he immediately spied the stylist he'd left Maddy with grinning broadly at the woman before her in the chair. A woman who, he thought in shock, was Maddy. Dear God, what had she done to herself?

He'd expected her hair to be shorter, of course—he'd told the stylist not to hold back with the scissors—but he hadn't expected the woman to chop it all off, either. The long mousy mane that had once trailed halfway down her back now barely brushed her chin and had been permed into short, flirty, becoming curls. Curls that were, unless his eyes were playing tricks on him, now reddish brown!

Stunned, Ace couldn't take his eyes from her. She'd put some kind of rinse on her hair, something that brought out the reddish highlights that he hadn't even realized were hidden in the dull brown mop. And the color looked damned good on her. In fact, she was more than a little pretty.

The thought snuck up on him unaware, surprising him. Frowning, he searched her face, telling himself it was a trick of the light and his imagination. A new hairstyle and rinse couldn't change the fact that she was still the same brown wren he'd pulled from Cement Johnny's car. If the angular lines of her face appeared softer, more delicate, it was only because the short curls that framed her features were such a stark change from her previous style. Sure she looked better. Considering how old-fashioned and plain her hair had been before, anything would be an improvement.

That didn't mean he was attracted to her, he assured himself as he started toward her. She was a job to him, nothing more. Someone he'd had to bring along because he'd had no other choice. Miss America beautiful, or ugly as a mud fence, it made no difference to him. He still didn't trust her and looked forward to the day he could wash his hands of her and turn her over to someone else.

In the meantime, however, he had to deal with her. Stepping up behind her, he studied her as she stared at her reflected image in wonder. He wanted to believe that it was an act just for his benefit, but she hadn't taken her eyes from the mirror since he'd walked in the door. Like a young girl who had just discovered she'd turned into a fairy princess overnight, she touched her hair, the nape of her neck, the sassy curls that brushed her ears and cheeks.

Perversely irritated by the soft, awed smile that played around the corners of her mouth, he said, "Okay, glamor queen, time to cut and run. The party's over."

"Ace . . ." Whirling in her chair, she jumped up, her eyes alight with happiness. "You've got to give this wonderful woman an incredible tip! Look what she's done to my hair! Isn't it great? I never knew—"

"Yeah, yeah," he said dismissingly as he jerked his credit card from his wallet and handed it to the stylist. "It's a work of art. Now let's get out of here. We're running out of time."

A blind man couldn't have missed the hurt that flared in her eyes, but dammit, what was a man supposed to do? They weren't best buddies—he didn't want to be someone she turned to when she was excited or happy or sad. The brutal truth was he didn't want to be anything to her or any other woman. They'd been thrown together by chance and now had to endure each other's company by necessity, and that alone created a bonding he intended to avoid like the plague.

Because of Sandra. His ex-wife. The woman he had at one time trusted with his life. The same woman who had an affair with his best friend and only came to him with the news because she was pregnant and he'd been gone too long on an assignment for her to claim the baby as his.

The old familiar rage that always stirred to life whenever he thought of her betrayal lodged like a ball of ice in his gut. Even after she'd stabbed him in the back, he would have probably found a way to forgive her if she'd come to him in tears and openly admitted she'd made a mistake. Instead, she'd blamed him for her infidelity! Because he was always off somewhere playing James Bond, it was his fault that she turned to another man out of loneliness. If he'd been home like he should have been, she'd claimed, nothing would have ever happened.

God, what a fool he'd been! All those times when it had torn him apart to leave her, he'd never once worried about what she was doing while he was gone. Like a naive idiot, he'd trusted her—and got his teeth kicked in for it.

Never again, he promised himself, his blue eyes hard and uncompromising. He'd sworn the day she came to him with the truth that he would never again leave himself open for that kind of betrayal, and for the past three years, he'd stood firm by that vow. Oh, there'd been women—he wasn't a monk—but he always kept things light and steered clear of ladies on the wrong side of thirty. It wasn't that he had a thing for sweet young things, it was just that the older a woman got, the louder her biological clock ticked. And the louder her clock ticked, the more she fantasized about the man of her dreams riding to her rescue while she still had time to conceive a child.

And that was something he wanted no part of, especially with a woman like Maddy. She might or might not be partners in crime with Sneakers, and that didn't begin to describe the complexities of the lady. For weeks now, he'd watched her from across the street from the newsstand, and night after night, she'd had her nose stuck in a book—an Ace Mackenzie book. And that told him everything he needed to know about the lady. She was a romantic, a lonely woman who looked for excitement and a man in the pages of a book. As far as he was concerned, that spelled trouble... *big* trouble.

Muttering a curse under his breath, he signed the credit slip after adding a generous tip for the stylist, then stuffed the receipt in his pocket. Without a word, he took Maddy's elbow to escort her out into the concourse.

Blinking back stupid, foolish tears, Maddy promised herself she wouldn't let him make her cry. The man was a cretin, a caveman with the sensitivity of a rock. In a matter of hours, he'd turned her life upside down and changed her so that she didn't even recognize herself anymore. Before he'd walked into the salon, she hadn't been able to stop staring at the pretty stranger in the mirror. She knew it was her, of course, but it was a her she'd never seen before. Her eyes looked bigger, her cheeks more sculptured, her eyes darker.

The new Maddy Lawrence would never be described as plain and ordinary, and that thrilled and amazed and petrified her. Suddenly, she didn't know herself. She didn't know this woman who looked at herself with Ace's eyes and wondered if he thought she was pretty. He made her feel . . . things. Things she'd never felt before. Things she didn't know how to deal with. Things that made her heart race and her palms sweat with panic. Things that made her want to run.

"I want to go home."

He heard her—she knew he did—but he just kept on walking, his grip on her elbow hurrying her along until it was all she could do to keep up with his long legs. Frowning, she repeated loudly, "I want to go home! Don't pretend you didn't hear me—I know you did—"

"Half the people in the place heard you," he retorted in a voice pitched deliberately low. His grip tightening on her elbow, he didn't so much as check his stride. "Quit acting like a child. You're not going anywhere until we find Sneakers."

"Yes, I am. I'm going home! Just stick me on the first flight out of here—I don't care where it's going as long as it's back to the States. I'll worry about getting a connecting flight to New York later."

"With what? Your looks? In case you've forgotten, sweetheart, you haven't got two cents."

"But you do. You could book everything from here and pay for it—"

"I could but I'm not going to," he said flatly. "Not until we find Sneakers."

He was so stubborn, Maddy wanted to scream. But she didn't, of course. For all of her life, her mother had drilled self-control and manners into her, and she cringed just at the thought of calling attention to herself. "But why?" she asked in bewilderment. "Why are you doing this to me? I told you I don't know anything about Mr. Lazear's illegal activities. Why can't you just let me go?"

For a minute, she thought he wasn't even going to bother to answer her. His jaw rigid, he didn't look at her as he hustled her down the concourse, the matter apparently settled as far as he was concerned. Then, just when she was beginning to think that she was dealing with a man who didn't have an ounce of compassion in that rock-hard body of his, he pulled her to a stop at the information booth, which was deserted at that hour of the morning. His sharp, knowing eyes searching hers, he said quietly, "It's not that simple. Don't you understand? If you really are an innocent in all this—and that's still a big *if* as far as I'm concerned—then there's no way I can let you go."

"But I don't know anything!" she cried. "I told you—"

"I know what you told me," he said patiently. "But you saw Sneakers stuffing stolen jewelry from that hidden warehouse in his pockets the same as I did. That makes you a witness, honey. And Sneakers doesn't like witnesses who can put him away for ten to twenty."

Maddy paled. "What are you saying? That he'd try to shut me up before I can talk to the authorities?"

"The man's got an international fencing operation set up behind that newsstand. Do you really think he's going to just sit back and let you expose that?"

"But he's on his way to Caracas. He doesn't know we're on his trail."

At any other time, Ace would have laughed at her naiveté, but if she was for real, that kind of innocence could get her killed. "Wanna bet? Men like Lazear don't leave anything to chance, Maddy. He knows we know about his setup at the newsstand—we saw him with the goods in his hands. For no other reason than that, he's got to eliminate us. You can bet that new hairdo of yours that the minute his plane was in the air, he was on the phone to one of his thugs ordering a couple of hits. If I let you go off by yourself, you'll never make it home alive."

"Then go with me," she pleaded. "You don't have to go after Mr. Lazear yourself. Just call the authorities in Venezuela and have them pick him up at the airport."

"Dammit, it's not that simple. We're not talking about a law-abiding citizen who crosses all his *t*'s and dots his *i*'s and always plays by the rules. He's a slippery son of a bitch who greases palms and pulls strings everywhere he goes. He won't wait for the police—hell, he won't even wait for customs. He'll slip out the back way and just disappear before anyone even knows he's there."

"And you're going after him."

It was a statement, an accusation, one that he didn't bother to deny. "You're damn right I'm going after him. He's headed for Carlos Barrera's place in the jungles—"

"Carlos Barrera!" the man who walked up behind them echoed in disbelief. "*Madre de Dios,* amigo, are you sure you know what you're doing? Nobody messes with Barrera."

His rough-hewn face breaking into a slow smile, Ace pivoted, his hand already extended for an affectionate slap of his friend's shoulder. "I was beginning to wonder if you were going to show your ugly mug. What took you so long?"

Josh gave him a pained look. "Not everything can be done at the snap of *your* fingers, my friend. Some tasks take more than a phone call. So are you going to introduce me to the pretty lady or do I have to do it myself?"

The smile he shot Maddy was boyish and wicked and guaranteed to steal a woman's heart on the spot. Ace had seen his friend turn it on unsuspecting females a hundred times before, always with phenomenal success. But he'd always gone after sophisticated blondes, gorgeous women who knew the score and were as experienced as Josh was himself. In no way, shape or form did that describe Maddy. Surely the idiot could see that. She was blushing, for God's sake!

Bristling, fighting an inexplicable urge to deck his friend, he gave Josh a frown that warned him to back off...or else. "Maddy, this joker is Josh." The amenities taken care of, he growled, "Did you get it?"

Rolling his eyes, Josh turned to Maddy with a grin. "Don't mind him. The man was born a grouch. Nice to meet you, Maddy. I believe these must be for you."

"Me?" Surprised, Maddy gingerly took the small brown paper bag and looked at it as if she expected a snake to jump out of it any second. "What is it?"

"Disposable contacts," he said. "Ace said you lost your glasses."

"Yes, I did. But how in the world did you manage to get these at this hour of the morning?"

Grinning, he winked. "I have my sources. It's safer for you if you don't know what they are. You ever had contacts before?" At the shake of her head, his eyes started to dance. "I made sure instructions in English were included, but maybe I should help you put them in—"

"I'm sure she can figure it out by herself," Ace said curtly, glaring at him. Nodding toward the rest rooms, which were almost directly across the concourse from them, he told Maddy, "You can put them in in there. Holler if you have a problem."

Unable to believe that he'd called out a friend at that hour of the morning just to get her contacts, she stared at him in wonder, a smile she couldn't contain stretching across her face as she clutched the bag to her as if it were more precious than diamonds. "I'll be right back," she promised breathlessly, and hurried away.

"She's not your usual style," Josh said into the silence left by her leave-taking. "You're not serious about going after Barrera, are you? And taking her with you? Are you crazy, man?"

"I haven't got much choice," he said disgustedly. In a few short, concise words, he gave him the facts of the case. "The most expensive thing Lazear made off with was a diamond belly-button ring that was once worn by Cleopatra herself, and I can only think of one man in this part of the world who would have both the interest and money to buy it."

"Barrera," Josh spit out in distaste.

"Exactly. And Lazear can't get to him fast enough. I've got to stop him before he does."

"Or before Barrera kills him for invading his space without an invitation." Shaking his head over the task his friend had set himself, he said, "Damn, amigo, are you sure you want to do this? Tracking someone in the jungle is a tough job even for you. But to take a woman with you! Are you out of your mind? She's a city girl, isn't she? She's going to freak the first time she sees a snake."

"Then she'll just have to freak," Ace retorted. "Because I don't have time to take her home. I've got to catch up with Sneakers before he gets behind the walls of Barrera's jungle fortress or that ring will never be seen again."

Chapter 4

By the time they reached Caracas, it was nearly lunchtime and the airport was bustling with activity. Bleary-eyed, unused to the contacts, Maddy followed Ace as he wove his way through the traffic crowding the concourse, her hands clutching at the belt loop of his new khakis under the tail of the outrageous Hawaiian-style shirt that stretched across his broad back. She, too, wore new clothes—jeans shorts that left her legs bare and a scooped-neck aqua T-shirt that was too low, too tight, too...sexy.

Resisting the urge to tug at the neckline, she was hit from all sides by a mixture of languages. Spanish, something that she felt sure must be an Indian dialect and a smattering of broken English that her tired ears simply refused to comprehend. It was wonderful and different, a kaleidoscope of color, foreign sounds and exotic smells. Normally, Maddy would have been looking everywhere at once, committing it all to memory, hoarding the images for a lonely rainy day. But she was just too tired. She'd gotten just enough of a catnap on the plane to make her sick with exhaustion, and all she wanted to do was find someplace out of the flow of traffic and lay down. Just for a minute.

Ace, however, showed no signs of slowing down. His eyes sharp and clear, his strides quick, he forged through the crowd like a man on a mission, apparently not the least affected by the time zones they'd traversed or the minuscule bits of sleep he'd managed to grab over the course of the long night and morning. If anything, he seemed to be stronger and more alert than ever, never once dropping his guard as he led her outside to a taxi stand. If she hadn't been so tired, Maddy would have found his whole demeanor extremely irritating. Did the man never run out of gas?

He hailed a cab with a sharp whistle, then gave the driver directions in a short spat of Spanish that might as well have been Greek for all it told Maddy. Tiredly, she slumped in her seat. "Where are we going?"

"Somewhere a cockroach like Lazear would feel right at home. The slums."

Her brain fuzzy, Maddy frowned, trying to find the logic in that, but at the moment she couldn't have added two plus two. "Why would he go there? I thought this Barrera character he's trying to find lives in the jungle."

"He does, but Barrera's not going to be sitting in plain sight waiting for him. He's the head of one of the world's largest drug cartels, and rumor has it he's got a regular fortress hidden in the rain forest somewhere, complete with his own army of mercenaries. Sneakers'll never find it by himself, and no legitimate guide who values his skin will go anywhere near the place."

Stretching out his long legs, he appeared relaxed beside her, but he automatically noted every turn the cabby made as they left the airport on the outskirts of town and traveled down the wide boulevards of the suburbs, then narrower streets where the houses were smaller. The area was still respectable, but all too quickly, the manicured yard of Caracas's middle class gave way to a maze of twisting, rutted streets that were crowded with run-down shacks that should have been bulldozed down years ago.

Ace didn't so much as bat an eye at the rampant poverty that they suddenly found themselves surrounded by. "Yeah, this is where he came looking for help. It has to be. A man would have to be desperate to even think about approaching Barrera's stronghold, and these people are desperate."

Half expecting Maddy to comment on the stark despair on the faces of the children who stopped their play to watch the taxi slowly cruise down the street, he glanced over at her and couldn't help but smile. Sitting stiffly erect, she was fighting for all she was worth to stay awake, but it was a losing battle. Her weighted eyelids were already at half-mast and, even as he watched, her head bobbed. She caught herself almost immediately, but seconds later, her head started to drop again.

The ease with which he spontaneously reached for her stopped him before he so much as laid a finger on her. Oh, no! he thought, quickly drawing his hand back. He wasn't falling into that trap again. He'd held the lady once before while she slept and found it an all too enjoyable experience. She wasn't his type, dammit! He liked women with some meat on their bones and a sexy twinkle in their eyes. Maddy Lawrence had neither. The only reason she was starting to look good to him was because she was the only female around and he was stuck with her. That didn't, under any circumstances, mean that she was available.

Reminding himself that he had a job to do and that didn't involve getting messed up with a woman who might or might not be an uptight spinster who'd probably never even been with a man, he deliberately left her where she was and turned to scan the neighborhood as they drew deeper and deeper into the slums. The hopelessness was more prevalent here, the cantinas and liquor stores more numerous, sometimes taking up whole blocks. It was, he decided, just the type of environment Sneakers would have felt right at home in.

Instructing the driver to pull over at the next corner, he glanced back at Maddy and sighed at the sight of her sinking like a wilting flower against the door. Damn. What was he going to do with her? He didn't want to wake her, not when he already knew how the lady came awake. Soft and disoriented, drowsiness darkening her big, unfocused eyes, she'd blink up at him with a delightful confusion that was damn hard to resist.

But he couldn't just leave her there while he went looking for a guide. Blaming her for this crazy tug she seemed to have on his hormones, he scowled at her. "Wake up, Maddy!" he said loudly. "We're here."

A soft snore was his only answer.

Unexpectedly, Ace couldn't stop the grin that started to curl the edges of his mouth. Who would have thought prim and proper Maddy Lawrence would snore? And she probably didn't even know it. Picturing her face when he teased her about rattling the windows, he reached over and gave her shoulder a quick, rough shake. "Come on, deadhead. I don't have time for you to loll around and snooze. We're already at least two hours behind Sneakers. If we're going to catch the bastard, we're really going to have to haul ass."

His gruff, grating voice pounded at the edges of Maddy's consciousness, needling her, dragging her kicking and screaming into wakefulness. Forcing her eyes open, she pushed herself erect and gave him a narrow-eyed look that warned him the self-control and good manners her mother had drilled into her as a child weren't inexhaustible. "Has anyone ever told you that you're an extremely annoying man?" she asked irritably.

"Frequently," he retorted, chuckling. "I've been told that that's one of my more endearing qualities."

She snorted, drawing a grin from him. "That wasn't meant as a compliment. And for the record, I don't *haul ass* for anyone," she said, wrinkling her nose in distaste at the expression.

"You will for me, Princess Di, or you'll get left behind."

The cabby pulled over at the corner then, and in the blink of an eye, he was all business again. Quickly instructing the driver to wait for them—they'd never get a cab in this part of town, otherwise—he turned back to Maddy, his expression stern. "This isn't exactly Central Park West, so I suggest you stick close, do as you're told like a good girl and leave the talking to me. Got it?"

Maddy had never considered herself one of those women who instantly took offense at some of the stupid, sexist things that seemed to come out of a man's mouth so naturally. But then again, she'd never met anyone quite like Ace before. Lord, he knew how to push her buttons!

Lifting her chin a notch, she looked down her nose at him with a superior haughtiness that was guaranteed to put him in his place. "You know, this might surprise you, but I'm neither stupid nor slow-witted. And I haven't been a child for a very long time now. For the record, my name isn't Princess Di or Cinderella or Sleeping Beauty. It's Maddy. I'd appreciate it if you'd use it. As for following your lead, I'll be happy, to. Not because I haven't got the brains God gave a turtle," she added huffily, "but because this is apparently your field of expertise and I'm smart enough to know when I'm in over my head. Now, Mr....Ace, have *you* got *that*?"

She faced him like a bantam hen with its feathers ruffled, ready to light into him if he so much as looked at her wrong, Ace thought, stifling a smile. Snapping his shoulders back, he gave her a teasing, militarily correct salute. "Yes, Maddy," he drawled. "Anything you say, Maddy, darlin'. I beg your pardon for underestimating you. It won't happen again. Okay?"

Not yet ready to back down, she studied him suspiciously. "Why don't I believe you?"

"Maybe because I can lie through my teeth with the best of them," he admitted baldly, grinning. "Now that we've got that settled, let's get out of here. The meter's running."

There was, regrettably, no question that they were strangers in unfamiliar territory. After spending more hours in the air than either cared to remember, they both looked the worse for wear. The new clothes helped their appearance, but in the slums of Caracas, they stood out like sore thumbs. From every barred window and shadowed doorway, they drew hostile, distrustful glances.

Feeling the eery, invisible touch of unseen eyes, Maddy shivered. "Now what?"

"Just stay close," he advised in a low voice, and turned to the nearest bar.

With Maddy practically glued to his side, Ace moved from one cantina to the next, each worse than the last, as he tirelessly questioned everyone he saw. Openly asking only about Sneakers, he also cautiously put out feelers about Barrera and the whereabouts of his hideout in the jungle. Of those who would talk to him, no one would touch the subject of Barrera. As for Lazear, maybe they had seen a stranger fitting Sneakers description, but then again, one man looked much like another.

Frustrated, Ace knew a brick wall when he saw one. Standing on the cracked sidewalk outside one of the better lives in the area, he stared unseeingly down the street, muttering curses under his breath. "He's been here, dammit! I can smell him. He walked in here, waving some cash around, and found some poor sucker looking for his next fix to take into the jungles to Barrera. And we don't even know which way they went. Hell!"

If he hadn't had Maddy along, he would have done what he always did in this type of situation—gone into one of the bars, pulled up a stool next to the shadiest character in the place and kept the liquor coming until his drinking partner loosened up enough to tell him what he wanted to know. But that would hardly work with Maddy standing nervously at his side, looking as out of place as a virgin in a whorehouse.

Losing her for a while was out of the question, though, so he'd have to try another tactic. "I need a drink," he muttered, and led her into another bar.

Inside, it was shadowy and warm, the pall of cigarette smoke thick in the air. Waiting near the door for his eyes to adjust to the poor light, Ace noted the position of the half-dozen people in the room, from the bartender who was drying glasses with a dirty dish towel to the grizzled old drunk passed out cold at a table in the far corner. A couple at the bar was wrapped up in each other and didn't spare them a glance. Everyone else, Ace noticed, looked him and Maddy up and down, then turned back to the serious business of getting drunk. All but one, that is. Sitting alone at the end of the bar, nursing a cold beer, a thin, wiry man watched Maddy's every move.

Irritated, Ace didn't like the looks of the man one damn little bit. What the hell was he staring at? Hadn't he ever seen a woman before? A *plain*, ordinary woman? All right, so she was looking pretty good right now in spite of the shadows under her eyes from lack of sleep. That didn't mean the jackass had to drool all over her.

Or that he, himself, had to stand there scowling like a jealous lover when there was work to be done and the means to do it was staring at Maddy from across the room.

Grabbing her arm, he hauled her over to a deserted section of the bar, pushed her down on a stool and leaned over her. "Listen close," he whispered hurriedly. "You see that guy at the end of the bar—no, don't look! Trust me, he's there, and he's looking at you like you're the candles on his birthday cake."

"What? Oh, God!"

"I want you to go over there and talk to him."

She couldn't have looked more shocked if he'd suggested she jump on a table and strip. "Are you out of your mind? Why would I want to do that?"

"Shh! Keep a lid on it, will you? I'd just as soon not advertise this to the entire bar, if you don't mind." Quickly glancing around to make sure that they hadn't drawn anything more than passing interest from anyone but the man at the opposite end of the bar, he sighed in relief when no one but Maddy's secret admirer appeared to be interested in their actions. Turning his attention back to Maddy, he gave her a hard look. "Remember our agreement? That this is my field of expertise?"

"Yes, but—"

"No buts. My gut's telling me that Casanova over there is the type who knows everything that's going on in his neighborhood. If Sneakers came in here, he saw him. And he's interested in you." Reaching into the front pocket of his jeans, he pulled out some crumbled bills and stuffed them into her hand. "Go over there and buy him a drink and flirt with him a little and see what you can get out of him."

Horrified, Maddy just looked at him. "I can't do that!"

"Why not?"

"Because..." Oh, Lord, how did she admit her inexperience to a man who'd probably never been innocent or unsure of his sexual prowess a day in his life? He was a gorgeous specimen of a man—and he knew it. Flirting seemed to be as natural as breathing to him. He would never understand what it was like to grow up knowing you would never be anything other than ordinary at best and being all right with that because you spent so much time with your nose in a book. Just the thought of walking up to a stranger and trying to sweet-talk him made her stomach turn over. Her mouth suddenly dust dry, she swallowed. "Because I just can't. Anyway, you're the expert, as you're so fond of reminding me. You go talk to him."

"What for? Look at him. It isn't me he can't take his eyes off of."

"I don't care. I'm not flirting with him or anyone else. You'll have to find another way to get him to talk."

"Why not, dammit?"

Goaded, resenting the pressure he was putting on her when he had absolutely no right, she blurted out the last thing she ever wanted to admit. "Because I don't know how, okay? I don't know how."

Caught off guard, Ace unwisely said the first thing that came into his head. "You're kidding. Everybody knows how to flirt. It's instinctive."

"Maybe for you," she retorted huffily, her chin lifted to a defensive angle as she turned away. "I wouldn't even know where to begin. I guess I have a defective flirting gene."

He wanted to believe this was another part of her act, but no one could fake the hurt he saw in her eyes. Dammit, could she really be involved with Lazear? He'd been so positive, but now he couldn't be sure. He'd never met anyone who had so little confidence in themselves when it came to the opposite sex. And it wasn't as if she were some baby teetering on the edge of womanhood and afraid to try her wings for the first time. She should have gone through all the uncertainties and awkwardness of adolescence decades ago.

Frustrated, not exactly sure how to proceed, he reached out to cup her cheek in his palm and gently but firmly turn her eyes to his. "It's not that hard," he said quietly. "In fact, flirting with this guy will be a piece of cake since he's already got his eye on you. You just go up to him and smile and buy him a drink. When you get him loosened up, I'll stroll over and ask him about Sneakers."

"But I don't speak Spanish!"

"Some things don't need words, sweetheart. All you have to do is give him a couple of slow smiles and a beer and, trust me, he'll get the picture." Looking her up and down, he frowned. "But first we've got to make a few adjustments." Before she could guess his intentions, he fluffed her hair, then moved his fingers to the top button of her T-shirt.

Her heart lurching in her breast, Maddy gasped and swatted at his hands. "What are you doing?" she squeaked. "Stop that!"

"Settle down. I'm just showing a little skin so you won't look so straitlaced," he assured her, struggling to hold back a smile. "Don't get all bristly on me. You'll still be well covered."

The top button slid free. Her mouth dust dry, her pulse thundering like a scared rabbit's, Maddy couldn't catch her breath as she watched his strong, agile fingers start to move another half inch down her chest. Suddenly she was hot and confused and her knees had this alarming tendency to just buckle. Like a steel trap, her fingers snapped shut around his.

Flushed, she pulled back, shaking her head, whether in denial of the strange feelings he stirred in her or of what he was asking of her she wasn't sure. "This'll never work."

His eyes dropped to the hollow of her throat. Barely an inch of skin showed—not even a shadow of cleavage. She wasn't exposed, she told herself. There was nothing to be embarrassed about. Then he drawled, "Some men like to do their own unwrapping. If you came up to me like that and bought me a drink, you could get anything out of me you wanted."

Every suggestive word was like a long, slow glide of his hands, stroking her, heating her, sending her blood rushing up her throat into her cheeks and down into dark, secret, feminine places. Transfixed, she should have buttoned her T-shirt at the neckline again and told him that the sun would turn green the day she asked him for anything other than a plane ticket home, but her tongue was stuck to the roof of her mouth, and she couldn't for the life of her think of anything but what it would be like to have him touch her— really touch her the way a man touched a woman he found attractive.

You're out of your mind, Maddy Lawrence. The humidity in this godforsaken place has fried your brain.

Shaken, she pushed his hand away and started to button the top button again. "I don't care. I can't do this—"

His fingers closed around hers, trapping them against her breasts as his eyes drilled into hers. "This isn't some kind of game, lady," he said tersely. "If you want to go home, if you really are as innocent in all this as you claim and you want to see your mother anytime soon, then you'll help me find out which direction Sneakers went. Because you're not going anywhere until we catch up with him. You got that?"

She wasn't dense—of course, she got it! But he didn't know what he was asking of her. "You don't understand. It isn't that I don't want to help. I'll just never be able to carry it off. He'll take one look at me and know I'm a fraud.''

She was serious, Ace realized with a jolt of surprise. She might be able to appreciate the change in her appearance, but deep down inside, she didn't think a man would. And for some reason that he couldn't understand, that irritated the hell out of him. Were the men in her life blind or what?

Making a snap decision he knew he was going to live to regret, he grabbed her by the wrist and headed for the door. ''C'mon.''

''But what about the man at the end of the bar—''

''He'll wait. This won't.''

And before she could say another word, he pulled her outside, around the corner of the building, and pushed her up against the wall. In the split second it took to lower his mouth to hers, he saw her eyes widen, heard her gasp, felt her stiffen, and still he kissed her.

It was, he discovered almost immediately, the biggest mistake of his life. Too late, he realized there was a big difference between kissing an experienced woman and one who didn't know squat about what she was doing. The former he could enjoy and find mutual pleasure with without once engaging his brain. The latter was a whole different ball game.

He hadn't expected her to be so vulnerable.

The minute his mouth touched hers, she went as still as a fawn caught in the cross hairs of a hunter's sight. She didn't move, didn't breathe, and he could have sworn he could actually hear the wild fluttering of her heart. Unable to resist, he ran his tongue along the tempting curve of her bottom lip, learning the shape and sweet contour of her, and just that easily she started to tremble.

Entranced, he tried to tell himself it wasn't with fear. Surely by now she knew she had nothing to fear from him. But deep down inside, he couldn't be sure.

Shut up! he fiercely ordered the doubts in his head and gathered her closer without even being aware of it. But while one side of his brain was quickly sinking into pleasure, the other was roaring at him not to be any more contemptible than he already had been with this woman. She was innocent, dammit! If he'd had any doubts whatsoever on the matter before, they were silenced now. What she didn't know about kissing could fill the Grand Canyon, and he was a man who'd always avoided innocence like the plague.

He should have released her immediately. He liked women, enjoyed their company, their delicateness, and took no pleasure in scaring one. But her chasteness, he was discovering to his shock, had an unexpected appeal. Protectiveness rose in him, along with a tenderness that completely undid him. His hands gentled, his mouth softened on hers, words of reassurance rising on his tongue. He wanted to go slow with her, teach her, sweetly tutor her in the art of lovemaking and all that she had been missing until she came to him willingly, eagerly—

Have you lost your mind, man? What the hell are you doing? We're talking virgin here. V-I-R-G-I-N! You put stars in this girl's eyes, and she's going to be expecting you to put a ring on her finger. Is that really what you want?

Stung, he jerked back like a man who had been goosed with a cattle prod and stared down at her with a confused frown, his gut clenching at the sight of her dreamy-eyed expression and the slight, enticing puffiness of her still-parted lips. Alarm bells clanging in his head, he realized too late that Maddy Lawrence was everything she appeared to be— a prim, innocent woman who had never done anything more risqué in her life than read men's adventure novels. And only an idiot kissed a woman who had spent most of her life in a mythical ivory tower waiting for a prince to rescue her from the tedium of her own existence. Hell!

His jaw clenching on an oath, he knew he had to do something, and damn fast, or the lady was going to be jumping to all kinds of wrong conclusions. Pushing her to arm's length, he looked her up and down and said with deliberate mockery, "You look at that guy in the bar the way you're looking at me right now, and I guarantee you you'll have him eating out of your hand in no time."

The intoxicating taste of him on her lips and her heart still doing flip-flops in her breast, Maddy gazed up at him like a wide-eyed baby owl that didn't understand a word of English. What guy in the bar? she wondered, dazedly.

Then she remembered.

Hurt hit her first right in her pride. Then mortification. The blood drained from her face, only to rush back into her hot cheeks again, dragging telltale color in its wake. Oh, God, what had she done? Without a word of protest, she'd let him kiss her and never thought to ask herself what a man like Ace could suddenly see in her. The new hairstyle and contacts might have done wonders for her self-esteem, but she was still the same plain-Jane woman she'd always been, still the shy, bookish woman who had been completely passed over by the sexual revolution and had never felt the loss. Until now.

"Is that the only reason you kissed me? So I c-could... *come-on* ...to another man?"

For a second, she thought she saw regret flash in his blue eyes, but then he was arching a brow in amusement at the familiar phrase that even he could tell sounded strange on her tongue. "You seemed like you needed a confidence builder," he retorted mockingly. "The way I see it, I was doing you a favor."

A favor, she thought dully. He'd knocked the earth loose beneath her feet with a single, soul-shattering kiss, and all he cared to label it was a favor. Her eyes stinging suddenly with a horrifying rush of tears, she blinked rapidly and whirled away. "Then I guess it's my turn to do us both one and do whatever I have to to get us out of here."

Not bothering to see if he followed, she stormed into the cantina, her angled jaw set at a determined angle. She could do this. She could march up to that man at the end of the bar and give him a smile that would knock his socks off. All she had to do was pretend she was the heroine in an Ace MacKenzie book. The fictional Ace liked his women spunky and daring and they wouldn't think twice about taking advantage of a man's interest to get information out of him. And neither would she!

Inside, eyes watched her from the smoky shadows, but the only man she was interested in was the solitary figure sitting alone at the far end of the bar. Heading straight for him, she lifted her chin to a proud angle, pasted on her brightest smile and reminded herself that this was going to help her get back home...and away from Ace. For no other reason than that, she'd find a way to get through it.

But as she drew closer to the middle-aged man who barely sipped from the nearly full schooner of beer leaving rings on the bar in front of him, doubts crept in, weighting her feet until she was all but dragging them. He already had a beer. Now what was she supposed to do? Just sit down next to him and hope a smile would start him talking? Oh, God, what could she have been thinking of to let Ace talk her into this? She wasn't one of Ace MacKenzie's gutsy women—she just didn't have it in her. She'd never even been in a bar before, let alone tried to pick up a man. She didn't have a clue how to proceed.

Her heart knocking out a frantic rhythm, she settled onto the stool next to the man, her fingers instinctively climbing to the neckline of her T-shirt and the tiny patch of bare skin that seemed to throb like a neon sign. Behind her, she was aware of Ace as he silently took the seat at a table within easy listening distance, but she couldn't spare him a glance. Nervous to the point of nausea, she should have at least smiled when she glanced over to her companion and found his eyes waiting for her, but even that simple task was beyond her.

"Señor," she began hesitantly, only to have her mind go embarrassingly blank. What could she possibly say to the man? she wondered wildly. And what would he understand? "Do you by any chance speak English?"

It was the height of arrogance to come to his country and expect him to speak her language, but she was desperate. And he obviously knew it. Giving her a forgiving smile, he nodded graciously. *"Sí, señorita.* What can I do for you?"

"Oh, thank God!" Her smile tremulous, she never consciously came up with a story of a woman done wrong, but suddenly it was spilling from her lips. "I'm looking for a man, sir. An American." Quickly and succinctly she described her former boss, unconsciously using the same words Ace had earlier. "He's short and round and pock-faced and looks like a weasel with a bad toupee. The last time I saw him, he was headed for Caracas, and I have reason to believe that he came to this area of the city to look for a guide. If he came in here, you couldn't have missed him. He would have been in a hurry and wearing a suit. Have you seen him?"

The man merely stared at her, his shuttered face giving nothing away. "Maybe. Maybe not. Why are you looking for him?"

"Because he's a liar and a thief! He—he used me...." Her cheeks burned at the admission that was nothing less than the truth, though not in the way she was sure the man next to her took it. She told him then of the hidden warehouse and the items that had been stolen from some of the most famous museums in the world. "If I had known what he was doing, I never would have worked for him. Please help me," she pleaded. "He can't get away with this. The things he took are very rare and valuable, and I've got to get them back."

For what seemed like an eternity, the man didn't say a word. He simply stared at her consideringly while the seconds dragged by. Finally, just when she thought his answer couldn't be anything but a no, he nodded, as if coming to a decision in his head. "He was here about four hours ago waving a wad of money around," he told her. "As you suspected, he was looking for a guide."

Without a sound, Ace joined them, taking up a position directly behind Maddy. "Did he find one?"

"*Sí.* Miguel Rodriguez." A look of distaste skimmed over the other man's craggy face. "He's a rodent. A roach. He promised to take the American into the jungle to the headquarters of Carlos Barrera." Worry lining his brow, he turned back to Maddy in concern. "You must not try to follow him alone, *señorita.* The jungle is dangerous, and Barrera is a vicious man. A drug lord. There are rumors that he imprisons anyone caught near his hideout. For your own safety, don't go anywhere near there."

His words sent a chill sliding down Maddy's spine. Glancing to Ace's set face, she said, "I really don't have much choice, *señor.* We have to recover what he stole. Do you know where we can hire a guide?"

The older man looked from Maddy to Ace and back again, openly studying them both. "Are you sure you want to do this? Surely whatever was stolen is not worth your lives.''

"It's not going to come to that," Ace said grimly. "I'll make sure of it."

There was no doubting his word. His blue eyes icy in his hard face, he had the look of a man who wouldn't back down from a fight with the devil himself. Reassured, the older man said, "In that case, I would be happy to act as your guide." Rising from his stool, he offered his hand first to Maddy, then Ace. "My name is Dominic Salazar. I grew up in the jungle and know it well. I can take you anywhere you want to go."

"Including Barrera's place?" Ace asked shrewdly after introducing Maddy and himself. "You know the location of his hideout?"

"*Sí.*"

"How? I don't imagine that's something Barrera wants known."

His eyes bored into Salazar's, but to his credit, Dominic didn't look away. "There are places in the jungle, *señor,* where it is common knowledge it is not safe to go," he said with quiet dignity. "Men who have tried to go in there have not returned. That is where Barrera lives."

"And you're willing to take us there? For how much?"

"Only to the boundary. I'll wait twenty-four hours there for you to return. After that, you're on your own." He named a sum that, while high, was not completely outrageous. "That fee will include my services, as well as two of my men to help carry the food and tents—"

"No," Ace cut in. "We only need one guide—you."

"But, *señor*—"

"One guide," he repeated curtly. "No more or the deal's off."

"But it's a long way," the older man protested. "And without my men, the three of us will have to carry the tents and supplies ourselves. I have no problem with that, and I doubt that you do, either, but the woman—she doesn't look that strong."

Insulted by that, Maddy stiffened like a poker. "I'm tougher than I look. I can carry my share."

"And if she can't, I can," Ace added tersely. "So will you take the job, *señor,* or do I have to find somebody else?"

Not a man who hid his emotions well, Dominic Salazar hesitated, his black eyes clouded with worry as they drifted back to Maddy's slender figure. The jungle was no place for a woman, especially one who was so fragile she looked as if she'd blow away in a good stiff wind. There was no question that the man could take care of her, but to go after Barrera! He shook his head just at the idea of it. Americans! They were either incredibly brave or stupider than dirt, he didn't know which. He just knew that he couldn't let them trust their fate to another guide when he knew for a fact that he was the best to be had.

"I will take it," he said with a heavy sigh, "and pray none of us live to regret it." Pushing his barely touched beer away, he rose to his feet. "If we're going to leave within the hour, I have much to do."

"Before you go, there's one more detail we need to get straight before we actually shake on this," Ace said in flawless Spanish, stopping him in his tracks. "It's about the woman. I saw the way you were looking at her when we came in—"

"No, *señor!*"

"Don't bother to deny it. I'm not blind...or a fool. And I can hardly criticize you for appreciating the lady's looks when I've done the same thing. But we need to get one thing clear right now. She's mine. Got it?"

A hot tide of color slowly flushed the older man's weathered cheeks. "You misunderstood, Señor Ace," he, too, said in Spanish. "The lady is attractive, no? But I'm not interested. I'm married!"

Not the least impressed with that argument, Ace merely arched a brow. "You wouldn't be the first married man to think the grass looked greener on the other side."

"But I love my wife," he insisted sheepishly. "And she would take the broom handle to me if she thought I even smiled at another woman. So please don't worry. Señorita Maddy is safe with me."

Her ears perking up at the mention of her name, Maddy wondered what the two men could be discussing about her that would make the color come and go in Dominic's swarthy face. Before she could ask, however, Ace nodded and said, "Good. I'm glad to hear it."

"Glad to hear what?" she asked suspiciously. "What are you talking about?"

His color higher than ever, Dominic couldn't even look her in the eye. "Nothing, Señorita Maddy. Nothing at all. Now if you will excuse me, I have to get our supplies."

He was gone before she could so much as open her mouth, hurrying away like a little boy who'd just been caught with his hand in the cookie jar. Puzzled, Maddy turned back to Ace. "What was that all about?"

"That's for me to know and you to find out," he retorted with a maddening grin, then took her arm and pulled her toward the exit.

Chapter 5

After arranging to meet Dominic at a regional landing strip where they would rent a private plane to take them to San Miguel, a small town near the southern border where Barrera was reportedly said to live, they had almost two hours to kill. Hustling Maddy back to their waiting taxi, Ace gave orders to the driver in Spanish, and within seconds they were once again rushing through the narrow, winding streets at a pace that left her clinging white-knuckled to her seat. When an old Cadillac convertible suddenly darted out in front of them at an intersection, she gasped and braced herself, sure they were dead. But their driver only laid on his horn and swerved around the Caddy with a quick jerk of the wheel that caused the taxi to rock on its wheels.

Seconds later, they were shuddering to a squealing stop. Sprawled out on the seat next to her, Ace chuckled. "You can open your eyes now. We're here."

"Here" turned out to be a small but elegant hotel. A hotel, for God's sake! Maddy thought, unnerved. After only one kiss he thought he could take her to a hotel? The nerve of the man!

Outrage stiffening every nerve in her body, she gave him a look that should have turned his blood to ice. "If you think I'm going in there with you, you're out of your mind."

Confused, he glanced over at the flowered entrance of the hotel, but it was the same place he'd stayed the last time he'd unexpectedly found himself in Caracas. First class, beautifully decorated, it was one of the finest establishments in South America. "The hotel? Why? What's wrong with it?"

Her brown eyes flashing with fire, Maddy couldn't believe his nonchalance. "What's wrong with it?" she exclaimed. "Do you actually think that after only one kiss, you can..." Flustered, she couldn't find the right words and tried again. "That I would just go along with this...this..." She waved her hand ineffectually, heat suffusing her cheeks, and let her breath out in a frustrated huff. "I'm not that kind of woman."

Biting the inside of his cheek, Ace just looked at her. "And what kind of woman might that be?"

"The kind who...one who..." Unable to force out the right words, she saw the glint of devilment in his eyes then and almost threw her sack of new clothes at him. "What are you laughing at?"

"Me? Nothing," he claimed innocently. "I just thought you might like to get a room and clean up before we meet Dominic and leave civilization behind. But if you've got sex on your mind—"

"I never said that!"

He arched a masculine brow at her. "Didn't you?"

He had her and they both knew it, but she'd have died before she'd have admitted it. "I told you—I'm not that kind of woman."

"But I'm that kind of man, right?" When she only sniffed, refusing to answer, he chuckled, opened the cab door next to him and started to step out. At the last second, however, he turned, his grin full of mischief, and leaned close. "You're damn right I'm that kind of man, sweetheart," he taunted softly. "And with the right man, you'll be that kind of woman."

Not giving her a chance to so much as sputter a response, he stepped out of the cab and turned to help her out. She wanted to refuse it—both his help and his claim—but as she stared at his strong, callused hand, she knew in her heart she could do neither. To ignore his hand would have been childishly rude. And to deny the truth in his words, she discovered to her chagrin, was quite simply beyond her. Without a word, she placed her fingers in his and joined him on the sidewalk, while deep inside, her heart started to throb.

She promised herself she wasn't going to say another word. She'd already put her foot in her mouth once, and that was her limit for the day. But standing beside him while he registered for a room that they only intended to use for a couple of hours was one of the hardest things she'd ever done. Painfully aware of the fact that the only thing they had that passed for luggage was the two sacks that held the items they'd bought in Mexico City, she watched the very distinguished-looking desk clerk glance past Ace to her and back again and could just imagine what the man was thinking. Her cheeks burning, she waited for him to inform Ace that this wasn't that kind of establishment, but he only handed him the key with a soft, *"Gracias."* Within seconds, she was trailing Ace down a carpeted fourth-floor hallway.

The silence was so thick it fairly vibrated. Resisting the need to twist her hands together, Maddy didn't show so much as a flicker of unease as she joined him before the locked door of room 410. There was, she knew, nothing to be nervous about. She wasn't some heroine in an Ace Mackenzie book, about to be seduced in some foreign hotel room. He'd only been teasing her in the cab, pushing her buttons to get a rise out of her. And it had worked. He couldn't have been serious about the kind of man he was.

Could he?

The doubt came out of nowhere, sneaking past her guard to eat at her self-confidence with an ease that was frightening. Too late, she realized she may have trusted him too quickly. After all, what did she really know about him other than what he'd told her? And could she trust that?

"Here we are, milady," he said cheerfully as he inserted the key into the lock and pushed the door open. "A room fit for a princess . . . for a couple of hours, anyway. Enjoy."

Her stomach knotted with apprehension and her overactive imagination going wild, she stood flat-footed beside him, her feet refusing to budge. This was it, she thought, unconsciously wiping her damp palms on her shorts. The moment of truth when she learned just what kind of man he was. She wanted to believe he meant her no harm—her instincts told her she could trust him with everything from her virtue to her life—but at this point, she was so confused, she didn't even know if she could trust her instincts. His was the only familiar face in a crowd of foreigners, and even though he, too, had been a stranger less than twenty-four hours ago, it was all too easy to think of him as a partner, a confidant, someone she could place all her faith in in a hostile environment.

The truth was, however, that for all she knew, he could be just as ruthless as her former boss and Cement Johnny. He was going to a great deal of trouble and expense to get his hands on jewels that weren't his, and she had to ask herself why.

Sick at the thought, she looked at the hotel room that lay just beyond the open door and knew she had to get this settled now. "Ace..." she began, but he was already proceeding down the hallway. "Where are you going?"

"Next door," he retorted. Stopping at the next room farther down the hallway, he unlocked the door and pushed it open, his grin mischievous as his gaze swung back to hers. "Why? D'you think I was going to share a bed with you?"

"No, of course not!"

Her answer was too quick, too outraged, her cheeks too hot. "Liar." He chuckled. Lord, she was easy to tease! She set herself up so beautifully, he just couldn't resist. "Sorry to disappoint you, darlin', but we don't have time now. We've got to meet Dominic soon, and I don't know about you, but I don't like to be rushed when I get in bed with a lady. Maybe next time."

Daring to wink at her, he hurriedly stepped inside his room and shut the door before she could find something to throw at him. Seconds later, something thumped against his door, drawing a laugh from him. Whatever Maddy Lawrence was—and he was still working on figuring her out— she had yet to be a disappointment. And there weren't many women he could say that about.

Refreshed and somewhat rested, they met Dominic at the regional airport at the appointed time and found him loading gear into a small twin-engine plane that looked as if it had been through both world wars and barely survived the experience. Backpacks and supplies filled the baggage compartment area and spilled over into the cabin area, leaving just enough room for Maddy in the back and the two men up front. Once they reached San Miguel, everything would be unloaded and packed into the Jeep that Dominic had already arranged to have waiting for them at the other end.

Eyeing the whole setup warily, Maddy couldn't help wondering if they'd made a drastic mistake in hiring Dominic. They were placing an awful lot of faith in a man they had picked up in a bar. How did they know he was on the up-and-up? Or that the plane, which had to be as old as her grandfather, would get them where they wanted to go in one piece? If the slightest thing went wrong on this expedition, they would not only lose any chance of capturing Mr. Lazear, but they'd have to make their way out of the jungle by foot. It could take weeks!

Ace, however, didn't seem to be the least bit concerned. He cast a quick, knowing eye over the lot and nodded in satisfaction. "Looks good. We should be able to handle everything between the three of us once we reach San Miguel. How far into the jungle do the roads go?"

"Forty or fifty miles where we're going," Dominic said. "From there we'll go upriver by canoe." Taking the wrinkled bags that served as their luggage, he added them to the things at the back. "It's a hard journey. We can make it in four days if we take it in stages, three if we really push it."

"We haven't got that long," Ace retorted. "Not if Lazear's already eight hours ahead of us and we're going to catch him before he reaches Barrera."

Dominic nodded, but his gaze was unconsciously doubtful when it drifted to Maddy, which bothered her no end. Just because she was the only woman in the group and had never done anything like this didn't mean she was going to hold them up! Lifting her chin, she coolly told both men, "If we don't catch Mr. Lazear, it won't be because *I* held you back. I want to catch him just as badly as you do so I can get back to my own life."

Leaving both men standing on the tarmac, she climbed into the back seat of the plane without waiting for help from either of them. Ace and Dominic looked at each other and started to grin. Both of them, however, were wise enough not to so much as chuckle as they took their places in the cockpit.

Whenever Maddy had pictured them foraging into the wilds of the rain forest, an old Tarzan movie had immediately sprung to mind. With no trouble whatsoever, she'd seen the three of them driving down a narrow dirt track that was hemmed in on both sides by huge, towering, vine-covered trees. The air would be thick with the scent of exotic flowers and damp from waterfalls that would put Niagara to shame. The image had been so real, so lush, that she'd almost heard Cheetah grunting excitedly from the foliage overhead.

The rain forest of South America, she discovered to her delight three hours later when they drove away from San Miguel in the Jeep that had been waiting for them at the landing strip, was all that and more. The trees—ebony and mahogany and what she thought was rubber—seemed to reach halfway to the sky and were as thick as ants in an ant-hill for as far as the eye could see. Sunlight searched for breaks in the canopy of greenery overhead, but the forest floor was bathed in shadows that were only rarely broken by sudden, surprising pockets of light. It was beautiful, intimidating, mysterious.

It was the noise, however, that caught Maddy completely by surprise. Parrots and toucans and hundreds of species of birds she had no names for chattered from the trees like old ladies at a bridge club catching up on the latest gossip. And then there were the monkeys who added their two cents to the cacophony, screaming and yelling at one another as they swung through the trees with ease on the vines that were everywhere, warning anyone who cared to listen that there were intruders in their midst.

Clinging to her seat in the back of the Jeep as they raced over a jarring, rutted road that was little more than a mud track through the undergrowth, Maddy couldn't absorb all the sights and sounds fast enough. The heat, oppressive and cloying, seemed to sit upon her chest like a lead weight, but she hardly noticed. She was really here, she thought dizzily, pinching herself. In the rain forest. And she loved it.

Wishing she had a camera, she paid no attention to the quiet conversation between Ace and Dominic in the front seat or the worsening condition of the winding road ahead until they went around a bend and Dominic suddenly slammed on the brakes. Unprepared and unbuckled, Maddy promptly slid into the floorboard with a startled cry.

"Sorry, *señorita,*" Dominic said quickly. "There's a log in the road."

"Make that a tree," Ace corrected. With a single step, he was out of the Jeep and reaching for her, helping her up and over the side onto the ground. "Looks like this is the end of the road. You all right?"

Distracted, she pushed her hair out of her eyes. "Yes, of course. What do you mean, this is the end of the road? We've barely gotten started."

"Tell that to the tree," Ace said dryly. "Unless you brought a chain saw along without telling me, we're not going anywhere."

"The road ends less than a half a mile from here, anyway," Dominic added. Out of the Jeep the second it had rattled to a stop, he moved to the back and started to unload their gear. "We'll have to portage the canoe a little farther, but that shouldn't be a problem between the three of us."

Before they'd landed at the tiny promise of an airport in San Miguel, Maddy would have sworn she didn't have the energy to lift her little finger, let alone help carry the canoe Dominic had rented from one of the villagers. But just the thought of actually getting a closer look at her surroundings had her moving to his side to help. "How far is the river from here?"

Dominic smiled at her eagerness. "A mile—maybe a little less. The real portaging will take place tomorrow."

That didn't sound all that far, but Maddy wasn't foolish enough to think she was just in for a little stroll in the park. Sweat was already popping out of every pore on her body and she hadn't done anything. She could feel Ace's eyes on her, watching her, studying her. If he thought she was going to be a liability, she knew he'd send her back to town so fast he'd make her head spin. Just last night, she would have jumped at the chance to get away from him. But she was no longer afraid of him, and she was in an honest-to-God rain forest and up to her ears in adventure for the first time in her life. She wasn't going to miss a second of it for anything.

Shrugging as if she didn't care if it was one mile or ten, she said, "That doesn't sound too bad. What do you want me to carry?"

"Try this for now," Ace said, separating items from the pile Dominic had already taken from the Jeep. "If it gets to be too much, just holler."

Maddy had no intention of doing any such thing. But the things he set aside for her to carry kept growing and growing and growing. Dismayed, she blurted out, "You want me to carry *all* of that?"

Chuckling, he assured her, "It's not as bad as it looks. Here, let me help you. Turn around."

It wasn't until she had her back to him and he was guiding her hands into one of the backpacks Dominic had provided that she felt the first faint stirrings of misgiving. His hands brushed over her with an almost casual indifference as he guided the straps onto her shoulders and adjusted them, but it was the first time he'd touched her since he'd kissed her, other than to help her out of the Jeep. Suddenly he was close, too close, leaning over her, his eyes on his hands as he made sure the backpack fit her right, and her heart started somersaulting in her chest.

Standing as still as a statue, she told herself not to be such a pathetic ninny. He was just helping her and only a foolish old maid would get all hot and bothered over such an innocent act. He didn't mean a thing by it . . . or the kiss he'd given her earlier. Men like Ace never did, especially with women like her. She wasn't his type; that was glaringly obvious. And unless she wanted to make a total fool of herself during this trip, she'd remember that.

In spite of the silent lecture, however, his breath was warm against the back of her neck, an unconsciously erotic caress that sent goose bumps tingling down her spine. Her throat dry, she knew she should tell him to stop, she didn't need this kind of help, but she perversely found a hundred reasons not to. He would think she was skittish and paranoid and probably laugh at her. And it wasn't as if she was making up excuses to get close to him—she couldn't load all the stuff onto her back by herself and Dominic was busy. Ace already had her backpack half-packed. If she lied and insisted she didn't need his help to finish the job, he'd know something was wrong and start asking questions she had no intention of answering.

"There. How's that?" His hands on her shoulders, he turned her to face him, his fingers testing the weight and balance of the loaded pack to make sure it was evenly distributed. "Think you can handle that?"

Staring up at him wordlessly, every nerve ending in her body starting to stir to life, she nodded because anything more complicated than that was simply beyond her. This would be so much simpler, she thought inanely, if the man didn't look so darn good.

"So what do you think?"

Lost in her heated thoughts, she looked up and saw herself reflected in his eyes and forgot to breathe. For the span of a single, endless second, time ground to a halt. His fingers tightened ever so slightly on her shoulders, and suddenly the air was humming between them. He felt it, too, that sudden kick of awareness that came out of nowhere. She could see it in the dark depths of his blue eyes, feel it in the way he kept touching her long after the pack was loaded and adjusted, as if he couldn't stop himself.

"Is there enough padding on the shoulder straps or do you want me to tie a couple of T-shirts around them?"

The deep rumble of his voice washed over her like the slow brush of his hands. Bewitched, she wondered if he could hear the uneven rhythm of her breathing. Feel the skipping of her pulse—

"Maddy?" Smiling crookedly, he pressed his palm to her damp forehead. "Are you feeling all right? I swear you haven't heard a word I've said. Maybe I should have left you in Caracas, after all. You're not used to this heat."

Snapping out of the fog that shrouded her brain, she stiffened in alarm. "No! I'm fine. Really," she said quickly when he didn't look convinced. "And the pack doesn't bother me at all. Anyway, I only have to wear it while we're portaging the canoe." Turning away before he could come up with another argument, she told him pointedly, "Dominic could use some help."

* * *

Ten minutes later, they struck out for the river with all the gear loaded into the packs on their backs. Carrying the canoe right side up, they suspended it between the three of them and tried to make the best of an awkward balancing act. It wasn't easy. Dominic lined up at the front on the starboard side, with Maddy behind him at the rear of the canoe. Ace, because he was the strongest, took the port side all by himself, positioning himself in the middle as they made their way over the muddy ground.

And the ground underfoot didn't help matters any. Slick and muddy from the rain that fell almost daily, it was as treacherous as a sheet of ice. Within the first twenty feet, Maddy slipped three times and just barely caught herself before the men noticed. Digging her feet more firmly into the mud to find some traction, she tried not to wince as the gooey stuff oozed over the tops of her shoes.

It was slow going and nearly forty-five minutes before they reached the river. Drenched in sweat, a blister already forming on her palm, Maddy helped ease the canoe into the water and sighed in relief. Finally! The last hundred yards had been the toughest. All downhill, she'd had to fight just to remain upright, and her legs were like noodles.

There was, however, no time to rest, not if they were going to catch up with Lazear. Their packs were quickly stowed in the canoe, and almost before she caught her breath, Maddy found herself seated in the middle with a paddle in her hand. And she didn't have any idea how to use it.

From his place in the stern, Dominic pushed away from the bank with his own paddle and said, "Watch Ace, *señorita.* You'll pick it up in no time."

The paddle felt heavy in her hands and awkward, but she did as he said and studied Ace. Not surprisingly, the man knew what he was doing. He sat with his back to her in the bow, facing forward, his left hand comfortably gripping the top of the handle, the other gripping the slender wooden neck just above where it widened into the paddle. With easy grace, he plunged it into the water several feet in front of him and made a long smooth stroke alongside the canoe that immediately propelled it forward. With a gracefulness she couldn't help but admire, he lifted the paddle from the water, turned it sideways so that it feathered a foot or so over the surface of the river as he brought it back out in front of him, then immediately began the procedure all over again.

Fascinated, Maddy couldn't take her eyes off him. There was a languidness to his movements that was surprisingly sensual for such a big, athletic man. Her gaze slowly trailing over him, she noted the power in his strong hands, the steeliness of his hard forearms, the rippling of his shoulder muscles beneath his shirt as he sank the paddle in the river again and again. Given the chance, she could have watched him for hours.

But she wasn't along for a free ride. Frowning, she copied the way Ace held the paddle, hesitantly sank it into the water and felt the pull of the wide, slow-moving river against her stroke as the canoe jerked forward. The beginnings of a smile played with the corners of her mouth. Watching Ace, she timed her stroke with his, and the forward motion of the canoe immediately turned into a smooth, powerful glide. Just that easily, she was in love.

Later, she couldn't have said how long they were on the river that first day, but it wasn't long enough. Once she caught the rhythm, paddling was like breathing—she did it instinctively—and she was able to turn her attention to her surroundings. Craning her neck, not wanting to miss anything, she soaked up the colors and smells like a sponge.

Over the course of the day, they passed a number of villages that had been hacked right out of the jungle on the edge of the river. Each time they came to one, they stopped so Dominic could go ashore and question the locals about Lazear. And each time he returned to the canoe, it was with the news that they were on the right track. Two men, one matching Sneakers's description, had been through there earlier in the day and had seemed in no hurry. They were still hours ahead of them, but Sneakers and his guide obviously had no idea they were being followed.

Encouraged, the three of them continued upstream with renewed enthusiasm even though they knew there was no way they would catch their quarry that day. They could, however, shave considerable time off the clock by pressing forward long after they should have stopped for the night. Dominic had warned them that they didn't want to risk setting up the tents once darkness fell or they might have to contend with snakes, but long after twilight fell, they were still on the water, pushing the envelope.

Finally, Ace called a halt. Peering through the thickening shadows up ahead, he said, "There seems to be a clearing on the starboard side about a hundred yards ahead. It looks like a good spot to pitch the tents."

Turning the bow of the canoe to the right with a simple flip of his paddle, Dominic sent them gliding toward the spot. "A trader used to sell his wares here," the older man informed them as the canoe bumped into the shore and Ace stepped out to drag it up onto the bank. "He would make the trip upriver once a month and set up a tent here until he sold out his inventory. He hasn't been seen for several months, however, and no one knows what happened to him. Six months from now, you won't even be able to tell he was ever here."

Taking a quick glance at the sky through the trees overhead, Ace frowned. "If we're going to get the tents set up before it rains, we'd better get a move on it. I don't like the looks of those clouds."

Bone tired but exhilarated, Maddy jumped to help. "I've never put up a tent before, but I'm game if you are. Tell me what to do."

"There's a hammer in my pack," he replied. "Why don't you get it while Dominic and I unpack the tents?"

With a speed that amazed Maddy, they had the first tent up in a matter of minutes. But before she could step back to admire their handiwork, the clouds overhead suddenly split wide open, sending a deluge raining down on their heads.

"Oh!"

"Quick! Inside!" Ace yelled. Pushing her into the tent, he and Dominic were right behind her, but it was too late. They were all three already soaked to the skin.

"My God," Maddy gasped. Flanked by the two men, she stood in the open doorway and watched the rain pour down in sheets. "If this keeps up, we'll be washed away. Shouldn't we do something? The canoe—"

"Will be fine," Dominic assured her, raising his voice to be heard over the thunderous roar. "Showers never last long in the jungle. It'll stop soon."

"You've got to be kidding. It's pouring!"

"*Sí,*" he agreed, smiling. "We are in a rain forest. But any second now..."

The words were hardly out of his mouth when the downpour ended as quickly as it had begun. Amazed, Maddy wouldn't have believed it if she hadn't seen it with her own eyes.

Flanking her on the other side, Ace chuckled. "I'd say the man knows what he's talking about, Maddy, darlin'. How long do we have before it's totally dark, Dominic?"

With the passing of the shower, the clouds had cleared, lightening the sky. Ace would have said they had at least forty minutes until they needed to break out the lanterns, but Dominic wasn't nearly as optimistic. "Twenty minutes," he said promptly. "No more."

"Then we'd better hustle," Ace retorted, ignoring the still-dripping trees as he stepped outside. "We've got a lot to do."

The second tent went up as easy as the first, but when Maddy looked around for the third, it was nowhere in sight. Tired, her wet clothes clinging to her and growing more uncomfortable with every passing moment, she watched Dominic throw his personal items into the smaller of the two structures and suddenly didn't like the look of things.

Turning, she confronted Ace. "All right, where's the third tent?"

As surprised as she, he shrugged. "I don't know. Maybe this was all he could get his hands on with such short notice."

Maddy might have accepted that if it had come from anyone but Ace. He was a man who liked women—he'd already made that more than clear. And then there was the little matter of a kiss that she knew was going to haunt her until she was old and gray.

"And maybe you put him up to this," she retorted in a low whisper that wouldn't carry to the other man. "I heard you speaking Spanish to him right before he left to get everything, and my name was mentioned. You told him we'd share a tent, didn't you?"

"Of course not!"

"Then what did you tell him?"

Caught between a rock and a hard place, Ace hesitated. Damn the woman, she wasn't going to like the truth and he'd be damned if he'd lie to her. "None of your business."

"Aha! I knew it!"

Goaded, heat stealing into his cheeks—dammit, he was blushing!—he snapped, "You want the truth, little girl? All right—here it is. I told him you were mine so he'd better keep his paws to himself or the deal was off. That must be why he only brought two tents. So there, Miss Nosy Britches! You wanted the truth, you got it. Now deal with it!"

Taken aback, Maddy just stared at him.

I told him you were mine. . . .

The words echoed in her head like a lover's whispered confession of love, teasing her, seducing her, once spoken impossible to ignore. Somewhere in the nether regions of her common sense, a voice was yelling at her not to be a fool— he probably used lines like that all the time on gullible women.

Why? she wanted to ask him. Why would you say such a thing to Dominic? But fear of his answer kept the words unspoken on her tongue. If this was his way of passing the time, of amusing himself until they got back to civilization, of giving the old-maid librarian a thrill for the first time in her life, she didn't want to hear it.

Lifting her chin, she said quietly, "Then the two of you can share this tent and I'll take the smaller one."

He nodded curtly. "Fine. You do that. And if Lazear gets wind that we're on his tail and sends someone back to take care of us, you're going to be a sitting duck. When I get back to the States, though, I'll notify your mother that she had a daughter she can be proud of. You died protecting your virtue."

Sneaky. Lord, the man was sneaky. The battle was lost before it had hardly begun. She would have given anything to call his bluff and insist on sleeping alone, but they both knew she was too much of a chicken to do that. Their eyes locked in a battle of wills, she had no choice but to retreat with as much of her pride intact as she could manage. "All right. We'll do it your way... for now. But I'm getting me a tent and gun of my own at the first decent village we come to tomorrow."

This far into the jungle, she wasn't likely to find such a well-stocked trading post, and even if she did, she didn't have any money, but Ace wisely refrained from pointing that out. "Have it your way," he said with a shrug. "Now that we've got that straightened out, I suggest we all eat, then grab some shut-eye. Tomorrow's going to be another long day and we're going to get started early."

"Oh, but I can't eat until I take a bath and get out of these wet clothes."

Amused, he laughed. "Good luck, honey. The nearest bathtub is sixty miles away."

"But I can't go to bed like this!" she cried, appalled. "Look at me!"

Taking her at her word, he did just that, then wished he hadn't. Thanks to the rain, her wet clothes were plastered to every feminine curve and tempting hollow. Just looking at her made him ache. For what seemed like the thousandth time since he'd kissed her, he reminded himself that she was an innocent and only a cad would take advantage of her in her present situation. But dammit, he wanted to touch her, to kiss her again and see if she was half as sweet as he remembered. God, what had he set himself up for by insisting that she share a tent with him?

"We're roughing it, remember?" he reminded her tightly. "If you're that desperate for a bath, you'll have to use the river. But I suggest you hurry. You heard what Dominic said about the snakes."

She paled, but he had to give her credit—she didn't back down. "Fine. But I'm not going off by myself. One of you will have to go with me with a gun."

Only a masochist would have agreed to such a thing, and self-torture had never been Ace's thing. He should have told her to do what she wanted, he was going to eat, but just the thought of another man watching her bathe was like a fist in his gut.

Dammit, he was jealous! he realized with a jolt of surprise. He'd never been jealous of a woman in his life, and it wasn't a feeling he cared for. What the hell was she doing to him?

He opened his mouth to tell her Dominic would probably be more than happy to watch out for her, but all that came out was a rough growl. "Then you'd better grab your soap and haul that little butt of yours. We're losing daylight fast."

Not giving her time to comment, he collected his gun from where he'd stored it in his pack and a flashlight from Dominic, and twenty seconds later he was escorting her downriver to a more secluded spot. After a quick reconnoiter of the place, he declared it snake-free and dropped down onto the bank with his back half-turned to the water. "You've got five minutes."

He should have been happy that he didn't have to tell her twice. Stepping out of sight behind him, she hesitated, and he could almost feel her eyes on him, her sudden doubts about stripping in plain view of anyone who cared to look. Her need for a bath, however, quickly overcame her need for modesty, and in a matter of seconds, he heard the whispered sound of buttons sliding free and the soft growl of a zipper. It was, he discovered too late, the most seductive sound he'd ever heard in his life.

And his conscience wouldn't let him sneak a peek.

A muscle jumping along his clenched jaw, he stared straight ahead at the darkening jungle and tried to concentrate on anything but the woman enjoying her bath just out of his sight behind him. But his mind refused to cooperate, and instead, he found himself listening for the next splash as she rinsed herself, her next sigh as she soaked sore muscles that were unused to lifting anything heavier than a book. She would be smiling, her eyes closed with pleasure, her skin ivory and softly flushed in the twilight, her breasts full and wet and pouting for a man's hands—

Suddenly hot and hard, he swore, cursing himself for a fool. "You've got two minutes," he said through his teeth. "Start wrapping it up."

"I'm almost finished," she promised breathlessly. Her hair full of suds, she quickly ducked underwater to rinse it, then burst to the surface with a smile on her lips. How could she have known skinny-dipping could be so invigorating? She'd never felt so free in her life! She wanted to laugh, to do the backstroke all the way across the river and back, to play like a child. But she was out of time.

Unable to stop grinning, she waded up onto the bank. "All finished," she called to Ace's back. "Just give me a second to dress and..."

She didn't see the snake that slithered out of the undergrowth and curled up on her clothes until she started to reach for her discarded shirt to dry herself. Freezing in her tracks, she screamed.

Chapter 6

"What the hell!" Scrambling to his feet, his pistol already in one hand and the flashlight in the other, Ace whirled and immediately spied the anaconda coiled on Maddy's clothes barely a yard away from her bare feet. The huge boa, nearly twenty feet in length, was facing away from her and couldn't easily strike from that position, but Ace was taking no chances. Lightning quick, he fired, shooting the snake right between the eyes. It wasn't until then, when he lifted his gaze and the flashlight to Maddy, that he realized she was as naked as the day she was born. "Are you all right?" he demanded hoarsely.

She nodded jerkily, her eyes huge in her ashen face as she stared unblinkingly at the now-still figure of the snake. "I—I didn't s-see it," she stuttered through chattering teeth. "I was reaching f-for m-my shirt a-and suddenly it w-was j-just...there."

From the camp, they heard a crashing through the underbrush and a muttered oath in Spanish as Dominic made his way toward them in the near dark, the beam of his flashlight bobbing as he ran. "Señor Ace? *Señorita?* Where are you? What's wrong?"

Cursing, Ace stepped over the shirt the dead snake lay coiled on, snatched up the clean one Maddy had brought along and whipped it over her shoulders. Snatching her close, he had her in his arms by the time the other man was close enough to pick them out of the deep shadows with his flashlight. "It was just a boa," he told Dominic gruffly. "A dead one now. Everything's under control."

The guide's eyes barely touched on Maddy's obviously naked figure draped in the shirt before they hurriedly moved back to Ace. "The *señorita* is okay?"

He nodded, his arms instinctively tightening around her as he felt her tremble. "She's just a little shaken up. I'll bring her back to camp as soon as she's had a chance to calm down."

Without a word, the older man quietly faded back into the night, leaving them alone. For the span of a heartbeat, the silence that settled around them was refreshingly complete. But the jungle was never quiet or still for long. An instant later, tree frogs croaked like musicians warming up for a performance, while katydids and other insects broke into song. High above the forest floor, the wind rushed through the tree crowns.

After the rain, the humidity was worse than ever. Ace never noticed. He couldn't remember the last time he'd just held a woman and comforted her. Damn, it felt good. *She* felt good. Soft and delicate and womanly. And she was crying.

She didn't make a sound, but he could feel her hot tears soaking his shirt as she buried her face against his chest and clung to him as if she would never let him go. Deep inside, something cracked in the region that had once been his heart. When she'd screamed, he'd thought… Hell, he didn't know what he'd thought, just that he'd kill anyone or anything that hurt her. Later, he knew that was going to keep him awake long into the night, but for now, he just wanted to hold her, touch her, reassure himself that she was really all right.

Stroking his hands down her back over and over again, he murmured, "It's okay, honey. You're fine. The snake's dead, and if you see another one, I'll kill it, too. Nothing's going to hurt you. Okay? Don't cry."

Maddy sniffed and managed a nod, but still she couldn't stop the tears that silently flowed down her cheeks and soaked his shirt. It was just nerves, she told herself, shuddering. A reaction to everything that had happened to her over the course of the past twenty-four hours. She'd been knocked out, kidnapped, shot at, dragged halfway across the world. And now nearly strangled by a snake as big as a house. And that was only the beginning. She was worried about her mother, and she couldn't remember when she'd had anything to eat that came close to resembling real food. That plastic stuff they'd served on the airplane and the trail mix Dominic seemed to have an unending supply of just didn't cut it. And then there were the aches that were beginning to make themselves known all over her body. Tomorrow, she'd be lucky if she could move. Tonight, she just wanted to stand there and absorb his strength.

The emotional roller coaster of fear faded quickly, however, and with its passing, her trembling gradually eased, and the last of her strength just seemed to fade away. Spent, hardly able to keep her eyes open, she sighed and slumped against him.

His hand lifted to her hair, his fingers soothing as he stroked her. "Better?"

Half-asleep, she hummed, "Mmm-hmm."

"Think you can get dressed by yourself? It's getting late and we need to get back to camp."

Her thoughts fuzzy, she frowned. What did he mean "get dressed"? Then it hit her. She was naked but for a shirt that barely covered her backside!

"Oh, God!"

"Now don't get all embarrassed on me," he warned quickly when every muscle in her body stiffened in alarm. "I don't know anybody who would stop to worry about their clothes if they found themselves that close to a boa. You did the right thing and screamed your guts out. Nothing else matters."

"That's easy for you to say." She groaned, pressing against him so he couldn't see anything. "You're not the one standing here in your birthday suit."

"No," he agreed in a voice laced with laughter. "But that could be arranged."

"Don't you dare!"

He chuckled. "Somehow I had a feeling you'd say that. I guess it's just not my day. Do you want me to get your clothes for you?"

And leave her naked before him? "No!"

"Okay, then you get them."

For a minute, he thought she was going to reject that suggestion, too, and then they really would have been in a fix. Because a frightened and unaware Maddy pressed against him was one thing. An appealingly shy and embarrassed one who was just as aware of him as he was of her was something altogether different.

"Don't look," she whispered softly. Lifting her hand, she blindly patted his face until she found his eyes and covered them with her fingers to make sure they were closed.

Going perfectly still at her first touch, Ace almost groaned at the innocence of her caress. He wasn't a kid.

He'd experienced the knowing, arousing hands of women from Singapore to Sydney, but nothing had ever stirred him like the artless brush of Maddy's fingers. He'd seen her naked and she knew it, yet she trembled at the thought of dressing in front of him on a dark, moonless night when he could hardly see her hand in front of his face.

Just yesterday, he would have called her a prude, too coy and repressed for his taste. If she'd pulled such a stunt last night, he would have accused her of playing some kind of game that he had no intention of falling for. But not now. Not after he'd kissed her this morning. Not after this. He didn't know how she'd managed it in today's jaded world, but she had somehow made it to the age of thirty-four without once being touched by a man.

Her modesty humbled him, touched him, made want to wrap her close and lose himself in her sweetness and an innocence that was as rare as snow in the jungle. But to do that, he would have to destroy that very purity that drew him like a bee to honey, he regretfully acknowledged. And that was something he couldn't do. When he finally took her home, come hell or high water, she would be as untouched as she was when Cement Johnny knocked her out and kidnapped her from the newsstand.

Fighting down the hot need rising like a tide in his body, he willed his eyes to remain shut and said gruffly, "Okay, they're shut. Scout's honor." Reaching for one of her hands, which was still lightly covering his eyes, he dragged it down and pressed the flashlight into it. "But the deal's off if you scream again. Take the light and find the rest of your clothes. And for God's sake, be careful!"

Her heart thumping madly, Maddy hesitated, a protest she didn't have the guts to voice hovering on her tongue. She didn't want to get dressed because she didn't want to leave the protection of his arms. Something had happened to her while he'd held her. Daring to study him in the weak light that bounced up from where she pointed the flashlight at the jungle floor at their feet, she tried to put her finger on what it was, and suddenly it hit her. Ace MacKenzie, or whatever his name was, was a fraud. He might pretend to be an irreverent, devil-may-care tough guy who didn't care about anything or anyone, but whatever else he was, he wasn't a man who would ever take advantage of a woman. And that made him a man she could trust.

They returned to camp a few minutes later to find a lantern burning brightly in the clearing between the two tents and the scent of something that smelled an awful lot like stew simmering in a pot over the small Bunsen burner Dominic had brought along. Dominic regretfully explained that it was only a dehydrated mixture that he'd simply added water to, but it wasn't trail mix, and in Maddy's eyes, that made it gourmet fare. Between the three of them, they consumed the entire pot in a matter of minutes, then finished off the meal with dried apricots as dessert.

After that, there was nothing to do but go to bed. But as her eyes drifted to the tent she would share with Ace, Maddy's heart kicked into high gear and she got this fluttery feeling in her stomach that had nothing to do with the food she'd just eaten. Nothing had really changed, she tried to tell herself. Yet everything had. She'd come to trust him, and that suddenly made him far more dangerous than he had been before. Because he was, she realized, shaken, a man she could lose her heart to without even trying.

"We've got an early start in the morning, gang," he said as he helped clear away the remains of the meal and put out the lantern. "Better get to bed and catch all the sleep you can. I'm setting my alarm for five."

"Sí," Dominic agreed as the night gathered closer. "Tomorrow's going to be more strenuous than today. We still have a long ways to go."

With a soft good-night, he headed for his tent, leaving Ace and Maddy behind in a silence that was suddenly crackling with tension. Hugging herself in the dark, she almost jumped when Ace asked in a gravelly voice, "Aren't you coming?"

"In a minute," she promised huskily. She needed some time to herself, some time to think. "You go ahead."

He wanted to argue with her—she could almost feel his disapproval, but just when she thought he was going to insist, he shrugged and turned away. "Have it your way. But I wouldn't stay out here too long by myself with the fire out if I were you," he advised. "Keep the flashlight handy."

The night swallowed him whole, and all too soon, Maddy found herself alone with her thoughts and a thundering heart that refused to behave. Staring at the darker shadow that she knew was the tent, she gripped the flashlight tighter and dragged in a deep, calming breath. This was not the time to let her romantic fantasies take charge, she reminded herself as the warm, steamy night pushed in on her from all sides. She and Ace were sharing a tent simply because Dominic had misunderstood their relationship. It was as simple and uncomplicated as that, and if she made the mistake of thinking Ace had some kind of romantic interlude planned, she was only going to end up making a fool of herself. And there was nothing more pathetic than an old maid who couldn't take her eyes off a man who wasn't interested in anything but a little harmless flirting that didn't mean a thing.

Wincing at the thought, Maddy didn't notice the frogs croaking on the opposite side of the river and in the trees. Then somewhere off to her right, something moved in the thick underbrush, leaving a wake of ominous, shimmering leaves. Suddenly from just beyond the clearing, something snarled, something big and hungry and wild. Maddy froze, every hair on her body standing at attention. A heartbeat later, she bolted toward the tent . . . and Ace.

She didn't stop to announce her presence but simply burst through the tent opening like the hounds of hell were after her . . . and caught Ace in the act of unzipping his pants. Startled, she gasped and dropped the flashlight, which immediately went out. "Oh! I—I'm sorry. I should have knocked . . . o-or s-something."

Not the least disturbed, Ace stepped out of his pants and laid them on top of his backpack. "That'd be a little difficult since there's no door," he said wryly as he threw himself down on top of his sleeping bag in just his shorts and rolled over onto his stomach. "Zip the tent, Little Red Riding Hood. We don't want any wolves visiting us during the middle of the night."

He'd slipped back into the irritating habit of calling her nicknames again, but Maddy was too flustered to protest. "Oh! Of course!" Her cheeks burning even though she hadn't seen a thing once she'd dropped the flashlight, she whirled and fumbled for the zipper tab at the tent opening and yanked it down, sealing them in. Behind her, she heard Ace move around in search of a more comfortable position, then his sigh as he found it and went still.

Such a simple thing, she thought, shaken, listening to a man prepare for sleep in the dark. She hadn't experienced it before and had never suspected how intimate it could be. Without her eyes to guide her, her hearing seemed to be supersensitive where he was concerned, picking up every nuance of his breathing, each whisper of his bare skin against the material of the sleeping bag as he settled down for sleep.

And in her mind, her imagination was going wild, teasing her with hot, restless images that stole her breath.

Her cheeks burning, she stiffened, suddenly realizing that if she could hear his every move, he had to be just as aware of her. And if she stood here much longer, he was bound to start wondering what the heck she was doing. Mortified, she quickly spun away from the tent entrance and cautiously made her way in the dark to the spot where she'd laid out her sleeping bag earlier.

She had no idea if he was watching her in the dark, but she had no intention of being caught without her clothes anytime soon in his presence. Contenting herself with stripping off her socks and shoes, she removed her contacts, dropped down onto the sleeping bag and stretched out with a tired sigh. She couldn't remember the last time she'd actually laid down in a completely horizontal position and it felt wonderful.

Every strained muscle in her body crying out for sleep, she closed her eyes and went limp. But the heat was oppressive, the humidity thick enough to cut with a knife. High above the tent, she could hear the wind in the treetops, but the air was utterly still on the forest floor, with not so much as a breeze to stir the bushes. And outside the tent, she heard again the snarl of the big cat that had sent her rushing inside. Only this time, it sounded closer, meaner.

Her heart in her throat, she glanced over to where she could just make out Ace's broad-shouldered form in the shadows. "Ace?"

For a moment, she thought he was asleep. He didn't move a muscle, let alone answer her. Then he stirred. "Hmm?"

"What was that?"

"What?" he mumbled.

The growl seemed to come from right outside the tent and sent her heart jumping into her throat. *"That!"*

He chuckled sleepily. "Just a jaguar."

"*Just* a jaguar?"

He laughed softly, an incredibly sexy, sand paper-rough sound in the darkness. "Don't worry. I won't let him chew on you. Scout's honor."

"You were a Scout?"

"You don't have to sound so surprised. I was a regular kid just like everybody else. Where do you think I learned my survival skills?"

She smiled at his defensive tone. "Somehow, I don't think they taught you how to dodge bullets in the Boy Scouts. I just assumed you learned all that stuff in agent's school."

She heard, rather than saw, him stiffen with wariness. "When did I say I was an agent?"

"Aren't you?"

For a moment, his only answer was dead silence. Then he said quietly, "There are some things a little girl shouldn't ask."

"I'm not a little girl," she said just as quietly.

"I know," he growled. "That's the problem." Turning on his side away from her, he presented his back to her. "Go to sleep, Maddy. You're perfectly safe."

Within seconds, his breathing was slow and steady and deep. Her pulse racing crazily, Maddy stared at his dark, still shadow. He wasn't as indifferent to her as he would have liked. That should have worried her, she thought as she flopped over on her back and closed her eyes. Instead, she couldn't seem to stop smiling.

Outside the thin net walls of the tent, the jungle was alive and restless in the night. Maddy reminded herself that Ace had a gun and she'd seen firsthand just how well he could use it. If he could shoot a snake between the eyes at the drop of a hat, there was no way he was going to miss something as big as a jungle cat. There was nothing to be afraid of.

But fear, she was discovering, had nothing to do with logic. Ace was less than six feet away, yet suddenly she felt alone, isolated, horribly vulnerable. If something decided to come through the flimsy material of the tent after her, it would be on her before she could manage a scream, let alone turn to Ace for help. And if he was a heavy sleeper, which he could be for all she knew, she could already be dead meat before he discovered something was wrong.

That's right. Maddy, a voice jeered in her head. *Scare yourself to death, why don't you? Then you'll really be able to sleep.*

Disgusted, she jumped up, grabbed her sleeping bag and quietly moved it four feet closer to Ace. Undisturbed, he didn't move a muscle. Close enough to reach out and touch him if the need arose, she laid back down, turned on her side so that she was facing him and closed her eyes. When the jaguar outside growled five minutes later, she was already asleep and didn't hear a thing.

When the alarm on Ace's watch went off at five, it was still black as pitch outside and the only time of the night or day when the rain forest was relatively quiet. Groaning, he fumbled for the button to turn off the alarm, cursing the damn thing when he finally found it. It'd been a while since he'd slept on the hard ground and he was feeling it in every bone in his body.

"You're getting too old for this type of thing, man," he complained in a gravelly voice as he dragged himself to his feet and reached for his pants. "Taking off into the wilds after scum was all right when you were a kid, but you're pushing forty, tough guy. You've gotten soft..."

In the process of zipping his pants, he frowned at the dark lump in the middle of the tent floor. What the hell was that? Scowling, he started to reach for the flashlight that should have been by his boots, then remembered that Maddy had dropped it when she'd come to bed last night. Praying that the thing in the middle of the floor wasn't a big, coiled boa, he stepped around it to where he estimated the flashlight had fallen and felt around with his foot until he found it.

He wouldn't have been surprised if it hadn't worked, but a couple of whacks with the heel of his hand did the trick. The light sprang on, illuminating every inch of the interior of the tent, as well as the lump in the middle of the floor.

Maddy.

She lay on her stomach, her face buried in the crook of her bent elbow and almost hidden from him by the sassy curls that just barely reached the curve of her cheek. Sometime during the night, the heat must have gotten to her. She'd stripped off her shorts and lay before him in nothing but a long-tailed shirt and the red panties he'd bought her in Mexico City.

His gaze fixed on the lacy elastic that just barely peeked out from beneath the hem of her shirt, he grinned. So she'd worn them. He'd wondered if she would. She'd been so shocked by the color and the cut that it'd been obvious that she'd never worn anything more daring than serviceable white cotton in her life. He hadn't dared tell her that there was something about a woman in red panties that he couldn't resist.

She looked damn good in them, he decided as his gaze slowly slid up and down the slender curves of her long legs. Too good. With no trouble at all, he could picture those legs wrapping around him, holding him close....

Just that easily, he was hot and hard and furious with himself. What the hell was he doing? He was here for one reason and one reason only—to catch Lazear before he reached Barrera. Once that was done, he was washing his hands of one Maddy Lawrence just as quickly as he could arrange it. If she was going to arrive home as innocent as the day she was born, he'd damn well better forget what the lady looked like in red panties!

But, damn, he wasn't cut out for sainthood. The minute he tore his gaze away from those beautiful legs of hers, it suddenly hit him how close her sleeping bag was to his. And since he hadn't moved his during the night, that meant she'd moved hers—to be closer to him.

Something streaked through him at the thought, something that a man with good intentions had no business feeling. His jaw rigid, he set the flashlight down, checked his boots to make sure they didn't hold any unwanted visitors and tugged them on. When he squatted down beside Maddy, his face was grim with purpose.

He started to reach for her, but she muttered something in her sleep just then and turned her head away without so much as opening her eyes. The devil sitting on his shoulder, Ace frowned down at her, fighting the sudden urge to lean over her and nibble at the back of her neck, the shell of her ear, the sweet, tempting corner of her mouth. If he set his mind to it, he could have her hot and needy and wide-awake in ten seconds flat.

Hell!

Cursing himself, he stripped off his watch, reset the alarm to go off again in sixty seconds and laid it right by her ear. When it went off, he was standing all the way across the tent.

Startled, by the sudden buzzing in her ear, Maddy jerked out of a sound sleep to find Ace dressed and glaring at her from the tent entrance. Confused, she said, "What? What's going on?"

"It's time to get up," he snapped. "Get dressed so I can take the damn tent down. It's already after five and we need to get moving."

Growling at her to check her shoes before she put them on, he strode out without another word, his face set in implacable lines, his eyes hard. Stunned, Maddy pushed her hair from her eyes and stared after him in bewilderment. Was this the same man who only just last night had killed a snake for her, then tenderly held her until she stopped shaking? The same one she'd felt so close to that she could have trusted him with anything, including her heart? Talk about getting up on the wrong side of the bed! He'd all but bitten her head off, and for the life of her, she didn't even know what she'd done.

Tears stung her eyes and lumped in her throat. How, she wondered, blinking rapidly, could she have misjudged a man so completely? She'd thought they were coming to like each other, but now that he'd had time to think about their closeness last night, he obviously regretted it and wanted nothing more to do with her.

The anger came out of nowhere, roiling in her gut like a summer storm sweeping in off the Atlantic. God, how could she have been so gullible? This wasn't a fairy tale where the princess got her man. She was a long way from a blue blood and Ace wasn't by any stretch of the imagination a knight who'd come charging to her rescue. Oh, he'd saved her, all right, but only because he'd thought she could lead him to her boss. He might have changed his opinion of her since then, but he'd just made it painfully clear that he didn't want to be friends or buddies or anything else with her. Her heart might kick in her breast whenever he was within touching distance, but when he looked at her, all he saw was a responsibility that he was stuck with until they returned to civilization.

Fine, she thought, snatching up her shorts and his watch, which she stuffed into her pocket. If that was the way he wanted it, she wouldn't make the mistake of thinking they could be anything more than civil to each other again, she assured herself proudly as she popped in another pair of the disposable contacts. She'd be polite ... and distant. And if there was a benevolent God up there somewhere looking out for her, she'd still have her heart when they went their separate ways.

Breakfast consisted of the hated trail mix that stuck in Maddy's throat and a silence that seemed unbreakable. His weathered face lined with confusion, Dominic kept looking from her to Ace and back again, trying to figure out what the problem was between the two of them, but he wisely held his tongue when no one seemed inclined to talk. Then it was time to load the canoe and head farther upriver, and they saved their energy for paddling against the current.

Dawn came as quickly as darkness had the night before. One minute, they were engulfed in a blackness that was so thick it seemed impenetrable, and the next, sunlight was bursting through the thick foliage and pushing back the shadows. Suddenly, the jungle was alive with life that, for the most part, remained just out of sight within the safety of the trees. Occasionally, they would catch a glimpse of something on the bank, the swish of a tail, the glint of watchful eyes, before it quickly darted back out of sight, and they couldn't be sure what they'd seen, if anything.

Seated in the middle again, with Ace in front of her and Dominic at the rear of the canoe, Maddy scowled at Ace's back, determined to hang on to her hurt and anger for as long as possible. But the unspoiled beauty of their surroundings soothed and fascinated her, and when Dominic quietly pointed out a family of turtles sunning on a dead log on the riverbank, she couldn't help but smile at the sight and long once again for her camera.

Later, Dominic drew her attention to a caiman, which resembled an alligator, all but buried in the water but for its watchful, unblinking eyes. Shivering, she eagerly asked him questions about it, and soon they were both chattering away about the jungle and all its mysteries. Ace, however, remained aloof. Staring stiffly ahead, he ignored them both for hours and only spoke to warn Dominic of a log or some other hazard farther upstream so that the other man could steer them around it.

And the longer Ace ignored them, the more annoyed Maddy became. She didn't know what his problem was, but whatever it was, it was no excuse for such childishness. They were all literally stuck in the same boat, and the least he could do was pretend to be friendly. But men, she was discovering, didn't feel the compunction to play nicey-nicey just to keep the peace the way most women did. What you saw was what you got, like it or not. It was downright irritating.

By midday, an uncomfortable silence had once again fallen, and this time, no one seemed inclined to break it. Then they heard a low roar that gradually grew louder and louder as they traveled farther upriver. Startled, Maddy glanced over her shoulder at Dominic. "What's that noise?"

"Diablo Falls, *señorita*," he said grimly. "Devil Falls. I've never been this far upriver, but I have heard it is one of the most dangerous spots on the river. We must be very careful."

Maddy started to ask him why, but within seconds, she could see for herself. They came around a bend, and suddenly the falls was right in front of them, towering two hundred feet into the air. With a roar that sounded like thunder that had no end, thousands of gallons of water poured over the cliff edge and crashed to the rocks below, creating a heavy mist that was as thick as fog.

Almost immediately, they were caught in the wild churning of the water caused by the falls. "Over there!" Ace shouted as the canoe began to rock back and forth. "We've got to get out of this current before it dashes us against the rocks!" Pointing to an area of relatively calm water that was protected by a small outcropping of land, he started to paddle furiously.

The thunder of her heart nearly as loud as the roar of the falls in her ears, Maddy quickly joined in as Dominic steered them toward the spot, but the current already had them in its grasp and started to drag them backward. The blood draining from her face, she looked to Ace for help and saw him dig his paddle deeper into the water, the muscles of his arms knotting as he pulled against the powerful river with all his strength. Tightening her grip on her own paddle, she did the same.

For what seemed like an eternity, they just hovered there, caught like a fly in a spiderweb, unable to make any headway whatsoever. Behind her in the stern, Dominic muttered something in Spanish. Her arms straining, her teeth clamped with purpose, Maddy paddled faster and prayed like she had never prayed in her life. And inch by slow, painstaking inch, they gradually nosed forward.

"Yes!" Ace yelled over the roar of the water. "That's it! Keep it up. We're gonna make it!"

Too breathless to manage so much as a yes, Maddy could only nod. Then they finally reached the smoother water of the little cove, where the strength of their strokes sent them shooting right up onto the bank. Laughing, tears of relief running down her cheeks, Maddy collapsed with a groan in the bottom of the canoe as the mist fell down on them like rain.

"*Madre de Dios!*" Dominic wheezed weakly, pushing his wet hair back from his brow. "That was too close for comfort!"

"You're damn right it was," Ace huffed. "If there hadn't been three of us paddling, we'd have been goners for sure." His gaze lifted to the thousands of gallons of water cascading from the top of the high cliff. "That's going to be a pain in the butt to climb. There's no other way around it?"

"Only if you want to go fifty miles out of the way," the older man said.

"Climb?" Maddy gasped, her eyes lifting to the rocky escarpment that rose like a rock wall before them. "We're going to climb *that?*"

"We have no other choice if you want to reach Barrera's hideout quickly, *señorita*. Going around will take you days out of the way."

"But what about the canoe? And all our gear?"

Tilting his head back, Ace studied the path to the top, looking for the easiest way. There wasn't one. "Damn, I don't like the looks of this," he said with a shake of his head. "But if there's no other way, the only way to go is up. Dominic and I will get the canoe, then come back for the packs," he told Maddy, glancing down at her. "You think you can manage yours by yourself?"

Manage? Maddy almost cried out. Manage what? To climb up the side of a moss-covered cliff like a lizard? No, she couldn't manage! Not this. Anything but this! She didn't do heights well. Ever. Not since the day she fell out of a tree in Central Park when she was seven and broke her arm. She'd had nightmares for months afterward, horrifying dreams of that heart-stopping moment when she'd realized that there was nothing beneath her feet but thin air. She hadn't even been on the lowest step of a stepladder since.

God, she couldn't do this. But she had to. What other choice did she have? "Yes," she said, forcing a smile. "Of course."

She thought she sounded confident enough, but something in her voice must have given her away. Ace's gaze narrowed sharply on her face. "Are you sure?"

"I can do it," she assured him firmly, and prayed she didn't live to regret those words.

His eyes searched hers for what seemed like an eternity before he finally nodded. "Just don't try to be Superwoman, okay? If you get stuck or think you can't make it, just sit there until Dominic and I get the canoe on top and I'll come back for you. Okay?"

If her stomach hadn't been sick with nerves, she would have laughingly told him he didn't have to worry. If she got in trouble, he'd definitely hear about it. The best she could manage, however, was a snappy salute and a smile that never reached her eyes. "Got it, kemosabe. Lead the way."

Standing well back out of the way, she watched as Ace and Dominic lifted the empty canoe and started up the cliff. Each step was a tricky one. The rocks underfoot were large, jagged pieces of granite that looked as if they had been tossed there by a careless hand. Appearing to barely cling to the side of the cliff, they were covered with wet, slick moss that thrived on the constant moisture in the air.

When the men were fifteen feet up, it was Maddy's turn. Her heart in her throat, she gingerly stepped onto the first rock. Above her, she heard Ace and Dominic grunt and swear as they struggled to lift the canoe over the sharp-edged boulders that offered the only path to the top, but she didn't dare spare them a glance. "Everything okay up there?"

"Peachy," Ace snarled as his foot hit a slippery patch and he almost went flying before he was able to grab on to a nearby rock and right himself. "Just peachy."

The near slip, however, sent the canoe jerking back toward Dominic and bumped him in the chest. Caught off guard, he staggered and cried out in surprise. A split second later, he sat down hard on the rock behind him, dragging his end of the canoe down with him.

Startled by the commotion and the string of oaths suddenly heating the air, Maddy had this sudden image of both men losing their balance and falling all the way to the bottom, taking her with them. Horrified, she looked up...and promptly lost her balance.

It happened so fast, she didn't have time to do anything but cry out and throw herself toward the nearest rock. But it was covered with sodden moss and she couldn't get a solid grip. Her nails ripped. Her raw fingers helplessly clawed at sheer granite. Strangling on a scream, she started to fall.

Chapter 7

"**M**addy!"

Somewhere on the edge of the fear that cloaked her mind like a black fog, Maddy heard Ace roar her name, but she couldn't unclench her teeth long enough to assure him she was all right. By rights, she should have been lying in a broken heap at the bottom of the cliff. Why she wasn't would forever remain a mystery to her, but she didn't dare question the whims of fate, not when the only thing between her and a long fall to the base of the waterfall was the slippery boulder she'd finally grabbed at the very last second. Clinging to it, she squeezed her eyes tightly shut and waited for the jackhammer beat of her heart to level off. But that wasn't going to happen, not when she only had a four-inch ledge to stand on that could, for all she knew, crumble at any second.

The furious curses that rained down on her from above were graphic, coarse and highly imaginative. "Hang on, honey!" Ace called hoarsely. "I'm coming. Just hang on!"

Already near the top, Ace and Dominic hurriedly shoved the canoe over the edge of the cliff, then scrambled back down the rocks to where Maddy clung like a burr to a boulder that wasn't nearly big enough for her peace of mind. "I'm all right," she said shakily as they half slid down to her. "Really. I just need a minute to catch my breath."

Hovering on the rock next to the one she gripped like a lover, Ace reached out to gently sweep her hair back from her ashen face. "You know, if you wanted to take a break, sweetheart, you didn't have to go out on a ledge just to get our attention. All you had to do was say something."

"Cute, MacKenzie. Real cute. For your information, I thought you and Dominic fell."

"So you jumped off the cliff, too," he needled, trying to draw a full-fledged smile from her. "Talk about being cute, Lawrence. That was a no-brainer. Do you think you can step over here to where I am?"

"No!" The cry bursting from her lips, she tightened her hold on the rock until her knuckles were white with the strain. One wrong step and she knew she'd be history. She wasn't budging.

"We won't let you fall, *señorita*," Dominic assured her as he took a position on the other side of her. "We're right here. There is no reason for you to be afraid."

"Easy for you to say." She laughed shakily and hugged her rock.

Studying her pale face, the almost desperate way she gripped the boulder, Ace frowned. "I know this isn't the smartest time to ask this question, but do you have a problem with heights, sweetheart?"

At first he thought she was going to deny it. Then she shrugged, a faint movement that was quickly checked. "Maybe a little."

He could have scolded her for not telling him sooner—he knew from the way she braced herself that she wouldn't have blamed him—but he only murmured to Dominic in Spanish that he would take care of Maddy while the other man got their backpacks, then leaned his shoulder against the cliff wall as the guide made his way down to where they'd left their supplies.

"Did I ever tell you about this little problem I used to have with small, closed-in places?" he asked quietly once they were alone. He knew perfectly well he hadn't—it wasn't a part of himself he shared with many people—but he saw her grip relax slightly, which was just what he'd hoped for. "When I was a little boy, I accidently got locked in a closet in the attic."

"Oh, no! How long were you in there?"

"Six hours," he said flatly. "My mother thought I had gone with my father, and my father assumed I was safe and sound at home. Which I was—I just couldn't get out of that closet and no one heard me screaming for help. No one even realized I was missing until my father came home and no one could find me. For years, I broke out in a cold sweat every time I found myself in a small locked room. Even a bathroom."

He had her attention now. She was watching him, the concern darkening her eyes more for him than herself. "You said you *used* to be afraid. How'd you get past the fear?"

"I was in Budapest a couple of years ago and got locked in a basement by someone I was trailing." His voice roughened just at the thought of it as he confided, "I went out of my head for a little while, but once I got control, I dug my way out of that hellhole."

His gaze directed inward on memories he didn't often take out and examine, he didn't see her cautiously reach out to him until her fingers traced the frown furrowing his brow.

"And that cured you of the fear?" she murmured. "Just like that?"

"No," he admitted honestly. "It's always there, waiting just beyond the shadows, but it's not as powerful as it was. Because I know now that no matter what kind of mess I'm in, I can get out of it if I just keep my head." Taking her fingers, he smiled at her. "I won't lie to you, honey. You've got a hell of a mountain to climb, but you can do it. One step at a time."

Her eyes locked on his, she saw an unwavering faith there...for her. Her fingers tightening in his, she didn't make a conscious decision, but suddenly she was in his arms and she had no memory of how she'd gotten there.

Snatching her close, Ace sighed in relief. God, she'd scared the hell out of him! When he'd seen her start to fall and knew he was never going to be able to reach her in time, his heart had stopped dead in his chest. He'd never felt so helpless in his life. Or so furious with himself.

He shouldn't have brought her here, dammit. Hell, he'd had no business dragging her out of New York. She was a city girl, soft and inexperienced and like a duck out of water once you got her out of the towering canyons of Manhattan. If he had any sense, he'd go the rest of the way by himself and send her back to Caracas with Dominic, who could put her on the first plane back to the States. She'd be out of his hair for good, and he could get back to the business at hand—catching Lazear before he was able to unload that belly-button ring.

But even as his gut told him that was what he should do, he knew he couldn't do it. He couldn't let her go—not yet. He tried to convince himself it was just a guilt trip that made him hold on to her—he was responsible for her safety, for personally delivering her back to her sick mother—but he wasn't a man who bought into guilt. Ever. So what the hell was going on here?

"Okay," she mumbled wryly against his shoulder. "You got me off that ledge. But I've got to be honest with you, MacKenzie—the view doesn't look much better from here. It's a long way down."

"Then it's a good thing we're not going down," he replied, keeping his tone deliberately light as he carefully set her from him just enough so that he could see her face. She was pale and there was definite apprehension in her eyes, but the terror that had held her on that ledge was, for the moment, thankfully under control. Taking her hand, he wove his fingers through hers and held her, palm to palm. "You ready to get off the side of this damn cliff now?"

He made it sound as easy as a walk in the park, but the second her eyes took the long, dangerous trip to the top, her stomach tilted sickeningly. "Maybe I'll just stay here by myself while you two go after Mr. Lazear," she said faintly as he started to step up to the jagged boulder just above them to the left. "I'm sure I'll be fine."

"That's one option," he agreed, dropping back down beside her. "But I don't think you'd like this place very much once it started to get dark. Of course, if you're really dead set against making the climb today, we could set up camp down at the bottom for the night, then do it tomorrow when you're steadier on your feet."

A class-A coward, she wanted to jump at that offer, but putting the climb off until tomorrow would only make things worse. And she knew as well as he did that if they quit this early in the day, it would kill whatever slim chance they still had of catching up with Lazear before he reached Barrera's stronghold. "No, we could wait a month and it wouldn't be any easier. Let's just do it and get it over with."

"There's another option," he said, watching her closely. "I could carry you."

On flat ground, she shamelessly admitted to herself, she didn't think she would have been able to deny herself the pleasure. But on that rocky cliff? "I don't think so."

His mouth crooked up at one corner. "Then what if we take it one step at a time? I'll wait until you're ready before I move on and I'll never let go of your hand. Okay?"

It was the best offer she was going to get and, unless she wanted to stay there by herself with the snakes and jungle cats and whatever else was waiting out there in the undergrowth for her, one she didn't have the luxury of turning down. In spite of that, she couldn't manage the single word that was going to take her higher up that cliff. Her throat tight, all she could do was squeeze his hand.

It was enough. He gave her a smile that warmed her all the way to her toes and tightened his fingers around hers. "Good girl."

Just as he promised, he took it nice and easy, never rushing her, making sure she was steady on her feet before taking her higher. The roar of the waterfall loud in her ears, she kept her eyes trained on Ace's booted feet, then her own, while in her head, she promised herself over and over again that if she could get through this, she could get through anything. Still, no one was more surprised than she when they actually took that last step that put them over the top.

Stunned, she looked up for what seemed like the first time in hours and saw nothing but level ground covered by the thick vegetation of the rain forest. Surprised, she laughed, elated. "We did it. My God, we did it!" she cried, and threw herself into his arms.

Chuckling, he wrapped her close. "Well, you don't have to sound so damn surprised. Did you think I was going to let you fall?"

"No, of course not, but..."

She drew back the tiniest bit to see his face, her eyes locked with his, and suddenly the exhilaration sizzling through her had nothing to do with the hurdle they'd both just climbed. She drew in a quick breath and the scent of him filled her. Her heart stumbled and picked up speed as she felt awareness make its way through his body. Seduced, she could hear Dominic making his way up the dangerous cliff face with their supplies. Any second now, he'd stumble over the edge and catch them in each other's arms.

She should move, do something, she told herself dazedly. But she couldn't, not when he was this close. Not when his mouth was just a heartbeat from hers. Not when it seemed like a lifetime had passed since he'd kissed her.

His gaze riveted to hers, Ace stared down at her and couldn't for the life of him look away. She had the look of a woman who needed to be kissed. Desperately. Her brown eyes were nearly black with need, her lips slightly parted in an unconscious invitation that only a saint could have had a prayer of ignoring. And God knew, he was no saint. He wanted her. There was no use lying about it to himself. She stirred a hunger in him that ate at him from the inside out and got stronger every time his eyes chanced to meet hers. And he ached, dammit! No woman had ever made him ache this way! All he could think about was dragging her down to the jungle floor with him and kissing every sweet inch of her until she was hot and panting and didn't remember her own name. He'd love her then, like she'd never dreamed of being loved, like he'd never allowed himself to love a woman...

He was already lowering his mouth to hers when he suddenly realized what he was doing. Cursing himself, he froze. What the hell was the matter with him? The lady was a virgin. A sweet, tempting virgin who didn't have a clue what she was inviting with those long sultry looks of hers. And that made her off-limits. Why was he having such a hard time remembering that?

His mouth pressed flat into an uncompromising line of determination, he never knew where he found the strength of will to put her from him. Especially when her eyes flashed with hurt. Dammit, hadn't anyone ever told her she wasn't supposed to wear her heart on her sleeve? he thought resentfully. Did she think this was easy for him? He knew what he was missing; she didn't. But he was trying to do the right thing for once in his life, and by God, he was going to do it even if it killed him!

"Dominic can't get all the packs up the cliff by himself," he said tersely. "Why don't you take a break? You look like you could use one."

He left her standing there and headed back to the cliff like a man who had just escaped a close brush with disaster. Feeling as if her heart had just taken a dive over the waterfall, Maddy stared after him long after he disappeared from view. The breath she hadn't realized she was holding escaped in a slow rush. She told herself she was glad he hadn't kissed her again. She couldn't handle it, couldn't handle what he did to her. He made her forget that this wasn't reality, that he wasn't and never could be the man she'd been waiting for all her life. Because he was a dream, as out of her reach as the fictional Ace MacKenzie.

The emotion that helped get her up the side of the cliff faded as Maddy settled in the middle of the canoe and they started upriver again. With her paddle in hand, she should have slipped right back into the rhythm with ease, but one by one, her muscles began to tighten up. Bumps and bruises that had until now been masked by the rush of adrenaline that had accompanied her near fall began to make themselves known.

She ached . . . literally everywhere. Even her teeth hurt. A dull throbbing in her head seemed to keep cadence with the beat of her heart, and she wasn't sure, but she thought she must have wrenched her shoulder. White-hot pain seared her every time she moved her left arm.

Casting a quick look at Ace's stiff back, she sent up a silent prayer of thanks that he was sitting in front of her instead of behind her. He never saw the grimaces of pain she couldn't quite hide or the careful way she shifted in her seat in an effort to get comfortable. But regardless of how she changed positions, nothing seemed to help.

And then there was her side. She didn't think it was bleeding, but from the way it burned, she must have scraped it raw against a jagged edge of rock when she'd thrown herself onto the ledge. She could feel her shirt sticking to it and didn't dare lean against the side of the canoe the way she longed to. She knew Dominic had to notice, but he was thankfully silent, and for that, she was profoundly grateful. Because if Ace suspected half of what she was feeling, he'd stop immediately, deal with her injuries and then send her back to Caracas to wait for his return. And in the process, he would lose precious time and probably any chance of catching Lazear.

No, she told herself silently, stifling a moan when she inadvertently moved the wrong way. She wouldn't let him lose Mr. Lazear because of her. After all, it wasn't as if she were dying. So she had a few scrapes and bruises, so what? She'd clean them up later when they stopped for the night and Ace would be none the wiser. By tomorrow, she'd be good as new.

It was a good plan, but by the time they stopped for the night, she was so stiff she could hardly move. If it hadn't been for Dominic quickly coming to her aid, she wouldn't have even been able to get out of the canoe.

Taking her hand as he helped her out, he said quietly, "Maybe you should sit down and rest, *señorita*. You don't look so good."

If she looked half as bad as she felt, that had to be a whopper if she'd ever heard one, but she couldn't help grinning at his blunt statement. "Gee, thanks, Dominic. Now I really feel better."

"Oh, but I didn't mean—"

"The *señorita* knows what you meant," Ace said dryly as he lifted the backpacks from the canoe and began unpacking the tents. "She was just teasing. And you're right— she's beginning to look a little purple around the edges." Turning his attention to Maddy, he frowned. There was no point in asking if she was all right—he knew her well enough by now to know that she'd have to be half-dead before she'd complain. "Pull up a log and sit down," he said gruffly. "Dominic and I can handle the tents."

"But I've been sitting all day. And look at those clouds," she added, lifting her eyes to the dark clouds gathering ominously overhead. "You'll never get the tents up before it rains if you don't let me help."

She had a point, one that he had no choice but to concede to if he was going to have her safely inside before the evening showers hit. But he didn't like it. She looked... fragile. Finding the hammer among the bag of tools he carried in his pack, he handed it to her handle first. "I'll take care of the heavy stuff. All you've got to do is hammer when I say hammer. Got it?"

It was an order, pure and simple, one she didn't miss. "Yes, sir. Anything you say, sir."

She didn't salute, but she might as well have. His lips twitching, he tried his damnedest to keep his expression stern, but he was fighting a losing battle. Little witch. "That's what I like to hear—a woman who knows her place," he drawled. Casting another quick look at the clouds gathering overhead, he estimated that they were only five minutes or so away from busting wide open. "We'd better get moving or we're all going to get soaked."

They didn't need a second warning. Jumping into action, they hurriedly started throwing the tents up. Four minutes later, with only a slight sprinkle for a warning, the skies opened up, and they still had one stake left to secure. Muttering a curse, Ace grabbed the hammer from Maddy and yelled at her to get inside, but her strained muscles refused to let her do anything fast. Already soaked, she turned toward the tent entrance, wincing in pain, as Ace gave the stake two powerful blows that sent it shuddering into the wet ground. In the next instant, he snatched her up into his arms and ran for the cover of their tent as Dominic darted into his own.

"Damn, I thought we were going to make it!" Shaking his wet hair out of his eyes, he laughed and bent to set her on her feet.

Every muscle in her body seemed to cry out in protest at the simple movement, but Maddy refused to give in to the discomfort. Pasting on a smile, she lifted a hand to her dripping hair and instantly regretted it. A hot pain shot out of her sore shoulder, stealing her breath. With a quiet hiss, she froze and squeezed her eyes shut.

The second she opened them a few moments later and found him watching her, she knew it was too much to hope that Ace hadn't noticed her pain. His gaze sharp in the shadows that slowly filled the interior of the tent, he frowned at her accusingly. "Why didn't you tell me you were in pain?"

"I'm not—"

"The hell you're not! You're as white as a sheet, and you can hardly move. I knew you'd be stiff and banged up, but this is more than that, isn't it? You're really hurt."

His tone was filled with a self-reproach that stabbed her right in the heart. "No! I'm not...not seriously, at least," she quickly amended. "It's just my shoulder—I think I wrenched it when I fell."

"And...?"

He waited for the rest, and she knew he wouldn't let up until she told him. "I scraped my side."

Ace swore long and hard then, wanting to shake her. "You little fool! This is the jungle, for God's sake! You don't walk around with open wounds all afternoon getting infected with God knows what. How bad is it?"

"It's n-nothing. Just a scrape."

She tried to shrug off his concern, but he knew he'd scared her—he could see it in the shadow of her eyes. And she needed to be scared, dammit. If she got some kind of jungle fever because of this...

"I'm going to have to take a look at it," he said huskily. "Which side is it?"

She started to give him an argument, but he gave her a fierce glare that warned her this was one fight she wasn't going to win. Pale, she turned her left side to face him and lifted her arm. Reaching out, he carefully lifted her shirt.

Her head turned aside, Maddy felt the touch of the damp air on her raw skin and braced herself for Ace's touch. But he only sucked in a sharp breath and gently lowered her shirt. And that's when she knew she must have hurt herself much worse than even she had suspected. He didn't yell at her or grumble about her foolishness; he just spoke in a quiet, controlled voice that was somehow much more unsettling than a shout of anger. "The first-aid kit's in Dominic's backpack. I'll be right back."

He strode out into the rain, leaving her to think what she would as the shadows gathered around her and her imagination ran wild. He would send her back for sure now, she thought, stricken. She'd left him no other choice. And she didn't want to go. He'd showed her a whole new world and a side of herself that she had never suspected existed, and for the first time in years, she felt alive, really alive. Her days had a vibrancy they hadn't had before, her nights an anticipation that left her breathless. All because of Ace. He'd dragged her kicking and screaming out of a dull, colorless existence, and just the thought of going back to that... and leaving him ... made her sick at heart.

With the rain a dull pounding against the roof of the tent, she didn't hear him return, but suddenly he was there in front of her, his face creased with lines of concern and his arms laden with supplies that included everything from the first-aid kit and a flashlight to the Bunsen burner Dominic had used to cook their supper last night. Frowning, she said, "What's that for?"

"To heat water." All business, he switched on the flashlight and hung it on the center pole of the tent, then quickly proceeded to set up the burner and start heating a small pot of water. His eyes on the task, he tore open the first-aid kit and started removing the items he would need. "Can you take your shirt off by yourself or do you need some help?"

Somewhere in the back of her mind, she'd known he couldn't very well treat her injuries with her shirt on, but the thought that she would have to undress in front of him never quite registered. Staring at him blankly, she said, "You're going to help me undress?"

He looked up then, his blue eyes dark with purpose and deadly serious. "This is no time for modesty, sweetheart. Your side's got to be cleaned and treated with antiseptic.

That means taking off your shirt. If you can't do it by yourself because of your sore shoulder, then I'll help you.''

There wasn't anything the least bit suggestive or out of line in his tone. He looked as professional as a paramedic, but her heart still had this crazy tendency to turn over at the thought of him undressing her. Hugging herself, she unconsciously took a step back. ''N-no. I can do it. Just give me a minute.''

He nodded. ''Take your time. The water's not warm yet, anyway.''

He turned his attention back to the first-aid kit, not sparing her so much as a glance as she lifted trembling fingers to the top button of the grass green blouse he'd bought her in Mexico City. Her throat dry, Maddy hesitated, feeling like a child and hating herself for it. He was right—this was no time for modesty. And it wasn't as if he'd never seen a woman without her clothes before. He'd probably been personally responsible for stripping hundreds himself. He'd gotten a good look at her last night at the river, so he wasn't likely to so much as blink at the sight of her in a bra.

Still, she presented him her back as she fumbled with the buttons, releasing them one by one. And in the tense silence that seemed to grow like spectators at the scene of an accident, her heart thundered like a runaway train.

Reaching the last button, her blouse hanging open like a wanton's, she dragged in a calming breath and assured herself that she could do this. All she had to do was act as if she wasn't the least concerned about standing before him in her underwear and he'd never notice her embarrassment.

But when she peeled the front sections of the garment back so that it could just slide off with only a slight shrug, her sore shoulder locked up tight, making only the barest minimum of movement possible. More on than off, her blouse just hung there. A silent groan lodging in her throat, she tried again...with the same results.

"Problems?" Ace asked quietly.

She hadn't heard him approach, but suddenly he was right behind her, so close she could feel his breath stirring her hair. She stiffened, feeling horribly exposed. In the revealing light of the flashlight, a blind man couldn't have missed the curve of her breast covered only by her bra.

Sudden tears thickening in her throat, she nodded. "I g-guess I need some help, after all."

Without a word, he carefully placed his hands on her shoulders and gently began to ease the garment off. His jaw as rigid as a block of granite, he sternly ordered himself to concentrate on her injuries, but from the moment he'd stepped up behind her and caught sight of her bra, it was all he could do not to groan. Red again. God, what had possessed him to buy her sexy underwear? He'd wanted to shock her, to shake up that prim and proper demeanor of hers and get under her skin a little, but he was the one who was constantly being thrown for a loop. Dammit, next time he bought a woman—any woman—underwear, he was getting plain-Jane cotton!

"Well?"

Jerking back to attention, he looked up to find that she'd turned and lifted her arm so that he could see her side clearly in the light. From the expectant way she was looking at him, her cheeks on fire with color, she'd obviously said something, but he hadn't a clue what it was. "What?"

"I said it must be pretty bad. You haven't said a word."

Only because he'd been too busy drooling like a young pup who'd never seen a woman in her underwear before, he thought irritably. "No, I was just...thinking," he lied huskily, and dropped his gaze to her nearly naked torso.

In the full glare of the flashlight, he was able to see that she was hurt much worse than he'd originally thought. Large patches of skin had been scraped away along her ribs, creating open wounds that had to sting like the devil.

A muscle bunching along his tightly clenched jaw, he lifted his fingers to an ugly yellow-and-black bruise that was just above the waistband of her shorts and as big as his hand. He knew battle-toughened men who would have gone to their knees with that type of wound, yet she hadn't so much as whimpered all afternoon. She'd let him lead her up the side of that cliff, then climbed into the canoe and paddle upriver for hours without a single break. How had she stood it?

Wanting to shake her, to take her in his arms and assure her that he would never let anything or anyone hurt her again, he said in a rough whisper, "I ought to turn you over my knee, lady, for not telling me about this. How do you think I feel knowing you must have been in agony all afternoon and you didn't trust me enough to tell me? What's the matter? Did you think I'd go on without you or what?"

"I didn't want to slow you down," she said with a quiet dignity that struck him right in the heart. "We've already lost too much time as it is. Mr. Lazear—"

"Screw Lazear," he growled. "He's not your problem—he's mine. And I'll deal with the bastard when I catch him."

Jesus, what kind of monster did she think he was? He'd get the damn ring somehow, but not at the expense of her health. Nothing was worth that. Turning away, he grabbed her sleeping bag and rolled it open with a snap of his wrist. "Come over here and sit down by the light," he told her gruffly. "The water's warm now."

Grabbing up her discarded shirt, she held it protectively in front of her and crossed to her sleeping bag, drawing a smile from him that faded the second she settled cross-

legged in front of him. He was going to have to hurt her—
there was no help for it. And it sickened him.

Tersely explaining what he was going to do, he dipped
gauze in the warm water and warned, "This is going to
sting. Yell if you want to."

At his first touch, Maddy stiffened like a poker, liquid fire
spreading out in waves across her ribs. She groaned—she
couldn't help it—and immediately felt Ace jerk his hand
back as if he was the one who burned. Curses—all directed
at himself—turned the air blue, drowning out the rain that
continued to pound the roof of the tent.

"Hell, honey, I'm sorry—"

"No!" she choked thickly. "Don't apologize."

"But I hurt you, dammit!"

"It'll hurt a lot worse if those scrapes get infected. Go
ahead. Do your worst. I can stand it if you can."

This time when he touched her, she told herself she was
ready for the pain. Her jaw locked and her mouth pressed
flat, she stared unseeingly at the dull green walls of the tent
and thought of ice. Mountains and mountains of ice surrounded by choppy seas and weeping skies that soothed her
fevered skin and chilled her all the way to the bone. There
was no heat there, no fire, nothing to burn her.

For all of two seconds, she was totally immersed in the
image, her concentration so fierce she actually shivered.
Then he swabbed another contusion with the gauze, and the
wintry scene vanished in a blast of red-hot heat. Sweat
popped out on her brow and her upper lip. Rigid, she felt a
groan swell in her chest like an expanding balloon, but this
time she didn't cry out. Not even when tears traced a silent
path down her ashen cheeks.

She never knew how long the torture lasted. Dazed, her
vision blurring, her body braced and all her attention focused on the next burning stroke, she lost touch with all

concepts of space and time. Nothing mattered but endur-
ing the never-ending agony with as much composure as she
could manage and hanging on until the moment when she
would finally cease to hurt.

Surprisingly, that moment arrived long before she expected it. One second, her nerve endings were crying out for
relief and the next, Ace was throwing the unused bandages
across the tent with a snarled oath. "There, dammit! I'm
through. If you want to haul off and hit me, I wouldn't
blame you."

Light-headed, she dragged in a deep, cleansing breath and
slowly let it out, but it was a long moment before she could
manage to say anything. "No," she said faintly, her smile
weak. "I'll have to take a rain check on that. If I tried that
right now, I'd fall flat on my face."

Ace chuckled, but there was little humor in the sound. At
the sight of the tears tracking her pale cheeks, something
clutched at his heart, something that was a hell of a lot
stronger than mere admiration, sweeter than tenderness,
more frightening than the near fall she'd taken off that
damn cliff. Where did she get her courage? he marveled.
And did she have any idea what it did to him? Beauty he
could appreciate but walk away from, but true courage was
a rare thing and stopped him in his tracks every time.

Unable to resist touching her, he cupped her face in his
hands. "You're something else, princess," he rasped, swiping at her tears with his thumbs. "You didn't have to be
brave, you know. You could have screamed this whole rain
forest down and I wouldn't have blamed you. Why didn't
you?"

"Because I was afraid if I started, I might not be able to
stop," she said with a sigh, closing her eyes. "And somehow, I don't think you handle hysterical women very well."

"I do when they've got a right to be hysterical," he retorted. "How's the pain now?"

"Better," she claimed, but she still didn't open her eyes.

He snorted, not believing that for a second. She was still pale, barely able to hold her head up, her brow etched with lines that hadn't been there the day before. Reaching for the first-aid kit, he dug up a couple of aspirins and uncapped his canteen. "Wake up and take some aspirins, sweetheart. Then I'll help you get ready for bed."

The fact that she didn't offer an argument said far more about her exhaustion than words ever could. She simply took the aspirins, swallowed a gulp of water and handed the canteen back to him as her eyes once again drifted shut. Rising to his feet, Ace found one of his T-shirts and returned to where she still sat on her sleeping bag and settled down in front of her, his knees just brushing hers.

Images of the night before flashed in front of his eyes, and all too easily he remembered her sweet insistence that he close his eyes while she dressed at the river, even though he'd already seen all of her there was to see. Hesitating, refusing to let his gaze dip below the level of her chin, he said huskily, "You can't sleep in those clothes, Maddy, honey. You'll be a lot more comfortable in one of my T-shirts. I'm going to slip it over your head, okay?"

Stirring to awareness, she frowned, "I don't think I can lift my arm."

"Don't worry about that. You just sit there and let me do all the work."

It should have been easy—she was already practically topless. But Ace hadn't counted on how much he would have to touch her just to get her ready for bed. When he pulled the T-shirt over her head and it settled around her slender frame with a soft whisper, she obviously couldn't reach around behind her to unhook her bra. It was left to him to slip his hands under the shirt and do the task for her. Too late, he realized he'd just made a big mistake.

Chapter 8

How he got through the next few moments without going quietly out of his mind, Ace never knew. With his arms around her under her shirt, her breath warm against his throat, he suddenly knew why the road to hell was paved with good intentions. His only thought had been to make her as comfortable as possible, but suddenly, he couldn't get his mind off the scent and feel and closeness of her. She was soft and so damn breakable right now. And she didn't have a clue what that did to him. His blood hot, his loins aching, he stared at her mouth and needed, just for a moment, to kiss her more than he needed his next breath.

But he couldn't, dammit! She was hurt and exhausted. Only a selfish, unfeeling bastard would think about taking advantage of her right now, he told himself savagely, and he hadn't quite sunk that low. She needed some TLC—nothing more. And by God, that was what he was going to give her even if it killed him!

Later, he would have sworn it almost did. Under her shirt, his fingers blindly found the back hook of her bra and gently released it. A muscle ticking along his jaw, he slid his hands to her shoulders and carefully eased the straps of the undergarment down her shoulders. She sighed, her head dipping to rest against his chest, and right then and there, he nearly came undone as the bra came away in his hands.

Heat curling low in his belly, he dragged in a cooling breath and tried to get a grip. Still, his voice was betrayingly rough when he murmured, "Better?"

She nodded, unconsciously rubbing her cheek against him like a cat. "Mmm-hmm."

A muscle ticking in his cheek, he bit back a groan. If this was God's idea of a joke, he wasn't laughing. Against his better judgment, he'd wanted the lady almost from the moment he'd come to her rescue, but she'd continually kept a brick wall between them. Until now. When he could touch her but he couldn't have her.

"This is payback time for all your sins, old man," he muttered to himself. And paybacks were hell—he hadn't realized just how much until he fumbled for her hands under the soft cotton of the T-shirt and brushed her thighs instead, then a breast. Sweat broke out on his brow. Damn, how much of this was a man supposed to take?

Growling a curse, he finally found her hands and carefully eased them through the sleeves that hung well past her elbows. Completely covered, she should have looked about as appealing as a frumpy teddy bear. To another man, she might have, but Ace knew what was under that T-shirt. And he still had to get her out of her shorts.

"We're almost finished, Sleeping Beauty," he promised hoarsely. "Just lay down and relax while I get rid of these shorts and boots. Then you can go to sleep."

She didn't wait that long, however. The second he helped her stretch out, she turned over on her stomach, pillowed her face on her uninjured arm and was out cold. "Oh, no," he moaned. "Not yet. Don't crash on me yet, honey. Give me a little help here."

His only answer was a deep, nearly silent sigh.

Setting back on his heels, he scowled down at her and was half tempted to just leave her the way she was. But the jeans shorts were still damp, and even as tired as she was, she'd have a miserable night if he didn't get her out of them. Swearing, his face grim with purpose, he straddled her hips and reached under the T-shirt for the snap of her shorts.

It took less than a minute to finish undressing her. But it was the longest minute of his life. Curses he'd picked up in some of the remotest areas of the world falling from his lips to rise on the close, steamy air filling the tent, he dropped the damp shorts on the floor next to her sleeping bag and swished the T-shirt down over the tempting curve of her scantily clad hips. It didn't help. Awake, asleep, too sore to move, too tired to keep her eyes open, she still had the power to make him want her more than any woman ever had.

He had to get out of there. His jaw a block of granite, he rose to his feet, switched off the flashlight and headed toward the tent entrance. Outside, the evening shower that should have stopped by now was still going strong and showed every sign of continuing all night. That was just fine with him. Stepping out into it, he lifted his face to the wet sky and waited for the rain to cool his heated blood.

Maddy slept for nearly two hours without moving so much as a muscle. Then she shifted slightly in her sleep, unconsciously turning on her side, and the scraped skin there instantly flared like a struck match. Startled, she jerked awake on a sharply indrawn breath, her heart pounding. Images from the afternoon flashed across her closed eyelids, vivid in every detail, and all too easily, she could feel the sick terror that had gripped her when she'd started to fall and for an instant there'd been nothing but thin air under her feet. The taste of coppery fear filling her mouth, she bolted straight up on the sleeping bag, gasping.

"You want some more aspirin?" Ace asked quietly from across the tent.

The low rumble of his voice reached out of the darkness to touch her, stroke her, steady her. Letting out a slow breath, she searched for him in the thick shadows but couldn't see him anywhere. "No, thanks," she said just as quietly. "I was just remembering..." A shiver slid down her spine. "What time is it?"

"Nearly nine."

He switched on the flashlight then, and she saw that he stood at the unzipped entrance to the tent and stared out at the rainy night like a man who would have given just about anything to be anywhere else but where he was. From six feet away, she could practically feel the tension rolling off him in waves. Frowning, she stared at his back. "What's wrong?"

"Nothing. You hungry?"

It was a deliberate attempt to change the focus of the conversation away from himself to her, and for the moment, she was willing to let him. "Not really, but I guess I'd better eat something or my stomach will think my throat's been cut. Did I miss supper?"

"If you want to call it that..." At the sound of her struggling to her feet, he turned sharply to face her, saw what she was doing and reached her in two strides. "What the hell do you think you're doing? Lay back down, dammit, before you hurt yourself!"

He was, she could see, going to be difficult. "I don't need to lay back down. It's not like I broke a leg or something. I just scraped myself up a little."

"A *little?*" he roared. "Have you looked at yourself?"

With a careless wave of her hand, she dismissed that argument and replied, "Anyway, it's too early to go to bed. If I sleep all evening, I'll be climbing the walls by four in the morning. I don't think you want that anymore than I do, so I'm going to get up, eat, walk around a little and find a way to kill the clock for a while. Okay?"

No, it was not okay, he wanted to growl. He was the one already climbing the walls, and it was all because of her. He'd spent the past two hours trying to steer clear of her and their tent by seeking out Dominic and discussing their route for the following day over a supper of rice and dehydrated vegetables, but he hadn't been able to concentrate. Afraid that he wouldn't be able to hear Maddy if she called out because of the thundering cadence of the rain, he'd checked on her every few moments. Just like a new mother peeking in on a newborn, he thought in disgust. Dominic hadn't said anything, but he'd seen the amusement glinting in the other man's eyes and had felt like a damn fool.

But she was right. He'd rather deal with her now than at four o'clock in the morning.

Without a word, he retrieved the bowl of food he'd brought back with him from Dominic's tent. "Here," he said curtly, shoving it into her hands. "It's not anything to write home about, but the nearest McDonald's is a long way away."

Turning away before she could drag him into a conversation he wanted no part of, he tried to ignore her by charting their course on a waterproof map of the area that he pulled from his backpack. And for a while, it worked. They'd made up for lost time that afternoon after Maddy's

near fall at the waterfall, and by the time they called it a
night, they'd reached the beginning of the final stage of their
trip. Tomorrow, they would leave the river and canoe behind at dawn and head south on foot through the jungle for
Barrera's secret stronghold.

Dominic, when pointing out on the map the area where
Barrera was rumored to live, had warned him it still wasn't
too late to turn back. Once they hiked deeper into the jungle, however, the drug lord's men could be anywhere, and
they might not be given a second chance to change their
mind.

Folding the map and returning it to his pack, Ace knew
the time for second thoughts—and turning back—had long
since passed. Lazear was out there, dammit! He hadn't been
this close to catching him since New York, and this time, the
snake wasn't getting away, by God! Before the sun set tomorrow, he'd have the bastard...and the ring...in his
possession come hell or high water.

"So what's on the agenda for tomorrow?"

Intent on just what he was going to say to the miserable
excuse for a human being when he caught up to him, he
hadn't noticed that Maddy had wandered over to see what
he was doing. She stood less than a foot behind him, her
hair mussed and his T-shirt engulfing her almost to her
knees, and didn't seem to be the least bit self-conscious
about it. Dammit, she was naked under that shirt except for
her panties! She should have been cowering under the
sleeping bag, not parading around in front of him like some
kind of fashion model without an ounce of modesty!

Cursing the sudden knocking of his heart, he scowled.
"Lazear," he said coldly. "We either catch him tomorrow
or there's no sense going on. Don't you have a robe or
something to put on?"

Surprised by the sudden change in subject and his fierce frown, Maddy glanced down in confusion at the T-shirt as if she had just now noticed it. What was he all in a snit about? she wondered, bewildered. The T-shirt covered her better than any gown she had at home and was about as provocative as a garbage bag. "No, you didn't buy me one. If it's bothering you—"

"Did I say it was bothering me?"

"Not in those words, but—"

"Then it's not bothering me. I've seen a woman in a T-shirt before."

Not caring for the image that that particular comment brought to mind, it was her turn to frown. "I'm sure you have," she said coolly. "But if you don't mind, I'd appreciate if you'd spare me the details."

"Details? What details? I just said—"

"I heard what you said. You don't have to repeat yourself."

"And you don't have to be so damn touchy!"

"Touchy?" she echoed incredulously. "You're calling *me* touchy? You've got to be kidding! Talk about the pot calling the kettle black. You've been acting like a bear with a sore paw ever since I woke up. And I'm getting damn tired of it!"

"Damn?" he repeated, his eyes narrowing dangerously. "Did you just say damn? I've never heard you say a curse word before. I don't like it."

As surprised as he, Maddy blinked. He was right. She'd actually used *damn*. She should have been horrified. She'd been raised to think that curse words were nothing more than a lack of vocabulary and, therefore, an insult to her intelligence, but she found the use of that simple four-letter word exhilarating. And what did he mean, *he* didn't like it? Who was he to tell her what she could and couldn't say?

"You don't have to like it," she retorted, lifting her chin proudly. "I can use any *damn* word I want, any *damn* time I feel like it, and there's not a *damn* thing you can do about it."

"I wouldn't be too sure of that, missy," he growled, glaring at her nose to nose. "Don't push me—"

"Push *you?* You've been pushing me for a fight for the past fifteen minutes! What's your problem, anyway? All I did—"

"All you did," he cut in furiously, grabbing her, "was parade around in front of me nearly naked."

"I did not! I'm decently covered!"

"You call that decent? It barely comes to your thighs. And any man with eyes can see that you don't have a damn thing on underneath it!"

She shouldn't have said it, shouldn't have even thought it, but the words just popped out. "Since you've got eyes and you're the only man in sight, I guess that means you've been looking."

"Of course, I've been looking!" he roared, pushed to the limits. "Dammit, woman, what do you think I've been trying to tell you?"

Too late, he realized what he'd admitted. Curses fell from his lips in a steady, uninterrupted stream. He saw awareness flare in her eyes, felt a sudden charge of energy between them that could have lit up the entire Southern Hemisphere, and should have pushed her away then and not touched her again until his head had cleared and he had a grip on his hormones again. But he couldn't let her go—hell, he couldn't even remember his name. All he could think of was how long it had been since he'd kissed her. It seemed like forever.

"Dammit, Maddy!" Her name a prayer, a curse, on his tongue, he glared down at her, his hands tightening on her arms as he fought to do the right thing. But the burning in his gut was hotter than the fires of hell and there were some things a man just couldn't walk away from. And she was one of them. Past thought, past reason, he dragged her up on her toes and covered her mouth with his.

The heat was immediate, intense, bone melting. Stunned, Maddy stiffened for all of two seconds, her thoughts in a whirl and her heart pounding out of control. Which was just what she felt like, she realized with a sob. Out of control. She shouldn't let him touch her, shouldn't let herself get caught up in the magic of something that was never going to last. Somehow, some way, she had to stop this. Now!

But when her hands came up to push him away, they touched the rock wall of his chest, and she found herself fascinated all over again with the differences between his body and hers, the strength and hardness and power of him. She wanted to touch him, taste him…everywhere. Just this once, she promised herself as her eyes grew heavy and her mind blurred. Just this once she was going to be like every other woman in the world and know what it was like to kiss a man senseless. Murmuring his name, she opened her mouth under his and threw caution to the wind.

His response was immediate, gratifying, shattering. With the same barely controlled impatience with which he'd snapped at her, he groaned, jerked her fully against him and slanted his mouth across hers with a hunger that left her weak with need. Elated, her heart slamming against her ribs, she went farther up on her toes and fit herself against him with a daring that would have horrified her only days ago.

Hard, throbbing, he felt like a man stretched tight on a torture rack. Need burned in his gut like a hot coal, a need to bury himself in her so deep that neither of them would know where one ended and the other began. He wanted to move in her and feel her shatter around him. Just once, he promised himself as his hands swept down under her T-shirt to cup her bottom. Just once before his common sense reminded him of all the reasons why he couldn't do this.

His breath hissing through his clenched teeth, he held her still against him, savoring the feel, the heat, of her. Wrenching his mouth from hers, he murmured endearments in her ear he hadn't even known he knew and scattered kisses across the curve of her cheek, the faint sweep of freckles across her nose, the soft, tempting skin of her neck. And all the while, his hands were blindly moving, seeking, caressing.

When his fingers slid up her ribs in search of the sweet fullness of her breasts, he was blind to everything but the desire heating his blood. Then he heard her moan, felt her stiffen, then shrink away from him, and the events of the day came flooding back in a rush. Swearing, he jerked his hands back, releasing her with a speed that would have been comical if he hadn't been so disgusted with himself.

"Dammit to hell! I didn't mean to hurt you. Are you okay? Honey, let me take a look—"

"No!"

She stepped away from him with a speed that was like a slap in the face, and suddenly he was furious—with himself, with her, with the entire situation. This had started out as a simple surveillance and tracking job. The kind he did all the time without breaking a sweat. How the hell had it gotten so complicated so fast? Cursing in seven different languages, he growled, "I don't know what you thought you were doing, but that was a stupid thing to do."

"Me? You kissed me!"

"I might have started it—because you pushed me—but you weren't just standing there like a piece of dead wood, lady. You kissed me back!"

It was a ludicrous accusation, one she immediately pounced on. "Well, of course I kissed you back, you big lug! Wasn't I supposed to?"

"Hell, no! I mean, yes!" Swearing, he speared an impatient hand through his hair. "Let's just get something straight right here and now, Little Miss Innocent. We might set off fireworks every time we touch, but that's as far as it's going to go. So don't get any ideas about me. Okay?"

It was a warning, pure and simple, a slap in the face he never meant to just blurt out. Damning his fool tongue, Ace opened his mouth to backpedal, but it was too late. Standing proudly before him, she somehow managed to look down her nose at him even though she was nearly a foot shorter than he was. "I beg your pardon?"

She was as snooty as a queen questioning a commoner, and even though he knew he was the one in the wrong, it rubbed him the wrong way. "You heard me," he snapped. "I'm nobody's hero. Is that clear enough? I may have saved you from Cement Johnny, but that's the closest I'll ever come to looking like a bloody knight on a white horse. So if you think a few kisses and a hot little romance in the jungle is going to lead to happily-ever-after, I've got news for you, baby. It's not ever going to happen. I tried that once, and once was enough."

He practically threw the words at her, but to her credit, she didn't so much as flinch. "You were married?"

"Oh, yeah," he said bitterly. "To a woman I was nuts about. I would have trusted her with my life. The only problem was I shouldn't have trusted her with my best friend." His mouth twisted in a travesty of a smile. "But, hey, live and learn, right? Believe me, honey, I learned. There's no such thing as Santa Claus or the tooth fairy or the twelfth of never. So don't look to me to put stars in your eyes and promise you forever. It's not going to happen."

He saw the hurt in her eyes and had to clamp his teeth together to keep from taking it all back. No, a good clean blow was always for the best, he decided grimly. If this didn't strip those rose-colored glasses from her eyes, nothing would. He was too hard, too callous, for the likes of her. He'd stopped believing in fairy tales a long time ago, and she was a woman who thrived on them. Anyone with an ounce of perception could see that she needed a man who could give her hearts and flowers. He wasn't that man. Better she see that now, than later, after she'd made the mistake of thinking herself in love with him.

Pale, each angry word striking her right in the heart, Maddy never knew where she got the strength to face him without crying. She just knew she couldn't let him see how he'd hurt her. Her eyes stinging but dry, she said stiffly, "I don't remember asking for forever or anything else. Just because I'm not as experienced as you obviously are doesn't mean I'm going to lose my head over a few kisses. And that's all they were...a few kisses. Nice, but nothing to write home about," she lied. "You might be a great lover—but frankly, I don't ever plan to find out for sure. Now, if you'll excuse me, I'm going to bed. Please put out the light before you turn in."

Ignoring the pain that flared in her side and shoulder—it was nothing compared to the one that squeezed her heart—she turned her back on him and dropped down to her sleeping bag. She heard him swear, but she only closed her eyes and waited for the oblivion of sleep. It was a long time coming.

Dawn was just a glint on the horizon the next morning when the alarm on Ace's watch woke them both. Outside, the rain had finally stopped, but the trees were still dripping, and there was no question that their trek through the jungle on foot was going to be a soggy one . . . and slow going. And they were already running short on time.

Grabbing his clothes, Ace tugged them on in the dark. "Breakfast is on the run this morning," he told Maddy tersely. "Get dressed while I make sure Dominic's up. We're leaving as soon as we can break camp."

He was gone before Maddy could even lift her head. Burying her face deeper into her arms, she groaned as every muscle in her body seemed to tighten in protest. "Good morning to you, too," she muttered huskily. "God, how am I going to get up?"

It wasn't easy. Her teeth clamped tight on a curse, her heart pounding and her palms damp, she inched her way up off the ground like an old man with rheumatism on a cold morning. It seemed to take forever just to sit up, but at least the contusions along her ribs weren't burning like they had last night. Now if she could just manage to hook her bra by herself, she'd have it made in the shade.

She'd just barely reached for the hem of the T-shirt Ace had dressed her in last night, however, when he burst back into the tent, cursing like a sailor. "He's gone! Dammit to hell, I should have known he was planning something like this last night. He all but told me—"

"What? Who? What are you talking about?"

"Dominic," he said flatly. "He's taken his tent and the canoe and just left us here high and dry."

"What? But he couldn't! He wouldn't do that."

Switching on the flashlight, he tossed a crumbled note into her lap. "Here. Read it for yourself. I found this in a plastic bag under a rock where his tent was. He must have left in the middle of the night after he was sure we were asleep or I would have heard him. Dammit, how the hell could he do this?"

Lifting the wad of paper with trembling fingers, Maddy smoothed it out and frowned down at the barely legible message that was a mix between a humble apology for leaving them in the lurch and a dire warning of danger. "It sounds like he was really terrified of Barrera. But if that was the case, why did he agree to be our guide in the first place? You would have found someone else if he'd turned us down."

Ace sighed in disgust. "Who the hell knows? Maybe he needed the money for his family and thought we'd turn back when things got rough. Or maybe he thought he could handle it. Last night, he told me this would be the last chance to turn back—once we left the river behind, we could run into Barrera's men at any time. I guess he got to thinking about it and decided that was a risk he didn't want to take."

Setting the note down, Maddy glanced up at him, her expression somber as her eyes locked with his. "So now what do we do? He left directions to Barrera's stronghold. Do we go after Lazear or head back upriver?"

"That's up to you."

She arched a brow at that. "Me? Why me?"

"Because you haven't had much say in any of this up to now," he retorted honestly, surprising her. "Yesterday, you could have been seriously hurt, and today things could get even dicier. For all we know, the devil could be just over the next ridge. You've got a right to say if you want to go on or turn back."

Her eyes searching his, Maddy hesitated, torn. If they turned back, her time with him would end as soon as they got back to Caracas and he could book her on a flight to New York. If they went on, there was no telling what kind of danger they would be walking into. She didn't doubt for a minute that he would protect her with his life, but as safe as she felt with him, he wasn't Superman.

"What would you do if I wasn't along?" she asked.

"That's beside the point."

"You'd go after Lazear." It wasn't a question, but a flat statement of fact that she knew he couldn't deny. He didn't even try. "Even knowing that you might end up in Barrera's hands, you'd go on."

"That's what I get paid to do. You don't. And, anyway, I've ended up in tougher spots."

Maddy couldn't imagine anything tougher than being in Barrera's clutches—his name alone was all it had taken to send Dominic scrambling downriver—but if anyone could handle him, it was Ace. She'd seen with her own eyes how he thrived on danger. Against all odds, he continued to outwit ruthless thugs who wanted nothing more than to put a bullet between his eyes. If he thought he could take on Lazear and Barrera single-handedly and still come out the winner, who was she to doubt him?

"And you lived to tell about it," she reminded him as she ignored her stiff muscles and pushed to her feet. "You will this time, too. Are we leaving the stuff here or taking it with us? We can move faster without the backpacks."

"Dammit, Maddy, don't do this because of me—"

"That's the only reason I'd do it," she said simply. Stepping around him, she put her hands on his shoulders and pushed him toward the tent entrance. "Give me a couple of minutes to get dressed and we can hit the trail."

Wanting to shake her, Ace dug in his heels and scowled over his shoulder at her. He shouldn't let her do this, dammit! She didn't have a clue what she was agreeing to. Even if they were able to catch Lazear before he sought sanctuary with Barrera, he wouldn't just throw up his hands and surrender like a good little boy. He'd fight like hell and wouldn't care who he hurt in the process if it meant getting away. And then there was Barrera. A snake in the grass if there ever was one, the man had a reputation for being a real bastard who had sold his soul to the devil long ago. No depravity was too low for him, no vice too sick. With more money than God, and an army of paid assassins to protect him, he was a virtual dictator in his little corner of the world.

Given his choice, Ace wouldn't have taken Maddy anywhere near either man. But he couldn't leave her there at camp alone while he went after Lazear, and Dominic had made it impossible for him to send her back to Caracas with him. He either had to let her go with him or give up. And *she* would fight him on that.

His jaw clenching, he told himself he could take care of her and prayed it was true. "Okay. We'll go on . . . on one condition. You carry a gun at all times, and if you have to, you use the damn thing."

Her eyes wide, she blanched. "But I've never even held one. I wouldn't know what to do with it."

"Just point the damn thing and squeeze the trigger. You'll hit something. Just make sure it's not me."

Ten minutes later, they took off into the jungle. Loaded down with nothing but food and water and all the ammunition they could carry, they took off at a brisk pace with Ace in the lead, following the directions Dominic left them. But as soon as they were out of sight of the river, just walking became a chore. So far from civilization, the jungle was virtually untouched by man. The vegetation was so thick it had to be chopped away with a machete, and because of the heavy rain overnight, they found themselves up to their ankles in mud. Forced to slow down, their chances of catching up with Lazear grew dimmer and dimmer as the morning dragged on.

Then they came across signs of a camp that looked as if it had just broken up.

"It had to be Lazear," Ace said as he knelt down to examine the vegetation that had been flattened recently by tents. "Nobody else would be stupid enough to come this far into Barrera's territory."

Her breathing ragged and her heart jumping in her breast, Maddy glanced around nervously, but the jungle around them seemed deserted. "How far ahead of us do you think he is?"

"Fifteen or twenty minutes judging from the condition of these plants," he said grimly, pushing to his feet. "He couldn't know we're behind him or he never would have left this for us to find."

Maddy closed her eyes on a quick prayer. The nightmare was almost over. "What about Barrera? How close is his place?"

"An hour, no more." Pulling his gun from where he'd shoved it into his waistband behind his back, he checked to make sure it was loaded, then shoved it back into place, this time within easy reach at the front of his jeans. He then did the same thing for Maddy, his eyes locking with hers as he eased the weapon between her waistband and stomach. "Keep your eyes peeled, Red. Things could get sticky fast. If you hear anything, see anything—hell, if you just get nervous—don't be afraid to draw your gun. Okay?"

Her mouth dry, the barrel of the revolver like a fist against her stomach, Maddy nodded. But deep inside, she was wondering what in the world had possessed her to think she could do this. She was a librarian, for heaven's sake! She didn't know anything about guns or men who handled them as casually as Ace did. She had no business being out here in the wilds of Venezuela pursuing anyone, let alone a man like Lazear who probably wouldn't think twice about shooting her if he got the chance.

But it was too late to change her mind. Ace had caught his quarry's scent and there would be no turning back now. Stiffening her spine, she forced a smile. "I'll shoot anything that moves...except you."

"I'd appreciate that," he said dryly, his mouth quirking in a smile. "Let's go."

He picked up the pace then, just as she knew he would, and it took all her concentration not to lag behind. Her sore muscles had thankfully loosened up with the exercise, but she had what felt like at least five pounds of mud caked to her shoes, weighting down every step.

Breathless, her legs starting to quiver, she glanced up to see how far ahead of her Ace was and took a step. In the next instant, her left foot caught on something and she went sprawling into the mud with a startled shriek.

Ace whirled, swearing, his gun already in his hand, to find her on her hands and knees, her clothes and face splattered with mud. "What the hell! Are you okay? What happened?"

"I tripped." Muttering at her own clumsiness, she lifted a hand to wipe a soggy blob away from her cheek and left a streak of mud instead as Ace shoved his gun back into his jeans and hunkered down beside her. "It must have been a root or something..."

They both turned to look down at her feet, but instead of finding a root or a branch hidden in the undergrowth, they saw a thin black wire that was stretched across the path and almost invisible in the vegetation.

"What the—" Not liking his sudden suspicions, Ace jerked out his gun. Something moved in the bushes. He fired, lightning quick. Instantly, six men materialized out of the shadows of the jungle as silently as ghosts. Dressed in camouflage and armed with the latest thing in semiautomatic weapons, there was no question that they were Barrera's men ... or that they had them surrounded.

Beside him, Maddy gasped and fumbled for her own pistol. "Oh, God!"

Just as it went off, firing harmlessly into the air, Ace wrenched it from her hands before she got them killed. Furiously, he cursed himself. He should have known that a man like Barrera wasn't going to let anyone just walk up to his stronghold without having traps and surveillance devices all over the place to warn him of intruders. Not even a rank amateur would have been that careless, and he had no one to blame but himself. When Maddy fell, he'd been so sure that she'd just tripped over a log that he'd let his guard down. And that was an unforgivable mistake.

Carefully inching his fingers around her gun, he murmured, "Don't panic. We might be able to talk our way out of this—"

"I wouldn't do that if I were you, *señor,*" a mercenary who seemed to be in charge said coldly in Spanish. "My men would have to shoot you, and then where would the *señorita* be? Your weapons, please."

It wasn't a request, but an order, one that Ace would have given anything to defy. But there was a time to fight and a time to step back and think reasonably. Beside him, he could feel Maddy start to tremble, then stiffen as she tried to hide her fear, but there was nothing he could do to reassure her. Slowly he started to hand over their weapons.

"What are you doing?" she cried, grabbing at his hand. "You can't just give them to them. They'll kill us for sure then!"

"That's what I'm trying to avoid, sweetheart," he murmured in a low voice that didn't carry beyond her ears. "You're going to have to trust me." For a second, her fingers tightened around his, her eyes pleading with his while the mercenaries surrounding them visibly tensed. She never spared them a glance. Then, just when he thought she was going to really create problems for them, she released her hold on his wrist.

Relieved, he let out his breath in a rush. "Good girl," he said approvingly, and helped her to her feet.

"Come," the tough-looking hombre in charge said coldly, and urged them down the path they'd been following only moments before. Surrounded, they had no choice but to do as they were told.

Chapter 9

Barrera's stronghold was like something out of a Steven Spielberg adventure movie. Built of stone, it rose up out of the jungle floor with no warning whatsoever, a huge, towering, impressive structure that was as silent and cold as a tomb. There were few windows, but there was little doubt that there were eyes watching from somewhere—the second their guards prodded them toward the fortress's narrow entrance, the solid steel gates blocking their passage silently swung open.

Maddy's hand tightly held in his, Ace looked around with pretended nonchalance, memorizing every door and possible avenue of escape. When he turned back to the burly, granite-faced man in charge, his grin was deliberately cocky. "Not a bad place you've got here, Bubba," he drawled mockingly in English. "A little cold for my taste, but I guess you sun yourself on the battlements just like the rest of the snakes whenever the chill gets to you."

The other man didn't so much as grunt in response. Only a fool would have missed the flash of resentment in his black eyes, however, and Ace was no fool. So the bastard spoke English. It was always nice to know what kind of garbage you were dealing with. Giving Maddy's cold fingers a reassuring squeeze, he continued to taunt their captor, though this time in Spanish. "Since you so graciously insisted on showing us the way, don't you think you ought to take us to the big man himself? I'm sure he's expecting us, and I've got a feeling he's the type who doesn't like to be kept waiting."

"You will shut your mouth and do as you're told," the man he'd dubbed Bubba replied coldly. "The *big man,* as you put it, doesn't waste his time on the likes of trespassers."

"Well, that's just too damn bad because we've got business with him, and he's going to want to hear what we've got to say. Get him."

It was a bold move, throwing orders at a hired gun who could shoot both him and Maddy in the back any damn time he felt like it. But pushing the perimeters told him a hell of a lot about a man and his position of authority. If Bubba was just a heavyweight who kept the guards in line, he wouldn't do anything without getting the okay from somebody higher up.

"Well, what are you waiting for?" Ace snapped when the man hesitated. "Go get him."

For a split second, he actually thought Bubba was going to fold like a deck of cards and take them to Barrera. Then his jaw hardened, his eyes narrowed with fury and he brought the butt of his rifle down on Ace's temple with a savage curse.

Caught off guard, Ace didn't have time to dodge the blow. Pain exploded in his head. Staggering, he felt his knees start to buckle and there didn't seem to be a damn thing he could do about it. Blackness crowded in, swamping him. The last thing he heard before he hit the ground and the lights blinked out was Maddy's scream. It seemed to go on and on and on.

The basement was humid and damp and filled with looming, threatening shadows. Grunge covered the walls and floors, and somewhere in a dark corner, water dripped in a constant cadence that was guaranteed to drive even the sanest mind over the edge. If she'd been thrown in there all by herself, Maddy would have been pounding on the door within seconds, begging for release. Ace was with her, though, and the terror that gripped her by the throat had nothing to do with whatever unseen monsters lurked in the dungeon's shadows. Ace had been out for ten minutes and showed no sign of regaining consciousness.

His poor head cradled in her lap, she leaned over him, rocking as tears welled in her eyes and spilled unchecked down her cheeks. "Please don't die," she whispered brokenly. With trembling fingers, she wiped frantically at the trickle of blood that oozed from the wound at his temple, but the blood kept coming and coming. Sick with fear, she tore a strip of material from the tail of her shirt and quickly pressed a makeshift bandage to the jaggedly torn cut. And all the while she prayed, she pleaded with him. "Do you hear me? You can't die. I won't let you. Dammit, Ace, open your eyes!"

She knew he didn't like it when she swore—why he thought he could and she couldn't she had yet to figure out!—but any hope that that would jar him back to awareness died a quick death. His breathing slow and shallow, his face colorless, he didn't move by so much as a flicker of an eyelash. Maddy had never felt so helpless in her life.

Despair weighting her heart, she sniffed back tears and told herself she couldn't just sit there and cry. She had to do something! Now! Carefully easing his head onto the moss-covered floor, she hurried up the steps to the bucket of water that had been left for them just inside the door by their jailers. Too worried about Ace to even spare it a glance until now, she peered into it suspiciously. It could, for all she knew, be laced with drugs or, worse yet, unfit for human consumption. But it was the only water they had, and Ace's wound needed to be cleaned. After his insistence on cleaning the scrapes on her ribs, she hadn't forgotten his lecture on the danger of letting wounds go untreated in the jungle.

Quickly carrying it down to where he lay sprawled on his back at the bottom of the steps where the guards had dumped him, she would have traded a ride back to the States for the antiseptic and ointments he had used to tend her injuries. But they'd been left behind at the camp. Choking on a sob, she dropped to her knees beside him and ripped the edge of her shirt with her teeth again, tearing off a ten-inch strip to use as a washcloth. Bending over him, she went to work.

She came to him in the dream, just as she did every night. Soft and warm and eager, she touched him with that same hesitancy that always knocked his legs right out from under him. His heart pounding, he bit back a groan, afraid to move, to make so much as a sound and risk scaring her back into the dark shadows that engulfed him. She was so new to this, so shy, so damn unsure of herself that it completely destroyed him.

Not for the first time, he told himself that her innocence shouldn't have mattered. This was the nineties and a woman had every right to seek her pleasure where she would without fear of judgment. And he didn't have a problem with that. In today's world, a man was a hell of a lot safer with a woman who knew the score and how to take care of herself.

But Maddy was . . . different. Sweet and wholesome and totally outside the realm of *his* experience. And every time he touched her, kissed her, the sensuousness that lay just beneath the surface of her virginal exterior hit him like a punch in the gut, robbing him of breath, of reason, until all he could think of was seducing her, loving her, charming her into falling in love with him so that she'd never think twice about another man, even her precious Ace MacKenzie.

God, he was out of his mind.

But even as the thought swam up through the unnatural darkness that clouded his subconscious, he felt her touch and started to reach for her. Pain exploded in his head like a flashbulb. Wincing, he groaned. What the devil was wrong with him?

"Ace? Oh, thank God! I was so scared. No, don't move!" she said quickly when he started to lift a hand to his pounding temple. "That Bubba idiot hit you in the head with the butt of his rifle."

"Son of a bitch! I didn't think he had it in him." Ignoring her efforts to hold him down, he ruthlessly pushed himself upright and paid the price as the grungy stone floor he sat on seemed to tilt under him and jackhammers went to work in his head. "Oh, damn, that hurts! Where the hell are we?"

"The basement."

From what Ace could see from the chains on the wall, it looked more like a dungeon or a torture chamber out of a house of horrors than a basement, but he had no intention of mentioning that to Maddy—she was already scared enough as it was, and with good reason. They were in a hell of a mess. He shot her a sharp look and even in the gloom couldn't miss the tears streaking her face and her unsteady fingers as she sat back on her heels and brushed the hair from her eyes. "Did he touch you? Did any of them touch you? By God, if they so much as laid a finger on you—"

"What?" Suddenly understanding what he was implying, she gasped, "Oh, no. No!" Launching herself at him, she buried her face against his chest and hugged him fiercely. "You were the one that Bubba character was furious with. He didn't even glance at me except to tell me we'd never get out of here alive. Then he had the other men drag you down here and he locked us in together. I—I thought they'd killed you."

The shaky admission was said so quietly against his shoulder that he almost missed it. Surprised and stupidly pleased by the notion of her crying for him, he grinned crookedly. "No kidding? And here I didn't think you cared. You should have told me, sweetheart. I would have been happy to do something about it."

"Oh, you...you..." At a loss for words, she wanted to hit him...and kiss the roguish laughter off his sensuous mouth. But she didn't have the heart to do the former when he had to still be woozy from the blow he'd taken or the guts to do the latter. Punching him in the shoulder, she couldn't help but laugh. "How can you joke at a time like this? Look at you! You're weak as a baby!"

He could have told her that all it took was one kiss from her and she'd see just how weak he was, but that was something he had no intention of admitting anytime soon. "It'll take more than a whack on the head to knock me out of the game, worrywart. C'mon, help me up. We've got to find a way to get out of here."

Drawing back, she looked at him as if he was crazy. "How? This place is like a bank vault. The only way out is through that door—" she nodded toward the three-inch-thick reinforced door at the top of the stairs "—and it's locked. They could leave us down here to rot if they wanted to, and there's not a heck of a lot we could do about it."

"What's outside that door? Did you notice the layout of the place? How many guards did you see standing around? And what about surveillance cameras? How many were there? And where?"

Struggling to his feet with her help, he threw questions at her as he moved to examine their holding cell, hardly giving her time to answer one before he was tossing another at her. "I don't know." Her fingers pressed to her temples, she closed her eyes and tried to remember, but she'd been so worried about him, there could have been a civil war going on around them and she didn't think she would have noticed.

"After that..." Struggling for an appropriate adjective, she blurted out, "... *jackass* hit you, everything happened so quickly, I didn't have time to see much. They took us down a narrow hall—it was to the left of the entrance hall where we came in, I think—and brought us down a back stairway to the basement."

"What about guards? And cameras?"

"There were several guards outside in the compound, but I only noticed one inside the main hall, and he was more like a butler than anything else. If there were any cameras, I didn't see them."

"With the state-of-the-art equipment Barrera's bound to have installed in this place, you probably wouldn't. That doesn't mean they're not here." Climbing the short flight of stairs, he examined the door that was their only way out, but it was sturdy as an oak and locked tight. Nothing short of a bazooka was going to get them out of there without the key.

Watching him probe every inch of their holding tank, Maddy knew as well as he did that they were effectively trapped and the chances of escape were slim to none. But the panic that should have been twisting in her gut like a snake by now just wasn't there. Ace wasn't going to take this lying down. If there was a way out, he'd find it.

He moved to the wall across from the stairs and stared up at the small window ten feet above their heads. Glancing over at Maddy, he arched a brow at her. "If you stood on my shoulders, you might be able to see out that window—if you didn't fall and break your neck. You game?"

Caught off guard by the grin curving his mouth and the glint in his eye, Maddy could only stare at him. He was enjoying himself, she thought with a shock of surprise. He'd just taken a blow to the head that would have put most men in the hospital, but he only shook it off and got right back into the hunt. How did he do it?

Shaking her head in wonder, she joined him beneath the window and looked up—way up. "I can't believe I'm even considering this."

"You've got more guts than you think you do. C'mon, up you go."

He held out his hand to her and braced his leg with his knee half-bent, offering her a step up. Too late, Maddy realized she had to climb up his body to get to his shoulders. Startled, her eyes flew to his.

Grinning wickedly, he taunted, "Don't chicken out on me now, scaredy-cat. We're just getting to the good part."

It was the needling nickname that did it. He'd done nothing but tease her since they'd left New York, and it was high time she paid him back. Her eyes locking with his, she closed the space between them with a single step and placed her hand in his. His grin never wavered, but for just a second, she could have sworn she felt him stiffen. Encouraged, she gave him a grin of her own. "Ready?"

"For anything you can dish out, babe. Go for it."

If she hadn't been so worried about falling, it would have been the most intimate experience of her life. She touched him, pressed herself against him, clung to him with a daring that set her heart slamming against her ribs. And all the time, he kept murmuring words of encouragement. "That's it, honey, you're doing fine. Easy, take your time. Don't worry about hurting me. You don't weigh more than a feather."

She knew that was an out-and-out lie, but by that time, she had reached his shoulders and had to focus all her attention on the barred window above her head. Holding her breath, she balanced herself on his shoulders and inched her hands up the wall until she could reach the bars. Latching on to them like a lifeline, she let out a huge sigh of relief and grinned down at him. "Now what was that crack about being a scaredy-cat?"

"I take it all back." He chuckled, wrapping his fingers around her ankles to steady her. "Every word. Can you see anything?"

Easing up on her toes, she sneaked a peak and gasped. "Feet," she whispered, quickly ducking out of sight. "There's a guard standing right in front of the window."

Ace swore. "Damn. I was afraid of that."

"He's facing the compound—I don't think he saw me." Inching back up, she pushed her nose just over the edge of the windowsill and carefully peered around the khaki-covered legs blocking half her view. "There's another one at the corner of the parapet. I think he's asleep. He's half-sprawled in a chair—"

Whatever she might have said next was drowned out by the scrape of a key in the lock to the basement door. Horrified, she looked helplessly down at Ace. "Somebody's coming!"

"Hang on," he whispered, and before she could guess his intentions, he stepped out from under her, leaving her hanging from the bars. "Okay, drop. I'll catch you."

She didn't think—she didn't have time. Willing her clenched fingers to unlock their fierce hold on the bars, she drew in a bracing breath and let go. A heartbeat later, she fell into his arms.

"Cry!" he muttered through clenched teeth, forcing her face against his throat as he wound his arms against her and sank to the floor. "Come on, sweetheart, give me some tears!"

Maddy had never been any good at pretending—she couldn't even tell a little white lie without looking as guilty as a thief caught in the act. But fear, she discovered, was a powerful motivator. By the time the door at the top of the stairs opened, she was crying real tears against Ace's hard, muscular chest.

His arms closing protectively around her, Ace held her close against him and glared at the man who stood on the landing staring down at them with contempt in his black eyes. Bubba. Great. "Come back for some more head bashing?" he taunted in Spanish so there could be no possible misunderstanding. "You'd better enjoy it while you can, big guy. My time's coming."

The other man's eyes narrowed slightly, but he only said, "Rooms have been prepared for you. Come. You will clean up and dress for dinner."

It was an order, not a request, but Ace had no intention of taking exception to anything that would get them out of the hellhole of a basement. "D'you hear that, Maddy, my girl?" he asked with a jaunty grin as he helped her to her feet. "We've been invited to dinner. Let's not keep the man waiting."

* * *

The chamber they were shown to was large and airy and surprisingly modern looking considering they were literally hundreds of miles from civilization. Suddenly conscious of just how filthy she was, Maddy stepped into the room first and glanced around, wondering if she would have time for a bath before Bubba came back for them. Behind her, she didn't see the stern-faced guard bring his rifle down in front of Ace, blocking his entrance into the room when he tried to follow her.

"This is the *señorita*'s room," he said coldly. "Yours is farther down the hall."

Alarmed, Maddy spun back around. "What do you mean, down the hall? Why can't he stay here?"

"The decision isn't mine to make," he retorted, and started to shut the door in her face.

"Then talk to Barrera!" she cried. Suddenly terrified at the thought of being separated from Ace, she clutched at the door. "Please, you can't do this—"

Ace swore and tried to muscle past Bubba, but the guard turned his gun on him, and all he could do was shoot him a murderous look and assure Maddy, "It's just for a short while, sweetheart. Trust me. There's no way you're going to be left in this mausoleum by yourself for long. I'll be back for you, and then we're getting the hell out of here."

The door shut in her face then, closing him out, locking her in. Her heart thundering, she pressed her ear against the door to see if she could figure out which room Bubba took him to, but the walls were a foot thick and apparently soundproof.

It was then that she became aware of the silence, the absolute quiet that seemed to push in on her from all sides and was broken only by the murmured whisperings of panic in her ear. Turning, she surveyed the large chamber and should have been reassured by its very ordinariness. There were no whips or chains, no drugs of choice on the bedside table to show that she was being held captive by one of the world's most notorious drug lords. Totally private, with its own bath, it appeared perfectly safe.

The walls could have eyes and ears, though. Her gaze zeroing in on the simple cotton blouse and skirt that had been laid out for her on the bed, she felt her stomach turn over at the thought of some perverted stranger watching her on a television monitor in some small dark room while she changed. Deep inside she started to tremble. No, she thought, shaken, hugging herself. She couldn't do this. She couldn't put on some stranger's clothes or sit down to eat with a man who was responsible for who knew how much death and tragedy and pretend to be civil to him. He was a monster, a devil, and just the thought of being at his mercy terrified her. For all she knew, he could have had Ace returned to the basement and even now could be torturing him to death. And locked away in this soundproof room, she'd never hear a thing. God, she had to get out of here! Go to him . . .

She was at the door, her fist raised to pound on it, when it hit her that she was on the verge of totally losing control. Horrified, she dropped her head weakly against the door and sucked in an agitated breath. Lord, what was she doing? If Barrera really was hurting Ace, she wouldn't do him any good by falling apart. She had to stay calm, think. Right this minute, Ace might need her.

There's no way you're going to be left in this mausoleum by yourself for long. I'll be back for you, and then we're getting the hell out of here.

His words came back to her as clearly as if he stood beside her. Strong, sure, fearless. Wherever he was, he was all right. And he would come for her. She knew it as surely as she knew her own name. As surely as she knew she trusted him with her heart and soul. As surely as she knew she loved him.

The truth hit her from the blind side, stunning her. Stiffening, she instantly rejected the idea. She couldn't love him. It wasn't possible. He might flirt with her, kiss her, even openly desire her, but he'd made it clear that once was enough for him as far as relationships were concerned. He'd loved one woman—he wouldn't love another. He wouldn't love *her*.

She winced, but there was no avoiding the inevitable. Some things weren't meant to be, and she and Ace were one of them. And that hurt. God, how it hurt! But if she could have gone back and changed that moment when he'd come into her life, she knew that she wouldn't have. Because not only had she learned just how much she could love a man, she'd tumbled into an adventure that she would remember to her dying day. Regardless of what happened, she couldn't regret that.

When Ace showed up at her door twenty minutes later accompanied by a grim-faced Bubba, he had changed into new jeans that fit him like a glove and a blue cotton shirt that darkened the color of his eyes. And he'd shaved! He *almost* looked civilized. His dark hair was neatly combed, his jaw a smooth slab of granite that her fingers itched to touch. Her pulse skipping, Maddy couldn't stop staring. How could she have forgotten what a good-looking man he was?

Her eyes met his and he gave her a rakish grin that was full of daring, and just that quickly, he was the same Ace who lied his way into two countries without a passport. Ignoring Bubba, he looked her up and down and whistled in appreciation. "You clean up real good, princess. I don't think I've ever seen you in ruffles before. I like them."

A blush stole into her cheeks, but her eyes sparkled up into his as she picked self-consciously at the ruffled neckline of the peasant blouse that had been left on the bed for her. "I bet you say that to all the girls."

Surprised, he blinked. "Are you flirting with me, Maddy Lawrence?"

She was, and she loved it. She loved *him*. And suddenly she wasn't the same old Maddy who jumped at her own shadow and was so unsure of herself that the only man in her life was the one she found between the pages of a book. Daring to slip her hand through the crook of his arm, she said saucily, "If you have to ask, I must not be doing it very well," and had the satisfaction of seeing him searching for a smart comeback for the first time since she'd known him. She was still grinning when they went downstairs.

The macabre dinner that followed was like something out of one of Maddy's worst nightmares. Barrera, who was waiting for them in the living room when they came downstairs, dismissed Bubba with a casual wave of his hand and proceeded to greet them as if they were honored guests. "*Señorita, señor,* welcome! Please, come in. It is a pleasure to have you in my home. Can I get you a drink? Wine? Iced tea? Whatever you wish is, of course, yours. Mi casa es su casa."

Maddy felt rather than heard Ace snort at that, but he only said, "Iced tea will be fine, thank you. This is quite a place you have here, *señor.* A little out of the way, though. I don't imagine you have many visitors."

Fixing their drinks himself from the elaborate drink cart that sat near the couch, Barrera chuckled, but there was little warmth in the sound. "That is true, Ace. I may call you and the *señorita* by your first names, *sí?* Formality is so boring, and you're right. We are quite isolated, which is why I'm so pleased to have you here." Crossing to them, he handed them each a glass of tea, then gave Maddy a smile that might have been charming if it had reached his eyes. It didn't. "Señorita Maddy, you must tell me what you think of our rain forest. I'm sure it's quite different from what you're used to."

Caught in the trap of his hard, all-seeing gaze, Maddy suppressed a shiver and forced a weak smile. "It's beautiful. But much more dangerous than I was prepared for."

"She doesn't like snakes," Ace added pointedly.

Not a slow-witted man, Barrera lifted an arched brow, the amusement that curled his thin-lipped mouth mockingly sinister. "I've been told it's an acquired taste. Shall we go into dinner?"

Maddy couldn't even swallow her tea—there was no way she was going to be able to force down food—but their host didn't appear to be concerned if she was hungry or not. Taking her arm, he led her into the dining room and pulled out a chair for her at the table that looked as if it'd come right out of a medieval castle. Dark and heavy and ornately carved, it was laden with enough food for an army.

Taking a seat right next to her at the head of the table, he motioned for Ace to take the place to his left so that he and Maddy were facing each other. "I've dismissed the servants for the evening so that we can dine in private, so please help yourself. I hope you like veal. It's one of my chef's specialties."

It was probably delicious, but when Maddy dutifully tasted it, it could have been shoe leather for all the pleasure she got from it. Ace, however, didn't appear to be having the same problem. He dug in with the enthusiasm of a man who didn't have a single worry on his mind. He chatted with

Barrera as if they were old friends, discussing everything from last year's Superbowl champ to the situation in Bosnia-Sergovia. But any fears Maddy had that he'd been taken in by the drug lord's smooth charm faded the instant her eyes met his across the table. He was just as on guard as she was and ready for anything.

Like the snake that he was, Barrera struck when they least expected it. One second he was arguing American politics with Ace, and the next he said coolly, "I know why have you have come, Ace, but I'm afraid you're too late."

Leaning back in his chair, Ace didn't even blink at the sudden change in conversation. His smile as easy as his host's, he merely lifted a brow in casual interest. "Oh, really? And what am I too late for?"

"The ring, of course," Barrera chided. "Come now, there is no need for you to pretend. I know you want the ring Mark Antony gave Cleopatra to wear in her belly button, and you know I have it. I bought it from Señor Lazear fifteen minutes before my men ran across you and Señorita Maddy on the path from the river. So you see, you have come all this way for nothing."

His tone was regretful, his manner consoling, but Ace saw the glee in the bastard's eyes and would have taken great satisfaction in punching his lights out. Unfortunately, that would have only brought the guards running, and that was the last thing he wanted.

Studying the other man shrewdly, he said lazily, "Well, maybe we did and maybe we didn't. I don't know how well you know Lazear, but he's got quite a reputation back in the States. You see, he's got a nasty habit of passing off fakes as the real thing, then keeping the original for himself. So you might have Cleopatra's ring and you might not."

"And I suppose you might know the real thing if you saw it," Barrera taunted. "Is that what you're angling for, Señor Ace? You wish to see the ring?"

Ace grinned. "If it's not too much trouble. As you said, we did come a long way."

For a tense moment, he thought Barrera was going to flatly refuse. But the drug lord could hardly do that and still continue to appear to be the congenial host, which, for reasons of his own, was a role he seemed to especially enjoy.

"Very well," the older man said with a lightness that was belied by the tight bunching of his square jaw. With a sharp flick of his hand, he rang the small bell that sat near his wineglass on the table and brought a servant running within seconds. "Bring me the rosewood box off my desk," he said in Spanish to the elderly woman who appeared in the doorway. *"Andele!"*

As silent as a wraith, she glided away and was back within minutes, this time with a small, antique rosewood jewelry box that she set on the table before him. Anticipation lighting his eyes, Barrera leaned forward eagerly and opened the lid. When he swiveled toward Ace, his smile was smug. "There you go, *señor.* Check it out for yourself."

Ace knew before he even touched it that the ring was genuine. He'd only seen pictures of it before, but he'd been told of distinguishing marks to look for, marks that weren't common knowledge or easily detected, and they were all there. Fighting the urge to palm the damn thing, he carefully returned the ring to its display box.

Glancing up, he shot the drug lord a narrow-eyed look that pinned him to his seat. "How much do you want for it?"

Truly amused, Barrera only laughed. "You must be joking, *señor.* In spite of Lazear's foolish willingness to part with it, some things are not for sale."

Ace had figured as much, but it was worth a shot. "Then it appears you're right, *señor*. Apparently we've barged in on you for nothing. I apologize for that and promise to get out of your hair first thing in the morning. So if you don't mind, we'll retire early tonight. It's been a long day, and we both could use some sleep in a real bed."

Acting as if he expected the other man's full cooperation, Ace actually started to push to his feet, but that was as far as he got. Again, Barrera laughed, but this time there was something decidedly evil about the sound. "Nice try, Ace, but I would have to be incredibly stupid to let you leave in the morning, and we both know I'm not a stupid man. You and Señorita Maddy will not be going anywhere. Ever."

"Ever?" Maddy choked, her gaze bouncing back and forth between the two men. "What do you mean *ever*? Surely you don't expect us to just stay here!"

"That's exactly what I expect, *señorita,*" he said coldly. "Only my most trusted friends and advisers are allowed to know the location of this compound, and you, unfortunately, are not one of those privileged few. If I let you leave here, you'd go straight to the DEA with that information. I can't allow you to do that, so I have no choice but to keep you here."

Unable to believe he was serious, Maddy just stared at him. "But we have lives back home, family, jobs—"

"You should have thought of that before you came barging in where you had no business sticking your pretty little nose in something you didn't understand."

Aware of Maddy's rising panic, Ace kept his voice deliberately calm as he chided, "Don't you think you're being a little paranoid here? I don't know why the DEA would be interested in your location, Mr. Barrera, but all we came here for was the ring. Since it's not available, there's no reason to stick around to talk to the DEA or anyone else—''

A pained expressed crossed Barrera's swarthy face as he held up a hand. "Please, sir, don't insult my intelligence. Mr. Lazear tried that, and he's now cooling nicely in the freezer. I would hate to consign you and Señorita Maddy to the same fate."

"Oh, God!" Maddy whispered faintly.

"Yes, it was quite sad," he said with little regret, "but he shouldn't have tried to play me for a fool. I'm sure the two of you will be much smarter." In the blink of an eye, his expression changed as he, too, rose to his feet with an easy smile and set the rosewood jewelry box on the sideboard. "But after such a trying day, I can understand why you would wish to retire early. I'll call Jose and he can show you back to your rooms. Tomorrow my men will retrieve the rest of your things from your camp in the jungle."

The man was mad, Ace decided, if he thought they were going to meekly accept his hospitality until he decided to either free them or kill them. His smile as shallow as their host's, he came around the table and pulled back Maddy's chair for her, slipping his arm around her waist as she stood. "Then if we're going to be your guest for some time, *señor,* I'd appreciate it if you'd allow Maddy to room with me," he lied brazenly. "We're lovers and don't sleep well apart."

Caught flat-footed, Maddy gasped, hot color singeing her cheeks. "Ace!"

"Don't be embarrassed, sweetheart," he teased, pulling her closer against his side. "I'm sure we haven't shocked Señor Barrera."

Amused, the other man laughed softly. "He's right, *señorita.* Don't be embarrassed—I understand perfectly. When a man is used to having a lover beside him in the night, he does not like to do without. Come, I'll show you to your room myself, then inform the guards that from now on, you are not to be separated.''

Her cheeks still hot and her hand tightly clenched in Ace's, Maddy didn't issue a single word of complaint. But the second they were left alone in Ace's room and the key clicked in the lock, she turned on him and muttered, ''I can't believe you did that! Did you see the way that sleaze was looking at me?''

Already methodically searching the room for a way out, he looked up and flashed her a grin. ''When you're dealing with scum, you've got to appeal to their baser instincts. It works every time. Once he gets to thinking about it, though, he's bound to realize putting us in together wasn't a very smart move. So help me search the place for a way out, Pollyanna. Tonight may be the only night we have together.''

Just the thought of being separated from him again was all the incentive she needed. Together, they went over the room with a fine-tooth comb, meticulously examining every nook and cranny for something that could be used to unlock the door and anything that could be used as a weapon.

Barrera, however, was no idiot. There were no coat hangers in the closet, no innocent pieces of wire that could be fashioned into a crude key for the lock on the door. That left the window as the only escape route. And while it didn't have any bars, there really was no need for them. They were on the second floor and in a tower room. The only way out was a sheer wall that led straight to the main compound . . . and the guards . . . two stories below. Even if they knotted the sheets from the bed together, they'd never reach all the way to the ground and they'd be easy targets for Barrera's men.

Staring down at the lighted compound below, Maddy swallowed, forcing moisture into her suddenly dry mouth. ''It looks like we're stuck.''

Beside her, Ace said, "Not necessarily. Just because we can't go down doesn't mean we're going to sit on our hands and wait for Barrera to stick us in the freezer with Lazear. One way or another, sweetheart, we're getting out of here. Tonight."

"But how?"

"We'll go up."

Chapter 10

"Up?" Maddy squeaked. "Are you out of your mind? We'll break our necks!"

"O, ye of little faith." He chuckled, clicking his tongue at her. "Would I let anything happen to you?"

"Not deliberately, no, but if we're dead, we're dead. What does it matter how we got that way?" Frowning, she lifted a hand to his brow. "That blow to your head must have really scrambled your brains. You're not thinking clearly."

Lightning quick, he trapped her fingers in his. "Will you stop that? There's nothing wrong with my head! It's harder than a rock. Now behave yourself and keep an open mind. Okay?" Laying an arm across her shoulders, he leaned out the window and turned her with him so that they were facing the side of the building instead of looking at the ground. Conscious of the guards down below, he said quietly in her ear, "All right, tell me what you see."

It didn't take an Einstein to figure that out. "The rock wall of the building."

"And?"

"And a rain gutter."

"Thatta girl," he said proudly, hugging her. "That's our ticket out of here."

He was crazy. Certifiable. For his own safety—and hers!—he should have been locked away a long time ago in a room with rubber walls so he couldn't hurt himself. And she loved him, God help her. So much that if he'd have told her he'd find a way to get her to the moon without NASA's help, she'd have tried her darnedest to believe him. Lord, she was in trouble.

"It's a gutter, Ace, not a ladder," she said pointedly in what she thought was a fairly reasonable voice considering the fact that her knees were already starting to knock. "How do you know it'll hold us?"

"Because it's been reinforced. Look at it. Go ahead," he encouraged when she just lifted a skeptical brow at him instead. "The brackets holding it to the building are just like the rungs of a ladder, and every one of them is cemented in place all the way to the roof. That thing would hold King Kong and never even shake. We've got nothing to worry about."

"Oh, really? And what do you call those bozos over there?" she asked, nodding to the men stationed at each corner of the parapet with automatic weapons.

He grinned. "A small technicality. They'll never even see us."

"And how do you figure that? Ace, I'm wearing white. The only way they're going to miss me is if they're blind."

"Look at the security lights," he coaxed patiently, pointing to where the floodlights were mounted at each corner below the battlements where the guards kept watch. "They're all directed outward, toward the jungle, not the compound. This place is a fort, honey, not a prison. It's designed to keep people out, not in. Nobody's paying any attention to what's going on up here.''

He sounded so logical, so sure of himself, that she couldn't help but believe him. But how could she scale the side of a building like some type of human fly? "I must be out of my mind to even think about doing this," she muttered to herself. "I'm a coward. A yellow-livered, crybaby, scared-of-her-own-shadow coward. I don't *do* things like this! Or at least I didn't before a certain someone kidnapped me and dragged me out of New York." Pulling her gaze away from the guards posted at the far corner of the parapet, she frowned up at him in irritation. "What have you done to me?"

"Woke you up, Sleeping Beauty," he said promptly, winking at her as he pulled her away from the window. "Whenever you want to thank me, honey, I'm ready, willing and able."

What he was was outrageous. His eyes laughed down at her, daring her. Just days ago, she would have blushed and stuttered and never had the nerve to call his bluff. But just days ago, she hadn't known what it was like to love him. It was so...so...exhilarating! So freeing. He made her feel as if she could do anything. Because with him she could.

Giving into the mischief he always seemed to bring out in her, she captured his face in her hands and brought his mouth down to hers. She didn't kiss him, though, not yet, not until she gave him back a little of his own teasing. Lowering her eyes to hide the laughter she knew was shining there, she dropped baby kisses on his chin, the deep slash of a wicked dimple, the corner—just the corner—of his mouth, and gloried in the groan that seemed to rumble up from his very soul.

With a muttered curse, his arms came around her with gratifying swiftness. "Dammit, Maddy—"

She laughed and lifted her gaze to his. "Something wrong, Ace?"

"If you're going to kiss me, woman, get on with it!"

"I thought that's what I was doing," she began playfully, but that was as far as she got. His hands tangled in her hair, and then he was kissing her like a man who had been pushed to the limits.

His mouth hot and hungry on hers, need tearing at him, Ace couldn't get enough of her. God, had there ever been a time he hadn't wanted this woman? If there was, he couldn't remember it. She was all he thought of, all he dreamed of. And the bed was just steps away. It was like something out of a fairy tale—a huge monstrosity of a bed complete with a feather mattress, mounds of pillows and a canopy. The moment he'd laid eyes on it before dinner, he'd known it was just the type of thing Maddy would love, and all too easily he could picture himself making love to her there, taking his time, gently teaching her, slowly awakening her to the pleasure they could find together.

With every passing hour, his need for her seemed to grow more intense. She'd come to mean so damn much to him, and he didn't even know how it had happened. Like a thief in the night, she'd slipped into his heart without him being aware of it until it was too late. She'd taken up residence there, and he could no longer imagine his life without her in it.

Dragging her closer, he felt her thighs against his, her hips cradling his hardness, and very nearly lost it. But as much as he burned for her, he hadn't forgotten for a second where they were.

Wrenching his mouth from hers, he buried his face in her hair, his breathing ragged as he held her close and waited for his blood to cool. "We've got to get out of here, honey."

"I know," she murmured huskily, and tightened her arms around him. "In a second."

Chuckling, he pressed a kiss to the delicate shell of her ear. "Does that mean you're going up the gutter with me?"

His tone was teasing, but when she drew back just enough to lift her eyes to his, she was dead serious. "If we stay here, Barrera's probably going to kill us, anyway. I'd rather take my chances with you than just sit here like a coward and meekly accept whatever he has in store for us."

The softly spoken admission came straight from her heart, a fact she made no attempt to hide. Staring down at her, Ace felt something tighten in his chest. Something that he should have been running like hell from instead of standing there like a man struck dumb. But the time for running was long gone and he didn't even know when it had happened.

Lifting a hand to her face, he traced a path of faint freckles across her cheek. "When we get out of here, honey," he said thickly, "I'm going to show you just what putting that kind of trust in a man does to him. You ready?"

"No," she said with a shaky laugh, nuzzling against his hand. "But I'm willing, and right now, that's about the most you can hope for. You'd better get me out of here while you can."

"Then let's do it. One word of advice, sweetheart. Don't look down."

That seemed a simple enough edict, but Maddy soon discovered that following it was easier said than done. Standing at the window with Ace behind her whispering instructions in her ear, she had to fight the need to look down and check the position of the guards below. Then it came time to actually climb out on the stone window ledge and step across to one of the brackets supporting the gutter, and all she could think about was how far down the ground was. If she slipped, it would be the last mistake she ever made.

"Don't think about falling," Ace growled in her ear, reading her mind. "You hear me? If I thought there was a possibility of that, we'd stay right here and take our chances with Barrera. You can do this, Maddy. Just pretend you're climbing up the ladder at the newsstand to get something off the top shelf."

It wasn't the actual climbing that worried her. It was taking that first big step. Her eyes locked on the metal pipe that seemed a thousand miles away, she knew she could reach it if she just leaned toward it the slightest bit. But her rigid body refused to cooperate. And every second that she stood out on the ledge, the greater the chance that someone would spot her.

Behind her, she felt Ace tense, then his voice came to her like a caress, a murmur that was no louder than a sigh on the wind.

"You're doing fine, honey. Just fine. Don't move until you're sure. That gutter's not going anywhere, and neither are we until you're ready. Just take your time and visualize that first step. You wait until the first frantic rush of your heart eases and your breathing is steady. That's it," he said with quiet approval. "The pipe is right there, closer than your favorite Ace MacKenzie book on your bedside table at home. You reach out—slowly—close your fingers around it, and take a step over to the first bracket as easily as if you're stepping into my arms."

Her heart knocking out a crazy rhythm, she never knew how long she stared at that gutter. True to his word, Ace didn't rush her.

Then, with no conscious decision on her part, she moved. Suddenly she was balanced precariously on a bracket that was hardly as big as her foot and clinging to the gutter with a grip Superman would have had trouble breaking.

"Look up, honey," Ace said firmly. "Focus on the next bracket and start climbing. Thatta girl! Keep going. I'm right behind you."

Hand over hand, she moved at a snail's pace, half expecting to get shot at any moment. But the guards, as Ace had promised, were too busy staring out at the jungle to notice the two of them making their way up the side of the building. Ace made no move to touch her, but she could feel his presence right beneath her feet. He was so close that if she bobbled the slightest bit, she knew he would steady her in a heartbeat. Reassured, her gaze focused unblinkingly on the dark shadows where the side of the building gave way to the roof, she climbed steadily upward.

The top, when she reached it, was a surprise. She didn't know what she had expected, but it wasn't a foot-high ledge, then a flat expanse of tar paper that didn't have so much as a guardrail or a light for the unwary. One moment she was reaching for the gutter's next brace, and the next, she was rolling over the ledge into dark, concealing shadows.

Stunned, she landed on her back, her arms spread-eagle, and stared up at the magnificence of the night sky while laughter bubbled up in her like water from a spring. A million stars winked down at her, and with no effort at all, she could imagine herself back in New York, stargazing on the rooftop of her building. She'd done it. By God, she'd done it!

Ace pulled himself over the edge and landed with a nearly soundless thud beside her, his grin flashing in the dark as he suddenly leaned over her, his face only inches from hers. "Excuse me, ma'am," he drawled in a soft, teasing murmur, "but are you sure you're the same lady who screamed

over a little snake only a couple of days ago? I think somebody switched women on me."

"I did it," she whispered, her eyes as bright as the con-
stellations as she looped her arms around his neck. "I didn't
think I could."

Tenderly, his hands brushed her hair back from her face.
"Honey, don't you know yet that you can do damn well
anything if you set your mind to it? I've known that for days
now."

He kissed her then because he couldn't help himself, because the adrenaline was still pumping and the need that was
always just under his skin whenever she was this close was
too damn powerful to resist. And for a precious moment in
time, when she tightened her arms around his neck and met
his descending mouth with a quiet sigh of pleasure, they
could have been the only two people for miles.

But it couldn't last, not when their empty room below
could be discovered any second. Reluctantly lifting his head,
he grinned down at her in the darkness. "How do you feel
about helicopters?"

Confused, she blinked. "What?"

He nodded to his left and the hulking shadows in the
darkness. "There's our ticket out of here, sweetheart."

Maddy followed his gaze to where the helicopter was
nearly lost in the darkness that engulfed the roof. Its long
blades still and quiet, it was all black glass and sleek lines
and appeared to be one of those new, high-dollar models
that looked like something out of *Star Wars*.

"Do you know how to fly it?"

"Piece of cake," he assured her as he helped her up.
"Let's see if the keys are in it."

Not surprisingly, they weren't, but Ace didn't bat an eye
at that. "I can hot-wire it and we'll be out of here in a mat-

ter of seconds. Go ahead and get in, sweetheart. I'll be right back."

"Back? Where are you going?" she demanded. But even as she asked, she knew. "You're going after that ring!"

"You're damn right I'm going after it. That's what we came for. And since Barrera was stupid enough to show me where he keeps it, there's no reason to leave it behind."

Maddy couldn't believe he was serious, but one look at the hard set of his jaw and she knew he had no intention of letting anyone or anything come between him and that ring. Still, she had to try. "Are you crazy? What do you call a dozen or more armed guards roaming the downstairs like ants? They'll blow you away the second they see you."

"Then I'll just have to make sure they don't see me," he said simply. "After all, it's not like they'll be looking for me. As far as Barrera and his men are concerned, we're still locked in our room. By the time they realize their mistake, we'll be long gone."

"But it's not that simple," she argued. "Barrera's not an idiot. He's not going to leave that ring just lying around in that fancy jewelry box for anyone to pick up. By now, he's probably got it locked away in a safe somewhere and you'll never find it."

"That's what I would do," Ace agreed, "but we're talking about Barrera, sweetheart. Haven't you noticed how arrogant he is? He doesn't even have a guard posted at the damn helicopter because he thinks we're no threat to him. He likes to flaunt what he's got, and putting that ring away in a safe place would be an admission on his part that this whole setup isn't quite as secure as he likes to think it is. Trust me, that ring is right where he left it on the sideboard."

"And if it's not? Then what?"

"Then we cut our losses and get the hell out of here."

He made it sound so easy, but just the thought of running into one of the guards when escape was right there at their fingertips chilled her blood. All for a stupid ring that was, as far as she was concerned, incredibly ugly and not worth anyone's life. Ignoring the helicopter's door he held open for her, she warned, "If this blows up in our faces, I'm never going to let you hear the end of it. You realize that, of course?"

He started to tell her that if that was the case, he wouldn't be around for her to nag, but then her words registered. "What do you mean . . . *our* faces? I'm the one who's going after the ring. You're staying here."

"And let you go back down there by yourself? No way. Who'll watch your back?"

He had to laugh at that. "Honey, I've been doing this sort of thing by myself for a long time. I don't need anyone to cover for me."

"Maybe not, but I'm going, anyway. You don't even know how many goons Barrera has wandering around down there. And you can't look for the ring and watch for them at the same time."

She had that stubborn set to her chin, the one that warned him nothing short of a bulldozer was going to move her. And he didn't have time to argue with her. "Stubborn woman," he muttered when she turned and started for the door that led downstairs. "Just hold on a minute! Damn, I wish I had my gun!"

Scowling at the dark interior of the helicopter, he leaned into the cockpit and started feeling blindly under the seats. "Barrera wouldn't go off in this thing without some firepower—he's got too many enemies. Half the world's major law enforcement agencies are after him—"

He broke off suddenly as his fingers encountered cold, hard steel. "Well, what have we here?" He drew out a 9mm automatic and grinned. "Bingo. Just what I was hoping for."

"Is it loaded?"

He checked and grinned. "Somebody upstairs is looking out for us, honey." Shoving it into his waistband, he urged her toward the rooftop entrance to the castle. "Stay behind me and be ready for anything," he said in a murmur that barely reached her ears as he cautiously pulled open the door. "This could get hot real quick."

The stairwell was as dark as pitch, but they didn't dare switch on a light. Down below, the place was quiet as a tomb, but Ace didn't believe for a moment that Barrera and his staff had retired for the night. It was too early, not even ten yet, and the drug lord had struck him as the night-owl type. He—and his men—were around there somewhere and could stumble across them any second.

Feeling his way in the dark, testing every step to make sure it didn't squeak before he put his full weight on it, Ace led Maddy down the single flight from the roof to the third floor where it abruptly ended at a closed door. In order to get to the first floor, they'd have to take the main staircase in the center of the building.

"Damn," he swore softly. "I was hoping this thing went all the way to ground level. I'm not looking forward to going down those main stairs."

"There might be a back way," Maddy said quietly. "This place is so big, it's bound to have more than one set of stairs."

"True, but even if we had the time to look for them— which we don't—it'd be just our luck that they'd take us right to Barrera's command center or something. At least we know where the main ones go." Leaning down suddenly, he started tugging off his boots. "Take your shoes off, princess. From here on out, we can't make a sound."

Images of the two of them sneaking down the hall in their stocking feet like a couple of cat burglars flashing before her eyes, Maddy reached for the ties to her boots with fingers that openly trembled. Unconsciously holding her breath as Ace slowly eased open the door, she braced for trouble, but there wasn't a soul in sight. Thank God! she thought with a sigh, and wilted in relief.

A single naked bulb glowed eerily at the far end of the hall, hardly piercing the darkness, but giving off enough light to reveal the ancient tables and heavily carved chairs that lined the walls like patients at a doctor's office. A storage area, she thought with a shaky laugh. They were using the whole floor for storage. The only time anyone probably came up here was to add another piece to the discarded furniture or to get to the roof. Even the air was musty and still and spoke of little use.

Obviously coming to the same conclusion, Ace relaxed slightly at her side. "Looks like it's all clear up here. Now comes the fun part."

Maddy could have thought of a hundred words to describe the possible nightmare they were on the verge of walking into, but *fun* wasn't one of them. Silently skirting the dusty furniture that littered the hall, they made their way to the main staircase, where they stopped in the near darkness at the top of the stairs and stared down at the second floor, which was better lit than where they stood but still bathed in muted light. Somewhere outside, a dog barked, then quieted, but that was the only sound from below. If anyone was milling about the stairs, they were being awfully quiet about it.

His face grim, Ace pulled out the 9mm. Leaning close so that he could speak directly in her ear, he said in a hushed whisper, "Once we start down, we're going all the way to the bottom unless someone is coming. If we run into someone other than Barrera or Bubba, act as if we've got every right to be there—the rest of his men may not know that we've been confined to our room yet. Do you remember where the dining room is?''

''Yes, but—''

''The kitchen's got to be just off that. If someone starts shooting, I want you to run like hell in that direction and slip out the back way. If you're lucky, the guards will come in from the front. I'll hold them off as long as I can.''

He was telling her to leave him. To turn her back on him and whatever trouble he was in and save her own neck while he faced certain death for her. Shooting him a wounded look, she asked, ''Do you really think I would do something like that?''

''You're damn right you'll do it,'' he growled. ''You'll do it because you love your mother and you know it'll kill her if you die down here at the hand of some lousy drug lord she didn't even know you knew. You'll do it so she won't have to hear the news from some poker-faced, tight-assed government official with ice water in his veins and a computer chip for a heart. You'll do it, all right. Or else.''

Or else he'd call the whole escape plan off right now and give them both up to Barrera before she had a chance to get hurt. He didn't exactly make the threat, but she knew him now, knew just how far he would go to do the responsible thing. Dear God, how could she have ever thought that he was just as crooked as Cement Johnny and her boss?

''All right,'' she grumbled, glaring at him. ''We'll do this your way. But if anything happens to you because you're trying to protect me, I'll never forgive you!''

Ace manfully struggled with a smile and nodded curtly. ''I wouldn't blame you, darlin', if you never spoke to me again.'' He would have given anything right then to kiss her, but that would have to wait until later. And there would be a later, he promised himself as his smile faded. He'd make sure of it.

They floated down the stairs on silent feet, their movements so smooth that they barely disturbed the air itself, two shadows that blended from one patch of darkness to the next like ghosts avoiding the revealing light of day. Barely daring to breathe, every muscle tense with expectation and their eyes constantly moving, searching, they reached the second-floor landing without mishap.

There was, however, no time to enjoy that simple victory.

With only a quick glance behind him to make sure Maddy was still close, Ace started down the last flight and was two steps from the bottom when he heard someone at the front door. The roar of his blood loud in his ears, there was no time to think, no time to do anything but grab Maddy's hand and haul her with him into a closet to the right of the entranceway just as the front door opened.

Darkness embraced them, hot and thick and all-encompassing. Just outside the closet door, they heard heavy footsteps in the front hall, then a quieter tread from the formal living room off to the right. It wasn't until the two men spoke, discussing the security for the night, that they realized they'd just missed running head-on into Barrera and Bubba.

Maddy didn't utter so much as a peep of sound, but she was plastered up against Ace in the crowded closet, her breast pressed intimately to his chest, her face buried against his throat, and he could feel the fear clawing at her and the need to bolt. But there was nowhere to run, not now. And there was nothing he could do to reassure her except cradle her close and pray that no one opened the closet door.

In the stifling darkness, it seemed as if they waited forever for the two men to conclude their business, but it was in actuality only a matter of minutes. They were the longest minutes of Maddy's life. Clammy, the food she'd forced herself to eat at supper now forming a riot in her stomach, she felt hot, sick. The edges of her control threatening to unravel any second, she had this crazy desire to laugh, to fight her way out of Ace's arms and run like a screaming madwoman for the concealing security of the jungle. God, she hated waiting! She just wanted this over with, one way or the other, so the suspense would quit tearing her apart.

But Bubba and Barrera showed no signs of concluding their business and retiring for the night. And then when they really did appear to be wrapping things up, they moved from the living room to the hall and seemed to take up residence right on the other side of the closet door. Horrified, Maddy felt her heart stop in midbeat. Sucking in a sharp breath, she froze, the pounding of her heart so loud she was sure the two men had to hear it even through the closed door.

If they did, however, they gave no sign of it. They continued to talk in Spanish as seconds stretched into minutes. Wanting to scream *"Enough already!"* Maddy barely managed to swallow the whimper that rose in her throat, threatening to choke her. The closet was too dark, too small, the air too thin. A cold shiver rippled down her spine. Out. She wanted out of there, *needed* out of there . . . now!

Ace felt her distress as clearly as if it were his own and didn't have to see her eyes to know that they were dark and dilated with rising panic. Tugging her tighter into his body, he wanted to reassure her that even if Barrera or his sidekick opened the door, he could take them both out before they had time to so much as blink, but he didn't dare open his mouth.

Then, just when he thought the two slimeballs would never shut up, Barrera gave Bubba an order to deliver to the guards outside. The front door opened and closed, then there was nothing but the sound of the drug lord's measured tread on the steps as he started upstairs, presumably to go to bed. Praying that he wasn't going to check on them to make sure they were still locked up tight, Ace had to tighten his arms to keep Maddy from bursting out of the closet then and there.

"Wait!" he rasped in her ear. "Give him time to get upstairs."

She nodded jerkily, but he didn't dare release her, not yet. Deliberately counting to twenty in his head, he cocked his head against the door and listened, but the silence that vibrated in his ear remained hushed and unbroken. "Now," he quietly murmured. Releasing Maddy, he opened the door inch by inch, until the opening was wide enough for him to cautiously poke his head through.

Nothing moved. Since they'd gone upstairs after dinner, the lights in the living room and dining room had been turned down low, and Barrera himself must have switched out the one in the entrance hall. It was bathed in dark shadows, making it impossible for anyone outside to see them through the glass panels that bracketed either side of the massive wooden door. A door that was, Ace noted with interest, fitted with a dead bolt that wasn't currently engaged. Stepping out of the closet, he reached over and shot it home with a quiet click, locking Barrera's men out.

"That takes care of Bubba and the gang," he said softly, flashing Maddy a devilish grin. "Now all you have to watch for is Barrera and the house staff."

The entrance to the dining room was just steps away. Pale faced, Maddy took up a position across from it so that she could see both the stairs and the hallway that led to the kitchen area. When Ace pressed the gun into her hand, she stiffened, startled, then closed her fingers convulsively around it. "Hurry," she whispered.

More aware than she of the passage of time and the fact that their chances of being discovered increased considerably with every tick of the clock, Ace nodded grimly and slipped into the dining room, his gaze immediately shooting to the sideboard where Barrera had set the jewelry box after dinner. It was still there.

A weight he hadn't even realized was sitting on his shoulders lifted at the sight of it. If one of the most famous rings in history had been in his possession, *he* would have had the thing under lock and key. But not Barrera. Oh, no. The arrogant bastard thought he was above that kind of thing.

Which made the taking of the ring all the sweeter, Ace thought with a smug smile as he flipped open the jewelry box. From the bed of rich red satin that it rested on, the ancient, priceless diamonds and rubies of Cleopatra's belly-button ring winked teasingly up at him. Every instinct he had urged him to hurry, but it would be just like Barrera to replace the original ring with a worthless imitation after he'd shown them to their room. Quickly examining it, Ace found the identifying marks almost immediately. In the time it took to blink, he pocketed the ring and set the jewelry box back where he found it.

"Got it," he told Maddy as he silently joined her and took the gun from her. "Let's get the hell out of here."

Shaking with nerves, Maddy didn't have to be told twice. Sprinting up the stairs in her socks, she found herself smiling and suddenly knew why Ace risked life and limb to do what he did. They'd done it. They'd snitched the ring right out from under Barrera's nose and by the time he discovered it was gone, they'd be far beyond his reach. Just thinking about how furious he would be then made her want to laugh.

They reached the second-floor landing, where they were forced to stop and check the hallway, but it was all clear.

One more floor, she thought, excitement sparkling in her eyes, then the only thing that stood between them and freedom was the dark flight of stairs that led to the roof. The way she felt now, she could fly right up them without touching a single step.

Delighted with the image, she pushed harder up the next flight, not caring that she was getting winded. Five steps above her, then four, the third-floor landing and all its dark shadows waited. She started to grin. They were almost there.

"What the hell! Stop!"

Barrera's roar of outrage came from below them, startling them both. Her heart shooting straight to her throat, Maddy stumbled and almost fell. "Oh, God, no! No!"

"Run!" Ace growled, grabbing her and pushing her the rest of the way up the stairs. Glancing over his shoulder, he took aim and fired without ever releasing her. "Go on!" he yelled over the deafening explosion of the 9mm. "I'm right behind you."

Sobbing, her breath tearing through her lungs and her ears ringing, she burst onto the third-floor landing like the devil himself was after her, which he was. Dodging the furniture in the hallway like a halfback running for the goal line, she ran toward the roof stairwell at the far end of the hall. It wasn't until she reached it that she realized that Ace wasn't with her.

Throwing himself behind the banister of the main stairway where it curved around onto the third floor, Ace fired down at Barrera again and had the satisfaction of seeing the bastard dive for cover. He was unarmed and screaming for his men in Spanish, and for the moment, Ace had him right where he wanted him. His mercenaries, however, were another matter. Far down below, he could hear them at the front door, shouting and beating on it. Any second now, they'd break it down and come running to their boss's aid with a full arsenal of weapons.

"Ace! My God, what are you doing?"

At Maddy's frightened cry, he whirled to find her hovering uncertainly at the door to the roof stairs with her arms clutched around their boots. "Go on!" he yelled. "Check the copter to make sure it's not tied down, then get in and strap yourself in. I'll be right there."

Down below, there was a loud crash as the guards broke through the massive front door. He'd just run out of time. Not checking to see if Maddy had followed his orders, he fired two quick shots at Barrera, then vaulted over the discarded furniture, throwing it into the path behind him as he sprinted for the roof stairs. Maddy was gone, and he could only pray that she'd followed his orders. Because if she hadn't, they were fried.

She'd left the door to the stairwell open for him, and he hit the open doorway at a dead run. Behind him, he heard the thunder of feet rushing up the main stairs, Barrera's impatient shouts as he reached the third floor and found his way blocked by an army of antiques. Then a shot rang out, shattering the wooden doorframe just inches from Ace's head. Swearing, he slammed the door behind him and lost precious seconds fumbling for a lock in the all-consuming darkness. When he found the simple catch, he knew it wasn't going to stop anyone for long, but all he needed was ten seconds to hot-wire the helicopter. Just ten damn seconds.

When he reached the roof, however, Maddy was waiting for him just outside the rooftop entrance. "Dammit, Maddy, I told you—"

"Everything's ready," she cut in breathlessly. "I found a piece of wood. It's not much, but I can wedge it under the doorhandle while you try to get the helicopter started." Not giving him time to argue, she jammed the wood in place as he ran for the copter.

"C'mon, c'mon," he said through his clenched teeth, fumbling around in the dark for the starter. Tension tightening the muscles of his shoulders and neck, he knew the second Maddy vaulted into the seat next to him and quickly buckled up, but he couldn't take his eyes from his task. "The gun's at your feet," he said tersely as he finally located the starter and jerked the wires from it. "Shoot the first man who breaks through that door."

Putting the ends of the two wires together, he grinned as the motor roared to life. "All right! Here we go, sweetheart. Hang on!"

Slowly, the huge rotors overhead started to spin, then pick up speed. His hand on the throttle, Ace waited impatiently for enough power to take off. "Almost there," he muttered to himself. "Come on, baby, you can do it."

The blades whirled faster, but not fast enough. Suddenly, before they were ready, they ran out of time. The door to the stairwell burst open and Barrera's men spilled out, their automatic weapons spitting bullets.

Chapter 11

Maddy screamed and ducked just as Ace hit the throttle that sent the helicopter leaping into the air like a black cat. "Shoot 'em, dammit!" he roared. "I don't care if you hit anything, just fire the damn gun!"

There was no time to think, no time to worry if she was really capable of killing another human being. Both shaking hands wrapped around the 9mm, she turned it down toward the men on the roof below, squeezed her eyes shut and pulled the trigger. The resulting blast nearly deafened her, but it was the kick of the gun in her hand that had her gasping in surprise. The force of it rippled up her arms like an earthquake.

"Again!" Ace yelled. "Keep it up until we're out of range."

Unable to manage a word for the lump of fear lodged in her throat, Maddy braced for the gun's kick this time and peppered the roof. Scattering, Barrera and his men scrambled for cover, firing all the while.

And they were good shots. Maddy felt the heat of a bullet as it flew right by her cheek, and Ace instinctively ducked and swore as one hit the windshield. Barrera, however, must have had the helicopter fitted with bulletproof glass because the bullet only ricocheted harmlessly off it. With a jerk of the control stick back and forth, Ace sent the copter swinging first one way, then another, dodging bullets in a deadly ballet in the sky.

They almost got away without a scratch. Then a slug slammed into the tail, and the jolt nearly sent them tumbling back down to the ground.

"Dammit to hell!" Swearing, Ace quickly recovered, but the sudden pungent scent of gasoline in the air told him that one of Barrera's sharpshooters had gotten lucky. He'd nicked a fuel line and it was only by the grace of God that they weren't a fireball right now.

His gut clenching, Ace knew their chances of flying all the way back to Caracas just took a nosedive. They were losing fuel at a steady rate. Another bullet anywhere near that gasoline, and they'd go up in flames. If by some quirk of fate they managed to avoid that, they'd be lucky if they managed to go fifty miles before he had to set down somewhere in the jungle. That wasn't nearly far enough. With all the high-tech computer gadgets Barrera had in his compound, it wouldn't take him any time at all to locate the downed copter.

"Ace? That smells like gas—"

"I know, sweetheart." He heard the shakiness in her voice, the apprehension she couldn't quite conceal even as she fired the 9mm like a seasoned veteran as they drew farther and farther away from Barrera's compound. "They got one of the fuel lines."

"Are we going to crash?"

"Not if I can help it," he said grimly. "It seems to be a slow leak, and that's in our favor. I'll keep her up in the air as long as I can, but you might as well know now we're going to have to set her down somewhere in the jungle, probably within the next hour."

"Barrera will come after us."

It wasn't a question but a flat statement of fact and he didn't insult her intelligence by trying to lie to her. "Yeah. But we're out of range now, and from what I can tell, he didn't have another helicopter in the compound. He'll have to follow us cross-country on the ground, and even with a Jeep, he's not going to do that with any speed in the middle of the night. We'll have at least an hour on him, maybe more."

Put that way, their chances sounded excellent, but Maddy wasn't buying it. Making up an hour was nothing to a man like Barrera. They'd tweaked his nose in his own house, and he wasn't the type who would forgive that. Or forget. Even if they somehow managed to evade him now and made it back to the States, he'd find a way to come after them.

Shoving the gun into the waistband of her skirt, she reached behind the seat to where she'd stashed their boots. "Then we'd better get our shoes on so we can hit the ground running," she said practically.

Grinning approvingly, Ace held out his foot.

Barely skimming the treetops, they flew in silence after that, tension thickening in the air with every beat of the huge rotors overhead. There would, Maddy knew, be no clearing in which to land the helicopter when the fuel gave out. In other parts of South America the rain forests had already been stripped to bare earth, totally destroying the delicate ecosystem, but not here. Barrera had too much power to allow that to happen in his neck of the woods, and the forest was still as thick and untamed as it must have been for centuries. So when they suddenly found themselves in desperate need of a spot to land, they would have no choice but to go in among the trees . . . and hope they survived the crash in good enough shape to escape into the undergrowth before Barrera and his men arrived.

"This is it!" Ace suddenly shouted over the noise of the rotor, startling her from her thoughts. "Put your face in your lap and cover your head with your arms."

Her heart stopping in midbeat, Maddy stared at him in confusion. "What do you mean this is it?" she yelled back, unable to detect any difference in the sounds of the motor. "The rotors are still—"

A sudden sputter, then a cough was all the warning they had. A split second later, the engine died and so did the rotors and they started to fall from the sky like a giant bird that had suddenly forgotten how to fly.

There was no time to scream, no time to even draw a bracing breath. Slamming her face down into her lap, Maddy covered her head with her arms, heard Ace curse and then all hell broke lose. They hit the trees—hard. Suddenly the windshield shattered, raining glass down on them. Branches flew at them from all directions. The helicopter jolted sideways, snagged on some more trees, and then they were pitching toward the ground. Before either of them was ready for it, they hurled into it with a bone-jarring crash.

The rear of the fuselage, where gasoline had been seeping for almost an hour, immediately broke apart, spilling gasoline everywhere. Swearing, Ace tore off his seat belt and Maddy's and hauled her clear of the wreckage. A split second later, the whole thing went up in flames, the force of the explosion sending them hurtling into the trees.

They landed twenty feet from the crash site face-first in the undergrowth, and for a good two minutes, neither of them moved so much as a muscle. Behind them, the flames danced and crackled and reached high into the night air.

Ace was the first to lift his head. "You all right?"

His voice sounded hoarse and strange to her ears . . . and oh, so dear. Half-afraid the earth would tilt under them if she moved too quickly, she cautiously looked up and found him lying less than a foot way, the concern furrowing his brow clearly revealed in the bright glare of the fire. A tree branch or a piece of glass must have gouged his cheek—a thin streak of blood trickled from a ragged cut—but other than that, he looked whole and healthy and wonderful.

Her heart kicking into gear again, she briefly considered all her aches and pain and dismissed them with a nod. "Yeah, I am," she said, amazed. "But you're hurt!"

She started to reach for his cheek, but he stopped her simply by catching her hand and tugging her into his arms. "It's just a scratch." The tension draining out of him at the feel of her against him, soft and whole and in one piece, he laughed suddenly and squeezed her tight. "God, honey, I thought we were goners for sure! The next time I want to go up in a helicopter, do us both a favor and give me a good hard kick where it'll do the most good, okay?"

"You can count on it. I've never been so scared in all my life."

The admission was murmured calmly enough against his throat, but Ace wasn't fooled. She was shaking in his arms and holding on to him for all she was worth, and he couldn't say he blamed her. That'd been a damn close call—he could still feel the heat from the blast singeing the back of his neck—and all he wanted to do was just hold her. But they weren't out of the woods yet—either literally or figuratively—and that was a luxury he couldn't afford. Not now, when Barrera was racing toward them, guided by the flames of the wreckage that glowed like a beacon in the night.

"Hey, what's this?" he teased, pulling back far enough so he could see the sparkle of tears in her eyes. "You're not going to fall apart on me now, are you, lady? The adventure's just begun."

"That's what I was afraid you'd say." She groaned. "Can't somebody call time-out or something, just till we catch our breath and regroup?"

"You'll get to rest," he promised, chuckling. "Later. After we put as much distance as possible between us and Barrera."

The drug lord's name sobered them both as nothing else could. Pushing herself out of his arms, she sat up. "Now what do we do?"

"We run," he said flatly. "As long and as far as we can and hope like hell that Barrera loses our scent somewhere along the way. If we're lucky, we'll come across a village where someone has a car and we can talk them into driving us to Caracas."

And if luck wasn't with them . . . they'd have to come up with another plan.

With no water to put out the burning wreckage, they had no choice but to turn their backs on it and leave it to burn itself out. For a hundred yards or so, the flames were bright enough to light their way, but then the wild foliage surrounded them, blocking out the light and encasing them in the thick, all-consuming darkness that was the jungle at night. Taking Maddy's hand to make sure he wouldn't lose her in the dark, Ace started jogging at a slow but steady clip that he could, if he had to, maintain all night.

With no flashlight and only the starlight high above the treetops to light their way, they tripped and stumbled over fallen logs and dodged branches that slapped them in the face, but kept on going, pushing themselves harder and harder, until their breathing was ragged and their steps heavy. And still they ran.

Maddy's hand tightly clasped in his, Ace knew she had to be tiring, but she hadn't issued a word of complaint. His own lungs were burning, and there was a stitch in his side that tightened with every step. Self-preservation urged him to keep going, but running them both into the ground would only allow Barrera the opportunity to catch them.

Stumbling into a small creek, he stopped in the ankle-deep water, gasping for air as he dragged her to a stop beside him. "We'll take . . . a break . . . here," he panted.

Unable to manage a word, Maddy nodded weakly and bent over at the waist, her breathing labored. God, she was dying! Another few steps and he would have had to drag her—that was all there was to it. Her blood felt like sludge in her veins, her brain mush. If she could just sit down—

But even as she started to sink right down into the water itself, a distant murmur carried on the night breeze had her turning to stone where she stood. Dogs. They were a long way off, but in the stillness of the jungle, sounds carried easily and the baying of hounds, even at a distance, was unmistakable.

Stricken, she looked up at Ace in growing horror. "My God, he's set dogs on us!"

Grimfaced, Ace cocked his head to the side and listened. "The fire led them right to us, but they're at least a mile back. That'll give us some time."

"Time for what? We can't outrun dogs!"

"No, but we can lose them in the creek." Squatting, he hurriedly cupped his hands in the water and took a long drink. As soon as Maddy had done the same, he took her hand again and turned upstream.

"Wait! I thought Caracas was the other way."

"It is. And that's just the way Barrera will expect us to go. So we'll go to Brazil instead."

Stunned, Maddy hurried after him, splashing water with every step, not sure if she wanted to laugh or cry. Brazil! Of course. Why hadn't she thought of that herself? she thought, swallowing a giggle that popped into her throat like an unexpected soap bubble. They had no clothes, no passports, no food—any other man would have seen that as a serious problem. But not Ace. Oh, no. They'd just hike on over to Brazil and get what they needed. Lord, what was she going to do with him?

They sloughed through the creek for hours, long after their feet had shriveled up in their wet shoes and they'd lost the energy to run, pushing themselves until they reached the stream's headwaters. And even then, they didn't stop. Boneweary, they backtracked numerous times to throw the dogs off just in case they tracked them that far. By then, Ace figured that they were well into Brazil, but he still didn't trust Barrera not to come after them. So they kept going.

So tired she could barely keep her eyes open, let alone walk a straight line, Maddy numbly followed wherever Ace led and never noticed the stars grow dimmer overhead. Suddenly, it was dawn and she had no memory of where the rest of the night had gone.

She thought he would stop then. They were dead on their feet. But he wouldn't even let her slow down. "Not yet, honey," he said as he wrapped an arm around her waist and half carried her through the trees. "I promise I'll let you sleep, but not out in the open. It's too risky. We've got to find some type of shelter first."

"But we're miles from any kind of civilization!" she protested, fighting tears. "And I'm so tired!"

The last came out as a wail that Ace could see she would have given anything to take back, but she was just too exhausted. Tenderness flooded his heart, a tenderness that no other woman had ever been able to pull from him. She was dirty and pale as a ghost, her cheeks streaked with the tracks of her tears, and all he could think of was that she'd never looked more beautiful, more precious.

His arms instinctively tightening around, he pulled her closer. "I know, princess. I'm dead on my feet, too. But there's got to be a village around here somewhere. Just hang on."

He was lying through his teeth—he didn't know if there was anything remotely resembling civilization anywhere within two hundred miles of them—but she only nodded and gratefully hung on, letting him lead her wherever he wanted. An hour later, when they stumbled across a small village that had been hacked out of the middle of the rain forest, no one was more surprised than him.

"Wake up, Dorothy," he murmured out of the side of his mouth as their unexpected arrival started to draw wary glances. "I think we just arrived in Oz."

Barely able to keep her eyes open, she only murmured, "Good. Find me the ruby slippers and I'll get us home. Can we sleep now?"

That was the sixty-four-thousand-dollar question. He wasn't letting his guard down long enough to fall asleep unless he felt sure that Barrera wouldn't be able to find them while they were out of commission. And despite the fact that they'd been walking all night and were now in another country, Barrera's stronghold was just on the other side of the border. He was a smart man with a long reach. For his own protection, he would have made connections in every little village and town within a hundred-mile radius.

"We'll have to see," he told her. "The locals don't look too friendly."

In fact, they looked downright hostile. Women stood in doorways of what were little more than huts, their children clinging to their skirts, and stared at them with eyes that were dark with suspicion. No one made a move toward them, but all work seemed to stop as Ace half carried Maddy down the muddy main street that cut through the center of the collection of primitive houses. And although the men weren't quite as overt in their scrutiny of them as the wives, Ace felt the touch of what seemed like a thousand pairs of eyes.

Frowning, he was just wondering how to proceed next when an older gentleman who had been lounging in the morning sun on the porch of what looked like a general store rose to his feet and slowly approached them. "We don't have many visitors from the north," he said in what Ace recognized as a dialect of Portuguese. "You and your lady have had trouble?"

Trouble didn't begin to describe what they'd been through, but Ace only nodded curtly. There was, he decided, no use beating around the bush. If Barrera had contacts in the village, he had probably already notified them of their escape, so they might as well find out now if these people were friends or enemies. "We escaped from Barrera," he said curtly in the little bit of Portuguese he knew. "You have heard of him?"

The weathered old man's eyes narrowed sharply. "No one ever leaves that devil's place without his permission. Are you sure you aren't a friend of his?"

Ace's mouth quirked. "We didn't exactly leave with his blessing," he said dryly. "Which is why he's been tracking us with dogs all night. That should tell you just how friendly we are with him. Can you offer us shelter?"

For a moment, he thought the man was actually going to say no. He studied them shrewdly, noting their ravaged clothes, the scratches and bruises they'd acquired when the helicopter went down, the exhaustion they couldn't hide. Abruptly coming to a decision, he turned to the other villagers who had crept closer and spit out a rapid series of orders.

When he turned back to Ace, he said, "Forgive our rudeness. But we are a small village and have no wish to do business with the likes of Barrera or any of his friends. Come, sir. You and your lady must be exhausted. I will show you to a hut where you can bathe and rest."

Maddy, already half-asleep, stirred as Ace suddenly swept her up in his arms and followed the old man to a small dwelling right in the heart of the village. Blinking owlishly, she looked around. "Are we still in Oz?"

"Yeah." Ace laughed. "But the flying monkeys'll never find us here." Thanking the old man for his help, he nudged the door shut with his shoulder and strode across to the rope bed that took up one corner of the hut's only room. "You can sleep now, sweetheart. We're safe."

That was all she needed to hear. With a low moan, she turned over on her stomach the second he laid her down. Before Ace could crawl in beside her, she was asleep.

Ace had only planned to sleep for four or five hours, but the bed was surprisingly comfortable and his tired body demanded more. With Maddy safely at his side and the villagers on the lookout for Barrera, he was finally able to relax his guard and just shut down. The morning gave way to afternoon, then the early-evening rains and nightfall. Lost in a deep, dreamless sleep, he never knew when the old man cautiously looked in on them to make sure they were okay, then left just as quietly as he'd come, leaving them alone.

He might have slept around the clock, in fact, if an unexpected thunderstorm hadn't rolled in around four in the morning. Lightning ripped across the night sky, but it was the sudden crack of thunder that sounded like the helicopter when it exploded that brought him awake with a jerk. His heart suddenly hammering, he lay perfectly still and stared up at the shadowy, unfamiliar roof of the hut, trying to remember where the hell he was when it finally hit him. Brazil. They'd made it to Brazil. They were safe.

Lightning flashed again, but this time, the thunder that followed seemed to shake the very ground itself. Curled up against him on her side, her back snug against his chest and her bottom nestled against his hips and thighs, Maddy jumped, coming abruptly awake with a frightened gasp. "Oh, God! What was that?"

"Just a thunderstorm," he said huskily, then almost groaned aloud when she innocently moved against him again. His jaw as rigid as granite, he clamped his arm across her waist and held her flush against him, stilling her unconscious movements. "Go back to sleep, honey," he rasped. "Now!"

He knew the second she realized what she was doing to him—she stiffened like a poker and sucked in a quick breath she forgot to release. Under his hand, he could feel the awareness that had every nerve ending suddenly humming, and it was all he could do not to let his fingers wander. She was a virgin, he reminded himself sternly and ordered his hand to stay right where it was. It did, but the effort cost him. Sweat broke out on his brow, and along his locked jaw, a muscle began to tick.

The rain started then, a soft but steady rain that pelted the roof in a regular cadence that was as soothing as a lullaby. His breathing slow and controlled, his blood growing hotter with every passing second, Ace closed his eyes and told himself she would sleep soon. He just had to wait her out. And then, by God, he was never crawling into bed with her again. He wasn't made of steel, dammit. There was only so much he could take.

But just when she relaxed under his hand and he thought she was out for the rest of the night, she broke the intimate silence that wrapped around them in the dark. "I don't want to go back to sleep."

She hardly spoke above a whisper, but in the quiet, her words sounded like a shout. Not moving so much as an eyelash, Ace tried to tell himself that she didn't mean anything suggestive by the remark—she'd just had her fill of sleep. But still, his voice was hoarse when he asked, "Then what do you want to do?"

Her heart thudding a dozen beats a second, Maddy couldn't even imagine what she wanted him to do to her. How could she tell him? She didn't have the words, the experience. But their time together was running out. She could feel it as surely as if the sands of an hourglass slipped between her fingers. He'd gotten what he'd come for—the ring—and he wouldn't waste any time spiriting it and her back to New York. When he left her on her doorstep, she wouldn't spend the rest of her life wondering what could have been between them. She would know.

Sliding her arm over his where it was drapped across her middle, she said faintly, "Touch me. I want you to touch me."

For what seemed like an eternity, he didn't move, didn't speak, didn't do anything but just lie there, his arm rock hard beneath hers while seconds gathered into minutes with painstaking slowness. Then, just when she thought he must be searching for the words to let her down easy, his hand moved abruptly under hers. Clutching her convulsively to him, he groaned like a man at the end of his rope.

"I can't just touch you and stop," he warned thickly, burying his face in her hair. "You know that, don't you? I want you too much to be satisfied with just that."

Her throat tight with emotion, she nodded as a slow smile spilled across her face. How could he have known how badly she needed to hear that when she hadn't even known it herself? Taking his hand in hers, she carried it to her mouth and pressed a kiss to his knuckles and suddenly the words she hadn't been able to say before were there. "I want you, too," she murmured. "Make love to me, Ace. It seems like I've waited my whole life for you to make love to me."

Her honesty struck him right in the heart, destroying him. He shouldn't do this—deep down inside, his conscience was ordering him to get the hell away from her while he still could. She was an innocent, for God's sake! He had nothing to protect her with, and even if he had, she deserved romance and candlelight for her first time, not a rope bed in a musty old cottage at the end of the earth. And she deserved the prince she'd unconsciously been waiting for all these years, that perfect, good-looking guy on the white horse who would sweep her off to paradise and the home in the suburbs with two point two kids that every woman seemed to want. He couldn't be that, couldn't give her that, and only a louse would let her think that he could.

But even as he struggled for the strength of will to put her from him, she turned in his arms to face him, and he knew he'd waited too long. A flash of lightning revealed her shy smile, the trust in her eyes, and he was a goner. In an agonized voice he hardly recognized as his own, he murmured her name and leaned down to take her mouth with his own.

He thought he had it worked out in his head how he would take her from innocence to pleasure. He was the experienced one and it was his job to see that she wasn't rushed or scared or in any way apprehensive. So he started with a kiss, a brush of mouth against mouth, a flash of heat, a tantalizing sample of the passion he would build with infinite patience even if it killed him. But the second he feathered his mouth whisper-soft across hers, she let out a shaky breath that was sweet and uncertain and so heart-twistingly vulnerable that the taste of her went right to his head. So instead of teasing her and slowly seducing her into forgetting her inhibitions, he lingered longer than he should have, drinking from the well of her mouth like a man who had been so long in the desert that he'd forgotten the fresh, heady taste of water.

The world slipped away, forgotten in the night, and there was only the two of them and the storm overhead that charged the air with electricity and seemed to set his very blood humming. Murmuring her name again and again, he kissed her until she was breathless, until her tongue came shyly seeking his and her arms slipped around his neck to hold him close, until they were both hot and aching and straining for more.

Driven by a blind, raging need to touch her, to kiss every soft, delectable inch of her, he swept his hands over her in a rush and encountered the ruffles of her blouse and skirt. Searching for buttons, he encountered nothing but an elastic at the waist and neck. Frustrated, he never noticed when his hands turned rough. With a muttered oath, he yanked up the tail of her blouse to pull it over her head. Now. He had to have her now or he was going to go out of his head.

Something stopped him. A slight gasp, an infinitesimal stiffening of her shoulders, an instinctive move, quickly checked, to grab his hands—it could have been any of those things, but suddenly the fog of desire clouding his brain lifted and he looked up just as lightning once again flashed outside. In the grayish light, she watched him with wide, apprehensive eyes. And then it hit him just how close he had come to taking her like a man possessed. And not once had he thought of her virginity.

He swore, spitting curses in Spanish that weren't fit for her ears. "Aw, damn, honey, I'm sorry!" he said, jerking his hands back from her blouse and rolling onto his back with a groan. "I didn't mean to scare you."

"You didn't—"

"The hell I didn't!" he growled, glancing at her sharply. "Look at you. You're shaking!"

She didn't try to deny it—how could she? But it wasn't just with fear. Until he'd almost ripped her blouse from her, she'd been as caught up in the moment as he had. Her pulse still hammering in her throat, her body aching with need, she turned on her side toward him and lightly laid her fingers against the hollow at the base of his throat. It pounded just like hers.

"It looks like I'm not the only one who's still shaken," she countered ruefully when he stiffened under her touch. "But somehow I don't think you're scared."

"Hell, yes, I'm scared!" he grated through his teeth, trapping his hand against her throat. "Feel what you do to me, lady. I'm wound up tighter than a broke clock and it's all because of you. I never came close to losing control with a woman before and it scares the hell out of me."

That admission alone should have alarmed her, but nothing could have thrilled her more. This was all just as new to him as it was to her. Trailing her fingers up to his mouth, she dared to trace the sculptured line of his lips. "Then let's be scared together," she whispered, and leaned over to kiss the pulse that thundered in his throat.

"Maddy... sweetheart..."

He groaned in protest, but she noted with a smile that his arms locked around her faster than a sprung trap. Chuckling, she wandered lazily up his throat, dropping kisses under the granite-hard cut of his jaw, the lobe of his ear, the proud plane of his nose, as she slowly made her way to his mouth. "Undress me, Ace," she murmured huskily. "Please."

She asked so artlessly that there was no way on earth he could have denied her. Tangling his fingers in her hair, he held her close for a sizzling kiss, then sat up, taking her with him as he reached for the hem of her blouse and slowly pulled it over her head. It landed with a nearly silent whisper somewhere across the room. For several thumps of their hearts, neither of them moved. Then his hand slid around to her back in search of the hooks of her bra.

Tension crackled in the air, sparking like lightning between them with every brush of his fingers against her hot skin. She never remembered holding her breath, but suddenly her bra followed her blouse and he was touching her, taking her breast into his palm, and she let out her breath on a sigh that ended on a moan when he suddenly ducked his head to kiss the nipple he quickly brought to a pout with his thumb.

"Ace!"

"Easy, sweetheart," he murmured, teasing her with his tongue. "I promise not to do anything you don't want. How does that feel?"

Taking her into the warm, wet heat of his mouth before she could answer, he suckled her with a powerful draw of his cheeks, startling her, delighting her. She whimpered, her fingers curling into his hair as a drizzling warmth shot straight from her breast to her loins.

"God, you're beautiful," he rasped. "So beautiful. So soft."

Chanting praise, he moved from one breast to the other, kissing her, caressing her, suckling her, until she was weak with desire and blind to everything but the need he stoked in her blood. Somehow she found herself on her back again, only this time, her clothes and his were gone. He leaned over her in the dark, the hard wall of his chest brushing over her wet, sensitized nipples, and she cried out in pleasure.

Easing down, he kissed her long and slow. "There's more love, so much more."

"Show me," she gasped, kissing him back hungrily. "Teach me."

On fire for her, Ace almost lost it then. Rock hard and close to bursting, he shook with the need to bury himself in her soft, welcoming heat, but he wouldn't rush her. Not this time. He took his hands over her slowly, then followed the fire he'd lit with his mouth, nuzzling the underside of her breast, her slender waist, the gentle slope of her belly, gentling her to his hands, his mouth, his tongue. And with every sigh, every ragged moan he drew from her, he burned hotter.

But still he would have held back even longer if she hadn't touched him. Suddenly she was the one stroking him with fingers that trembled, learning what made him gasp and buck under her hands, and it was all he could do not to explode right then and there. His hand snaking out to trap hers between their bodies, he glared fiercely down into her eyes. "Put your hand back on my shoulder, sweetheart. Now!"

A skittish virgin would have jumped to obey, but her virginity was just a technicality now, an encumbrance that stood in the way of loving him as she wanted to. He wouldn't consciously hurt her if he could help it. If she needed any proof of that, she only had to look into his face and see what holding back was costing him. Her heart swelling with love, she moved her hand, but not back to his shoulder.

Sucking in a sharp breath, he growled, "Maddy, I'm warning you—"

Whatever threat he would have made next was lost in a strangled groan as her fingers closed around him. Before he could stop himself, his hand was closing around hers, teaching her how to please him. God, how long had he dreamed of having her hands on him? His jaw locked tight, his breathing harsh, he rested his forehead against hers and endured the pleasure as long as he could. "Enough!" he said through his teeth and pulled her hand safely back to his shoulder.

But the little minx had gotten a taste of what she could do to him with just a touch, and after that, there was no stopping her. Delightfully drunk on her own power, she touched and rubbed and kissed wherever the mood struck her and proceeded to quietly drive him out of his mind. He tried to tell her that this wasn't smart—he was the one who was supposed to be seducing her, not the other way around—but she wouldn't listen. She wanted him unstrung, out of control, as crazy for her as she was for him, and she could, he discovered to his delight, be damned insistent about it.

As need coiled tight in his belly, he wasn't, however, completely lost to the care he needed to take with her. Murmuring hoarsely whispered words of encouragement and instructions in her ear, he stroked her with growing urgency, parting her legs to find her hot with arousal and weeping for him at the heart of her desire. She gasped at his touch and lifted her hips against his hand, and it was all he could do not to surge into her. With slow, languid movements that nearly killed him, he rhythmically stroked her inner warmth, stoking the fire higher and higher, until she was mindless to everything but his touch at the core of her. He felt her quicken, that first revealing shudder, and then with a keening cry, she was coming undone in his arms.

Something broke in him then, something sweet and clean and free. Covering her mouth with his in a smoldering kiss, he surged into her with a single controlled stroke, cursing himself for having to hurt her. But she only stiffened for a moment, then her arms and legs were closing around him as if she would never let him go. Lifting his head, he found her staring up at him with heavy-lidded eyes that were dark with wonder. As he watched, a slow smile blossomed on her kiss-swollen lips and completely stole his heart.

Suddenly he wanted to laugh, to shout with joy. Grinning, he leaned down and kissed her again. "Maddy, girl, you never cease to surprise me. What am I going to do with you?"

"Love me," she said against his mouth as her hips lifted to his. "Just love me."

No more able to resist her than the tides could resist the pull of the moon, he did.

Chapter 12

Long after the thunderstorms rumbled off to the east, they were still in bed, still in each other's arms. Sated, content to just hold Maddy close and savor the feel of her against him, Ace could have lain there all day and never felt the need to move. The world, however, had other ideas and intruded with a quiet knock at the door.

Half-asleep, Maddy jumped, startled. "It's okay, sweetheart," he said softly, pressing a quick kiss to her lips before reaching for his pants. "It's probably just the old man coming to see if we're still alive in here. Go back to sleep."

Quickly zipping his jeans, he checked to make sure Maddy was decently covered in the bed before he crossed the hut on bare feet and eased open the door. As he'd guessed, the old man who had escorted them to the hut yesterday morning stood on the small porch, his weathered face lined with worry. His gaze narrowing, Ace stepped outside and shut the door behind him. "There a problem, *señor?*"

The old man nodded. "Men in Jeeps have arrived from the north. So far we have been able to keep them out of the village by claiming that we are suffering with the plague, but I doubt that will hold them for long. You must hurry. I have a car waiting."

"To take us where?"

"Manaus," he replied promptly. "The driver will take you cross-country through the forest. From there you can find an ocean-going ship that will take you out of the country. Barrera will be looking for you at the airport."

Ace nodded. It was a good plan, one that he should have thought of himself. "We'll be right with you, *señor*. Give us five minutes."

Turning, he stepped back inside, wondering how the hell he was going to break the news to Maddy that Barrera had somehow managed to catch up with them, but she was already up and tugging on her clothes. "I heard," she said in a muffled voice through her blouse as she pulled it over her head. Jerking it down into place, she looked up, her face pale. "Barrera's found us."

There was no point in denying it. "It looks like it, but he's not going to catch us, sweetheart. Even if he brought the damn dogs with him, there's no way he's going to be able to track us once we drive out of here. The old man'll make sure of that."

After all that they had been through, Maddy wasn't sure she wanted to put their safety in the hands of a total stranger. "Barrera's bound to be offering a reward," she said as she quickly stepped into her skirt. "How do you know the old man won't turn us in?"

"If he was going to do that, he never would have warned us in the first place," he replied confidently. Snatching up his shirt from the floor, he pulled it on and quickly stepped into his boots.

As together as she could be considering the rush they were in, Maddy glanced around to make sure nothing was left behind to show that they'd been there, only to have her gaze catch and linger on the bed. After the most wonderful night of her life, this wasn't the way she had pictured the morning after. They should have had hours together yet, precious moments stolen out of time to explore each other in the soft morning light. Instead, they were forced to run for their lives again and they'd barely kissed each other goodmorning.

Reading her mind, Ace moved to her side and slipped his arm around her waist. "By tonight, Barrera will have bigger problems than us to worry about, and we'll be on a ship heading out to sea," he said quietly. "We'll put out the Do Not Disturb sign on our stateroom door and just dare anyone to bother us. So don't look so sad, baby. You've got clean sheets and champagne and me to look forward to. From what I've heard, you haven't lived until you've made love on the ocean."

She laughed—she couldn't help it—and grinned sassily at him. "Wait till tonight and I'll let you know."

"I'm counting on it, sweetheart. I'm counting on it." Twining his fingers with hers, he winked and led her to the door.

The driver the old man of the village entrusted them to was, Maddy decided, either a daredevil who thrived on taking chances or a sadist who got a cheap thrill out of watching them try to hang on. As soon as he had them captive in his pre-World War II vehicle that had once passed as a Jeep, he left the village behind and immediately struck out across the jungle at a speed that left them both gasping and grasping for handholds. Every hole and rock seemed to hold a special fascination for him, and with no seat belts to hold her in, Maddy was nearly bounced out of the back twice.

"A-a-a-ce!" she called in a wobbly voice as they hit a particularly rough spot. "Do-o-o somethi-i-i-ng!"

Through the rush of the wind in her ears, she heard him speak sharply to the man, who gave him a gape-toothed grin and the universal shrug that said he didn't understand a word of what he was saying. Bobbing up and down on the shot springs of the passenger seat, Ace glanced over his shoulder at her and laughed, his blue eyes dancing with rueful amusement. "Sor-ry, h-hon-ey, but we seem to h-have a slight c-communi-ca-tion problem. I think he just s-said we're in f-for a hell of a ri-i-ide!"

That turned out to be an understatement of gargantuan proportions. Their driver, who Maddy dubbed Fred, took them over every rough stretch of shallow river bottom and rocky hillside he could find in Brazil and laughed while he did it. They were jostled and shaken and jarred, but one thing they were not was followed. Looking back over her shoulder for what had to be the thousandth time, Maddy had to grin when she saw nothing but the undisturbed greenery of the forest behind them. If Barrera's men were back there somewhere, they'd lost them miles ago.

Manaus, when they finally reached it hours later, appeared out of nowhere. One minute they were bouncing over a level, forested plain, and the next, the trees gave way to narrow, crowded streets teeming with people and vehicles of every make and description. The city was awash in color... and noise. After listening to nothing but the harmonious sounds of the jungle for days, the blare of horns and shouts of vendors sounded caustic to her ears, which amazed her since she'd grown up surrounded by similar sounds in New York.

Looking and feeling like something that had been blown in by the wind to some exotic port of call, she drank in the sites with wide eyes. She wouldn't forget this, she told herself fiercely as they arrived at the docks on the Amazon and she saw one ocean-going ship after another lined up like soldiers along both banks. When she was old and gray and still shelving books at the library, she would look back on this and hug the memory to her breast with a smile.

Ace grinned as their driver pulled up with a flourish and stopped—actually set the brake—for the first time all day. "Looks like this is the end of the taxi service, sweetheart. It's something to see, isn't it? Come on, let's go find us a slow boat to China."

"A slow boat to... wait!" she cried, but it was too late. He bodily lifted her out of the Jeep, waved a cheerful goodbye to their driver and hauled her with him down the dock. "How are you going to get us on a boat? In case you've forgotten, we don't have any money."

Grinning, he arched a brow at her. "Have you ever known that to stop me before?"

"No, but—"

"No buts." Amusement glinting in his eyes, he pulled her to a stop at the first phone booth they came to. "Stand right there, honey, and watch a pro at work."

Ignoring the activity on the dock around them, he turned to the phone and punched zero, then a long series of numbers. Moments later, he glanced over at her, winked, then said into the phone, "Philip! How the hell are you? Yeah, I'm alive! What'd you think? I'd let Barrera whack me? You ought to know me better than that."

Amazed, Maddy listened to him chat with *Philip*, whoever he was, then give him detailed directions to Barrera's stronghold and the small village where they had spent the night. "Pick him up," he said flatly. "No, Lazear won't be a problem. From what I understand, he's in the freezer—literally. And I've got the ring right here in my pocket. I'm expressing it to you as soon as I get off the phone.''

Suddenly looking up, his eyes met Maddy's and he reached for her, grinning. ''Miss Lawrence is just fine, Philip, and still in one piece, so quit worrying. She would appreciate it, though, if you'd book a cabin for two on the next ship out of Manaus and pull some strings with customs here and at home. My passport got left behind in the jungle and there's no way in hell we're going back for it.''

He chuckled then at something the other man said, let him put him on hold for a while and spent the time kissing Maddy senseless before she could so much as open her mouth to ask him a single question. She should have been miffed with him, but with nothing more than a single kiss, he rekindled the magic of the night, and she was lost.

When he abruptly let her up for air when his friend came back on the line, she was breathless and his eyes were dark and slumberous with passion. ''Yeah,'' he said thickly, keeping an arm snug around her waist as she buried her face against his chest. ''The *Amazon Queen,* cabin twelve. Cash has already been wired to the captain and passports will be waiting for us in New York. Thanks, buddy.''

After promising to check in as soon as he got home, he hung up and immediately turned and hurried Maddy down the dock. ''C'mon, honey, our ship leaves in forty-five minutes. We've got to find a post office.''

Maddy couldn't believe that Ace would just drop something as priceless as Cleopatra's belly-button ring in the mail, but that was exactly what he did. Laughing at her horrified gasp, he assured her that the small package would never draw a second glance because he'd labeled the box Fertilizer Samples, and no one in their right mind would expect to find anything of value in a pile of manure. Maddy wasn't so sure; he didn't give her time to argue. They only had fifteen minutes to find their ship and they had to run all the way back to the docks from the center of town, where they'd finally found the post office.

Out of breath, they arrived back at the *Amazon Queen* and soon discovered that the ship wasn't nearly as elegant as its name. Once a top-of-the-line cargo ship with a few cabins for passengers, it was now a rusty bucket of bolts that was used to haul bananas from Cape Horn all the way to New York.

In spite of that, the sheets were clean, as Ace had promised. The captain personally showed them to their cabin and seemed honored to have them aboard. After assuring them everything they needed would be provided for them, he managed to scrounge up a dusty bottle of champagne from somewhere in the bowels of the ship to celebrate a pleasant voyage. Then he wisely left them alone.

Heat singeing her cheeks, Maddy leaned back against the door and couldn't seem to stop smiling. When Ace started to reach for her, she wanted nothing more than to go into his arms. But they had so little time left together, and if she was ever going to get any answers out of him, she had to do it now, before he touched her.

"Hold it," she said, holding a quick hand to ward him off. "I've been through hell with you, Ace MacKenzie or whatever your name is, and a couple of times, I thought we were goners for sure. After all that, I think I'm entitled to a few answers, don't you think? Who was that Philip character you called? And who's paying for all this—"

"Philip is...my boss," he said with a crooked grin. Taking the hand that she'd planted against his chest, he dragged it around his neck and pulled her against him to nuzzle her neck. "And as for who's footing the bill, let's jus say it's a little-known but very powerful department of the U.S. government. Honey, do we have to talk about this now?''

He trapped her against the door, and from her neck, he moved up to her ear and lazily worried the sensitive lobe with his teeth. Heat shot through her in a dizzying rush. Shuddering delicately, she leaned back weakly against the door and tried to remember why it was so important for her to know more about him, but with his warm, moist breath in her ear and his tongue teasing her, she couldn't fight her own needs, let alone his.

"Later." She sighed as she closed her eyes and leaned into him. "We'll talk . . . later."

"I think that's an excellent idea," he murmured, kissing his way to her mouth with deliberate care. "I want to take a shower. With you."

That got her attention. "A . . . sh-shower?"

"Mmm-hmm. I want you wet and naked and so damn hot for me we steam up every porthole on the ship." Slowly, softly, he brushed her lips with his—once, twice, a third time—until she was languidly moving with him, instinctively lifting her mouth to his each time in a sensuous dance of give and take, seeking him, kissing him, dreamily loving him. "What do you say, honey? Are you game?"

For an answer, she reached for the buttons to his shirt.

The loving that followed was like something out of a dream. She should have been nervous. Making love in the middle of the night was one thing, boldly stripping and stepping into a tiny shower stall with him in broad daylight was quite another. But somehow their clothes just seemed to melt away and she was too busy marveling over the wonder of his hard, sinewy body to worry if her own was a disappointment to him.

With the water pounding down on them and the rising steam swirling above their heads, they lost all sense of time, of reason. There was only need and an ache that grew more fierce with every touch, every brush of mouth and tongue. He murmured love words to her, praising her, worshiping her as he kissed his way down her body and back up again with a painstaking thoroughness that left her shuddering and every nerve ending tingling.

He could have taken her then, pushed her right over the edge with no effort at all, but he only laughed softly when she arched against him with a strangled cry. "Oh, no, sweetheart. Not yet. We're supposed to be taking a shower, remember?" Taking her hand, which lay limp upon his shoulder, he closed her fingers around a bar of soap and flashed her a grin. "If you see anything you like, feel free to touch."

Dazed, her blood rushing hotly through her veins, she looked up from the soap and found his eyes waiting for hers and alight with daring. Lifting a delicately arched brow, she started to smile. "Anything?"

He nodded, his grin broadening. "Anything."

Entranced by the wicked laughter in his gaze, catching his suddenly playful mood, Maddy rubbed the soap slowly back and forth in her hands and had the satisfaction of knowing she had his undivided attention. But instead of accepting the dare and touching him where he obviously expected her to, she suddenly stood on tiptoe and lifted her soap-slickened hands to his wet hair. The move, catching him off guard, brought her breasts against his chest and her hips snug against the hard evidence of his arousal. And with every slide of her hands in his hair, her wet, naked body rubbed against his.

Her eyes, dark and sensual, smiled into his as she deliberately moved against him again. "How's that?"

A groan ripped from his throat, and with a muttered oath, he clamped her tight against him. "You're killing me, honey. Don't stop."

Her heart thudding, she laughed and traced a slow finger around his ear. A split second later, sudden mischief sparking in her eyes, she pulled his head under the pulsing shower head.

"Aaargh! Dammit, woman, what are you trying to do? Drown me?"

"Don't be such a whiny baby," she chided, chuckling. "I was just getting the soap out of your hair."

"Baby? Me? I'll show you who's a baby," he growled with mock fierceness, and swiftly reversed their positions. She was still laughingly sputtering when he shoved her up against the shower wall and covered her mouth with his.

Heat. It was instantaneous, raw, untamed, licking between them like the roaring flames of an inferno, and suddenly neither of them was laughing. He rubbed against her in the same way she had against him, melting her knees. She moaned, reaching for him with fingers that weren't quite steady, and with no effort at all broke what was left of his control. His mouth rough, his hands blindly fumbling for the faucets to the shower, he shut off the water and swept her up in his arms.

"Ace, what—"

"Shh, sweetheart. I'm just carrying you to bed."

"But we're wet—"

"So we'll dry off later," he muttered against her mouth, and carried her down to the bed with him.

After that, there was no time for words, no time for anything but the fire they'd lit in each other's blood that threatened to burn them alive. His breath straining through his lungs, need tearing at him, he moved over her like a man possessed, driving her over the first crest before she could do

anything but sink her nails into his shoulders and gasp. Wit
a single stroke, he drove into her to the hilt, all the whil
telling himself he had to slow down, give her time, find th
control he needed for the tenderness he ached to show her
But then her hips eagerly lifted to his, setting a franti
rhythm that he found impossible to resist.

Feeling as if he were on the edge of dying, he moved i
her, with her, meeting her thrust for thrust, every muscle i
his body straining for release. Not yet, not yet, he chante
grimly to himself, his teeth clenched tight with the effort t
hold back. But then he felt the first faint rush of pleasur
deep inside her, the shudders that started to rack her slen
der frame, and it was his name she called, his name on he
lips that pulled him over the edge. The searing heat insid
him exploded, and with a strangled cry, he tumbled after he
into the ecstasy.

Replete, Maddy never knew how long she lay there in hi
arms, her eyes closed to savor the tiny sparks that flashe
inside her like star bursts, a smile of contentment perma
nently etched on her lips. In what felt like the distant part o
the universe but was actually the nether regions of a brai
that had turned to mush, she was vaguely aware that the shi
had set sail soon after they had ended up in the shower. Bu
not even the knowledge that she was actually sailing dow
the Amazon like a heroine in an Ace MacKenzie book coul
tempt her to stir from her lover's arms. She was right wher
she wanted to be—the Amazon would have to wait.

It could have been minutes, an hour, later when a soft
infinitely gentle kiss brought her eyes fluttering open
Looking up into Ace's dear, rugged face, she started t
smile, but his eyes were somber and searching hers, his ex
pression serious. Her heart twinging with the first fain

twitches of alarm, she lifted her hand to his cheek. "What? What is it?"

"I love you."

Startled, Maddy blinked, stunned speechless. He loved her! And all this time, she hadn't allowed herself to dream...to hope. Tears of joy blurring her eyes, she started to smile, only to hesitate as it suddenly hit her that he'd blurted the words out like a man who had just been hit over the head with a sledgehammer and was still reeling from the surprise of the blow.

Suddenly as unsure as the untried girl he had rescued from Cement Johnny, she said carefully, "I love you, too. Is that a problem?"

He laughed shortly, the strangled sound a mixture of self-deprecating amusement and amazement. "I always thought it would be," he said half to himself, his eyes focused on the past. "Sandra taught me a valuable lesson about women—love 'em and leave 'em before they can stab you in the heart. And I learned it well. Nobody came close to tying me in knots...until you came along."

He blinked, his gaze once again locking with hers as he looked at her, really looked at her, for what seemed like the first time. "I thought I could handle you, handle what you did to me, but you weren't like Sandra or any other woman I'd ever met before. You were so damn innocent. And when you finally decided to trust me, you did it heart and soul. I don't think you have any idea what that does to a man when a woman places that kind of trust in him, honey."

"I knew you wouldn't hurt me," she said huskily. "There was no reason to be afraid."

"See? That's what I mean. You gave yourself to me when you had to know that I planned to take you back home to your mother when this was all over. *I* thought that's what I was going to do. But now that we're safe and New York is just a long boat ride away, I don't want it to end. I don't want *us* to end."

Cupping her face in his hands, he gently brought his mouth to hers and kissed her until her senses were swimming in pleasure and the blood was thrumming in her veins. "Marry me, Maddy," he urged thickly when he finally, reluctantly, let her up for air. "Marry me and I promise the next fifty years will be the ride of a lifetime, Maddy Lawrence. I'll take you to Rome and Sydney and Timbuktu if you like. Anywhere. Everywhere! Just say the word. Say yes, honey."

Stunned, Maddy searched his face for some sign that this was all just a wonderful, fantastic dream that couldn't possibly come true. But the man lying in bed with her wasn't a figment of her imagination. He was warm and hard and real. His heart was in his eyes, his expression dead serious, the love he made no attempt to hide from her softening every fierce, handsome feature. He was offering her all the things she had ever wanted. All she had to do was say yes.

In spite of her love of adventure from afar, she'd always prided herself on being a practical woman. She'd known that Indiana Jones was never going to charge into her life and sweep her off to God knows where in search of lost artifacts and gold, and she'd told herself she could be happy just reading about such bold deeds. But now, looking up into his handsome face, she knew that most of her adult life had been nothing but a lie. She hadn't been happy—she'd just been existing, waiting for the only man in the world for her to come along and turn her life upside down.

And here he was, asking her to marry him. In the real world, she told herself, things like this didn't happen. But it was.

"Yes," she whispered huskily. "I'll marry you."

"Yes! She said yes!" A broad smile spreading across his mouth, he swooped down for a fierce, ecstatic kiss. "When?" he demanded hoarsely. "I want a date, lady! I need to know when you're going to be mine."

Caught up in his excitement, she laughed and looped her arms around his neck. "Whenever you like."

"Today, then," he said promptly, stunning her. Giving her one last lingering kiss, he pulled her arms from around his neck, planted a quick kiss in each palm, then rolled away and reached for his pants. "I've got to talk to the captain, see about making the arrangements. And you need a dress. Every woman wants a new dress on her wedding day. I'll have to see if there's some kind of shop on this floating rattletrap."

Already caught up in the arrangements, he tugged on his shirt and headed for the door before he stopped, suddenly realizing she hadn't said a word. Pivoting, he frowned at her. "You didn't want one of those big elaborate fancy shindigs, did you? I mean, I know most women dream of that sort of thing from the time they're little girls, and if you've really got your heart set on it..." He shrugged, his grin rueful. "Hell, honey, if that's what you want, you're the only one I can think of I'd wriggle into one of those penguin suits for. Just say the word, and we'll wait till we can throw it all together..."

He would do it, she thought, sudden tears stinging her eyes. He'd go through all the hassle of planning a wedding when that was obviously the last thing in the world he wanted...just for her. If she hadn't already loved him before, she would have fallen for sure after that.

"Oh, no, you don't," she said with a quick grin as she wrapped the sheet around herself and stepped from the bed and advanced toward him with a purposeful glint in her eyes. "Now that I've finally found you, there's no way I'm waiting to make you mine...or giving you a chance to change your mind."

He gave her a wounded look. "Sweetheart, I wouldn't do a thing like that to you."

"Good," she said promptly. "Then there's no reason why we can't be married today." Standing on tiptoe, she leaned up to give him a kiss that promised a lifetime of hot nights of love and seduction. "I can't imagine anything more romantic that being married on the Amazon," she whispered dreamily against his mouth. "Go make the arrangements."

Dazed, he nodded...and just stood there like a man who couldn't remember what he needed to do next. Laughing in delight, Maddy pulled open the door and pushed him gently through it. "This way, darling. Hurry. I'll be waiting for you," she promised, and promptly shut the door in his face.

Long after she heard him make his way down the narrow passageway, she leaned back against the door, hugging herself. Lord, she loved him! So much that she, who had never had a man in her life, wondered how she'd lived without him all these lonely years. He'd made her believe in fairy tales when always before she'd believed they came true for everyone but herself.

And as soon as he could pull whatever strings needed to be pulled, he'd be back...to marry her. Dear God, she had to get ready!

Her thoughts rushing ahead to what she was going to do with her damp hair, she stepped away from the door and forgot all about the sheet that was wrapped around her like a mummy's shroud. She tripped just as the ship rolled slightly under her feet. Gasping, she jerked at the sheet that had somehow gotten tangled around her legs, but too late, she realized she was standing on it. She started to fall and never saw the closet door swing open. She hit the floor hard just as the motion of the ship brought the door swinging back in the opposite direction. It slammed into her head, right at the temple. Stars exploded behind her eyes in a white-hot flash of pain, then there was nothing. Nothing but blackness.

Ace was there, just beyond her fingertips in her dream, grinning down at her from the billowing softness of a pristine white cloud, beckoning her to join him. Everything she wanted—love, happiness, adventure—could be found in his arms. She knew that as surely as she knew she loved him with all her heart. All she had to do was take his hand and let him lift her up and she would be home, with him, where she belonged.

"I'm not going to let you slip away from me, sweetheart. Do you hear me? So if you're thinking about checking out on me, you can just think again. I won't allow it. Dammit, Maddy, don't do this!"

From his perch on the cloud, he leaned down to her, his extended hand reaching for hers, silently begging her to just trust him enough to place her fingers in his, but even as she hesitated, it was too late. Before her eyes, the distance between them slowly stretched into a dark, bottomless chasm that was impossible to cross. Helplessly, she watched him drift away into the clouds, fading from sight until there was nothing left of him but his hoarse cry for her to come back to him. And even that disappeared when the blackness descended again, blocking out the light and dragging her down into the soothing depths of oblivion.

After that, time, the world, ceased to exist. There was only the darkness and the aching sense of loss that gripped her every time she even thought about opening her eyes and leaving Ace behind in her dreams. She couldn't do it. She wouldn't! He would come back for her if she just waited long enough.

In the end, however, she was never given a choice in the matter. One second she was lost in the shadows that shrouded her brain, and the next she was struck first by the feel of clean sheets against her body, then the antiseptic scent that was unique to hospitals and clinics that teased her nose. Her eyelids fluttering against the sunshine that seemed to be hitting her right in the face, she blinked once, then again, and, with no conscious intention on her part, opened her eyes.

Manhattan.

The city skyline, larger than life and as familiar as the lines in her hand, was right outside her bedroom window. Puzzled, her head starting to throb, she frowned as she noted the utilitarian bed and stark white walls decorated with a generic watercolor print. No, this wasn't her bedroom, she thought fuzzily. She was in a hospital... in New York.

A dream. From the moment that magazine rack had come tumbling down on her head at the newsstand and knocked her out cold, nothing else had been real. Especially Ace and his love for her. It was all just a dream. Nothing but a dream.

No!

The silent cry echoed without end through the bruised canyons of her head. Slamming her eyes shut, she squeezed back the tears, furiously trying to reject the reality before her. But it was a wasted effort. The silent tears of acceptance were already streaming down her cheeks. Ace. He'd never been anything but a dream, a fantasy, the wishful thinking of a lonely woman who could only find love and adventure in the pages of a book.

Pain lanced her heart. Devastated, she heard the door open to her small, private room, but she couldn't bring herself to open her eyes and face the city and a life she didn't want to go back to. Not yet. Not without Ace. She just needed a few more minutes to cling to a dream that was never going to be.

"Maddy? Honey? Dear God, are you awake? Can you hear me?"

Of course she could hear him. When, she wondered wildly, had her imagination become so good that she could recreate every nuance of his husky voice with no effort whatsoever? If she hadn't known better, she would have sworn he was standing right beside her. Lord, she was losing it.

Then the mattress dipped and she opened startled eyes to find him bending over her, his rugged, unshaven face haggard with worry. Dazed, she could only stare at him in confusion.

"Thank God!"

At the relieved sigh that burst from his lips, she frowned in confusion. "How did I get here? I thought you were a dream...that everything that happened was just a dream. But you're here...you're real..."

"Hell, yes, I'm real, honey! It's the past three days that have been the nightmare!"

"Three days? I've been out for three days?"

He nodded, his blue eyes somber as he reached for her hand and pulled it to his own cheek. "I thought I'd lost you, sweetheart," he rasped. "When you didn't regain consciousness on the ship, I had you flown home. I thought if you were on familiar ground, it would help. Your mother's been here constantly—in fact, she's down in the cafeteria right now—"

"Mother's here? But she's not supposed to be walking yet! Her hip—"

"Is just fine," he assured her. "I talked to her doctors myself. They've been trying to get her to exercise that hip for over a week, but she was so upset over your disappearance that she wouldn't even get out of bed. The second she heard you were in the hospital, though, she was up and dressed and down here to see you before I could even send a cab for her. She's been worried sick about you, sweetheart. We all have."

"We?"

"Your friends from school, your neighbors. They've all been here. When the doctors couldn't find any medical reason why you wouldn't wake up, your mother called everyone she could think of who might be able to reach you. You've got some great friends, honey. The minute they heard you were in trouble, they came to see you. But nothing seemed to help. You didn't respond to any of us."

Amazed, Maddy just stared at him. What he'd just described sounded like something out of *It's a Wonderful Life*, and she hadn't been aware of any of it. Except him. Tears constricted her throat. "I heard you," she choked. "I heard you calling to me, but I couldn't reach you. That's when I thought I must have imagined everything. It was horrible. I was afraid if I woke up, I'd lose you."

"Aw, honey." He reached for her then, pulling her into his arms, against his chest, locking her close. "That's never going to happen. I'm real. *We're* real. Dammit, I love you! Surely you don't think you dreamed that? Dreamed this?"

He kissed her then, a hot, scorching, desperate kiss that told her more clearly than words just how much she meant to him and how terrible the past three days had been for him. No, she thought, swallowing a sob as she threw her arms around him and kissed him back. She hadn't dreamed this, hadn't dreamed him, hadn't dreamed the love that she felt in his every touch as his hands swept over her in a rush to reassure himself that she was really okay.

He was shaking. The same tough, fearless man who had boldly followed her up a rain gutter right above the heads of Barrera's armed guards without breaking a sweat was shaking like a leaf in the wind . . . for her. Against her breast, the wild thunder of his heart was slamming against hers, filling her with wonder and a sweet, sweet urgency that she'd never felt for any other man but him.

He loved her!

If she'd still had any doubts about that, they would have died the second he framed her face in his hands and pulled back just far enough so that his gaze could meet hers. Naked love burned in his eyes. "I never thought I would ever find anyone like you. I've dragged you halfway across the world, taken you away from everything that's familiar to you and given you every reason to hate my guts. When I asked you to marry me, you didn't ask me my real name or who I work for or even where we were going to live—"

"I knew we'd get around to all that stuff eventually," she said, grinning. "Once you said the *L* word, nothing else mattered."

"Sweetheart, I plan on spending the rest of my life whispering the *L* word in your ear, but just for the record, I want to clear the decks now so we can get on with the more important stuff—like when you think you might feel up to a very small, very private wedding right here in your room. No," he said, chuckling, when she opened her mouth, "first things first." He held up his index finger. "Number one—I can live anywhere as long as you're with me. Two—as for my job, I don't really have an office, but I'm officially assigned to the Smithsonian. That makes me plain old civil service."

"The Smithsonian!"

"Yeah." He laughed. "Surprised? My job title is Tracker, and that's pretty much what I do—track down stolen artifacts for our government and anyone else Uncle Sam loans me out to. Every once in a while, I run into some real hard asses like Barrera—who's in custody, by the way—but most of the time, it's pretty routine. As for my name . . ."

"Yes?"

His grin turned rueful at the thought of the stiff and stuffy name his very rich parents had put on him. Alistair. God. One day he'd tell her, but not now. "Let's just say I've gone by a variety of nicknames all my life, but the latest was given to me by one of my co-workers who's really hooked on a series of books by an author by the name of Susannah Patterson Rawlings."

Her eyes wide with disbelief, Maddy said, "You're putting me on!"

"I swear to God I'm not," he assured her, holding up his hand like a witness called to testify before a judge. "It seems Ace Mackenzie and I have a lot in common besides our nickname. You love us both. So you see," he continued, gathering her closer, "from the very beginning, we couldn't have fought what was between us even if we'd tried. It was fate."

He leaned down and dropped a kiss to the corner of her mouth. "Kismet." A second kiss followed, this time to the opposite corner of her mouth. "Written in the stars," he murmured, lingering to explore the full sensuous curve of her bottom lip. "You were looking for someone to love in the pages of a book with my name on it, and I was right across the street, just waiting for the chance to rescue you."

Light-headed, glowing with happiness, she clung to him. "What was that you were saying about a private wedding?" she asked huskily.

He laughed softly. "I thought you'd never ask. You just lie here and take it easy and I'll take care of everything."

He started to ease her arms from around his neck, but she quickly locked them tight. "Oh, no, you don't!" she gasped. "The last time we tried that, I didn't wake up for three days. This time, I'm not letting you out of my sight until the deed is done."

His grin crooked, he shifted her in his arms and crawled right into bed with her. "We'll probably shock the hell out of your mother, but she might as well get used to seeing me around. I'm not going anywhere without you. Give me the phone, sweetheart. I've got some calls to make."

Laughing, she did as he asked, her eyes sparkling at the thought of the changes he was going to make in her life. Things were never going to be the same. She couldn't wait.

* * * * *